Shifting Sands

Barry Litherland

Published by Barry Litherland, 2020.

This is a work of fiction. Similarities to real people, places, or events are entirely coincidental.

SHIFTING SANDS

First edition. May 16, 2020.

Written by Barry Litherland.

Chapter 1

'I'm telling you, man, this guy was butt-naked, walking down a country lane at two in the morning and whimpering for someone called Bunny. Scared the shit out of me, I can tell you. I mean, it's not what you expect, is it? There I am outside this big house, minding my own, and I'm edgy enough, if you know what I mean, when I hear this weak, tinny voice coming out of nowhere. I don't believe in spirits or ghosts or any of that shit, but I tell you, man, at that moment...

'"Bunny! Bunny!" he calls. "Bunny!"

'Then he emerges from the darkness like a ghost, hasn't an item of clothing to his name, and he's got his hands out like he's reaching for something, like a little kid who's just learned to walk, and he's repeating over and over, "Bunny! Bunny!"

'Okay, Winston, I get the picture. Can you just lower your voice a little? People are staring.'

We're in Maggie's café in the precinct, sitting by a window which looks out into the pedestrian area. It's crammed with tourists, it being summer, and the school holidays being underway. The café is full, and most of the customers have spent the last few minutes listening to Winston. I mean, you don't have much choice. Winston is loud. It's as if he's unaware that there's anyone else in the whole world, as if there's just you and him. He doesn't suffer from embarrassment. He never has.

I do.

Not for the first time, I want him to shut up or lower his voice or maybe just go away.

Yeah, going away would be good.

Only Winston has never learned to take a hint. You could drop a hint by clubbing him with a cricket bat, or you could scream in his face. It'd make no difference. He's always been the same. A nuclear warhead would bounce off Winston.

'Hey, man, what are you worried about? It's a great story for that paper of yours. You should be thanking me. But I haven't told you the best bit.'

He snorts with laughter and leans forward as if he's going to whisper, but then he doesn't.

'I mean, whoever this Bunny is, this guy is really hot for her, if you know what I mean. He's got a dick like that leaning tower — what do they call it?'

'Pisa,' I whisper, 'the Leaning Tower of Pisa.'

Winston rolls back his head, opens a cavernous mouth, and roars with laughter. 'Well, that's appropriate. This guy is signposting heavenward with the most enormous...'

'Okay, Winston, okay. There's no need to get graphic. I've got the picture.' I glance round, and heads turn away instantly. 'Everyone in the room has got the picture.'

A couple of older women leave their afternoon tea with haughty looks and head for the door, but plenty more remain over empty cups and plates. They're listening and pretending not to, and suddenly I'm on a stage and we're improvising this scene and I've no idea what's coming next or how it's going to end, and everyone is waiting for my contribution.

Then I see Maggie over by the counter and I know exactly how it's going to end and what I have to do. She's formidable even when she's smiling, but she's not smiling now. She's dusting her heavyweight hands on a tea towel, flexing her muscles, preparing for a fight. She isn't even looking at the old guy who's talking to her. Her eyes are trained on Winston and me. I look at my chest, imagining a little red light targeting me.

It's understandable, I guess. Winston isn't her regular type of customer. This is more of a middle-aged, middle-class, genteel, tea and cakes sort of establishment — the sort of place my mum likes. Maggie doesn't care for tourists, and she can't abide anyone with children. She looks at anyone under the age of 50 as if they're about to spring a trap. She only smiles at them when they're leaving and that's more out of relief than anything else. Winston is in a category shared by drunks, dog owners, and people who don't pay. She looks at him as if he's trodden both feet in something unpleasant with the sole intention of bringing it into her café.

When she hears his latest outburst, she's had enough, and now she's rolling our way like a lumbering, doom-laden cloud.

'Come on, Winston, it's time to go.' I drag him to his feet and head for the door. 'Sorry, Maggie,' I call over my shoulder. 'We're leaving.'

He's still trying to cram the last of his cream cake into his mouth as I push him through the door and into the stream of pedestrian traffic.

'And don't come back!' Maggie shouts after us. 'We don't want your sort in here.'

Winston looks back with an enormous grin.

'Is it a race thing?' he calls.

If she was holding a knife, she'd throw it, I swear.

I steer him round a couple of corners and only slow down when I'm sure no one is looking at us.

'What the hell, Winston? I could be a column in my own newspaper tomorrow.'

'No one reads newspapers anymore. No offence.'

'My mum and dad do. And what do you mean, "Is it a race thing?" Do you know how many times I've heard you say that?'

'Shuts them up though, don't it?'

We're walking slowly now, getting jostled by tourists in a hurry to get nowhere special. I direct him to a seat that a large woman with an even larger shopping bag has just vacated. There are flowers in a circular bed just behind the bench, contained by a low, brick wall — part of the town centre improvements. My boss, Liz, says they're incongruous. She says it's like sticking a candle in a turd.

'What do you think of my story?' Winston asks. 'Is it worth a few quid?'

'No disrespect, Winston, but I'd need more than your word before I wrote a story about a naked rambler. I'm sure you've got a lot of admirable qualities, but honesty isn't the first that springs to mind. You'd lie to your mother.'

'Yeah,' Winston grins.

'Besides, I can't help wondering what you were doing on a country lane at two in the morning. Hardly your scene, is it? I mean, when I think of you, I don't really picture nocturnal nature walks. What were you doing there?'

'Just a bit of private enterprise.'

'Alone?'

'Nah, with Benny.'

'Benny Jarrett? Jesus, Winston, you mean you were burgling the house?'

'Me? No. I was just standing at the end of the road, waiting for Benny. I was his driver, man. He lost his license, you know.'

'Yeah, that happens when you drive at ninety down the promenade and swerve into the concrete seating. They reckon if he hadn't been drunk, he might have killed himself.'

'That's always been Benny's trouble. He likes a drink, and he likes cars. But at least it wasn't his car. Every cloud...'

'He likes burgling remote houses too, doesn't he?'

'Benny's okay. He never hurts anyone.'

'I'm not sure his victims see it that way. Did Benny see your mysterious nudist?'

'I don't know.'

'What do you mean you don't know? Didn't you discuss it on the way back? I mean, it's the sort of thing you might mention. "Hey, Benny, guess what I just saw..." that sort of thing. Wouldn't it make an interesting conversation, even for a couple of dough brains like you and Benny?'

'He was in there for ages. After the naked guy turned up, I figured I'd split before someone came looking.'

My head is starting to spin at this point, and I'm in danger of following Winston's stream of consciousness towards a cliff edge. I think maybe I'll keep to the important points.

'So where were you when all this happened?'

Winston hesitates as his fine-tuned, automated instinct for self-preservation kicks in.

'Maybe it's better you don't know,' he says.

'Come on, Winston, I don't betray my sources, not even when they're thieving bastards like you and Benny.'

He relaxes, and the big smile returns. You can't offend Winston. God knows I've tried. I used to think if I was offensive enough often enough, he'd get the hint and leave me alone. He didn't.

'We were out towards Westleigh, a few miles after the railway crossing. There's this house behind the trees — Westleigh Lodge — that has single-glazed windows in a couple of rooms round the back. I mean, shit, man... in this day and age... don't they know there are thieves about? I mean, it's like an invitation.'

'Yeah, I know the place; it's near Westleigh Hall, isn't it?'

'Yeah.'

'So this guy...'

'Yeah, just like I said — "Bunny! Bunny!" It was weird, man.'

'So what did you do?'

'What do you mean?'

'You've just seen a naked man walk past you on a country lane calling out for this...'

'Bunny! Bunny!'

'Will you stop doing that, Winston — putting on that simpering little voice? It's getting really irritating, and people are looking.'

'Hey, chill, man.'

'You've just seen this helpless guy walking down the lane. Forgive me for stating the obvious, but did you call the police?'

'Hell no. Think of Benny, man.'

'Ambulance?'

'Nah.'

'What *did* you do?'

'I figure someone will see him sooner or later. Then I think maybe I'd better get out of there before the police arrive or someone sees me and starts asking questions. Like you say, it's not easy to explain being up there at two in the morning. And with Benny up there at the old house... you catch my drift?'

'With both hands, Winston, with both hands. So you get in your car and drive off, leaving Benny and the naked rambler to sort themselves out.'

'Pretty much.'

'You're all heart, Winston. You know that?'

'Yeah,' he grins again.

'Did you pass the guy on your way back to town?'

'I went the other way. I didn't want to meet anyone coming to throw a towel over him. It took ages, and I nearly got taken off the road by this four-by-four. You don't expect it on a country lane, do you? The bastard thought he owned the place.'

'There are a lot of things you don't expect to see on a country lane at that time of night. You're pretty high up the list yourself.'

'Yeah, I guess.'

'What did Benny think when he came out with his sack of loot to find his driver had done a runner?'

'I haven't seen him. I'm keeping a low profile till he calms down.'

That grin is starting to really irritate me. I think it's time I took my leave.

'Yeah, I can see the sense in that. I've got to go, Winston — work, you know.'

'Yeah, see you, man.'

I stand up and head towards the promenade. I figure I'll walk for a while and get Winston out of my system. Only, I don't get far before I hear him calling after me.

Everybody within a hundred yards hears him.

'He had electrodes all over him too, and he was covered in gel,' he shouts, 'head to toe. Even his...'

I turn a corner but not my head and walk towards the fresher air of the Sefton seafront. The word follows me, and I imagine heads turning, watching me all the way to the sea.

Chapter 2

I've got to admit I'm intrigued by Winston's story. I think maybe it's worth a few phone calls — the hospital, the police — just to see if someone more compassionate than Winston phoned in about this guy. I mean, someone must have seen him eventually, even at that time of night. There's usually someone around with a camera phone nowadays. No tragedy would be complete without some desensitised moron making a few quid from his crap picture. We even get them at The Evening Post.

Hey, I've got a picture of those kids who burnt to death. They're standing at the window screaming. It's a great picture. What's it worth?'

They just don't get it.

You'd think someone would have missed this guy by now though, wouldn't you? He must be from somewhere, some house, some clinic. Someone must have noticed something — an empty bed, an open door or window?

Mustn't they?

Only, they haven't. The hospital is a blank. No one matching that description has been admitted to the hospital during the night, and since he'd be pretty hard to miss, I guess that's a dead end. I try the police. The desk sergeant knows me, but he still sounds like he thinks I'm winding him up.

'Naked, you say?'

'Yes, totally.'

'I see and it's — what time did you say?'

'About two in the morning.'

'Near Westleigh Lodge?'

'Yes.'

And... er, gel, you say?'

'Yes.'

I think he's trying not to laugh, and I haven't even reached the funny part yet. I take a deep breath.

'He was calling out for someone called Bunny and....'

No, I just can't tell him.

'You saw this yourself, did you?'

'No, it was... a friend.'

'Could you tell me his name?'

Winston is well known. If I mention him, this guy is going to laugh out loud.

'No, I'm afraid I can't.'

'I can understand that,' the sergeant says. He pauses, probably writing notes, maybe for an after-dinner speech. 'What was your source doing out there at that time of night?'

I start to feel uncomfortable.

'He was just driving home.'

'Had he been drinking or indulging in recreational drugs, do you think?'

He's fighting back laughter; I can hear it. I bet he's got tears running down his cheeks. I'm really glad I didn't mention the naked guy's most distinctive feature. Someone should remind this guy that taking the piss is only funny when you're both laughing.

'Can you let me know if you hear anything?' I ask.

'You'll be the first to know,' he tells me, 'I promise.'

As I close my phone, I feel my face glowing with embarrassment. I can just see him now, calling to his colleagues.

'Hey, guys, you want to hear a good one?'

Shit. He'll probably phone Slattery too. They were mates back in the old days.

I head to the office and bury myself in work until my emotions stabilise and my colour returns to normal, but the story is still niggling away at me. It's not something I'd admit publicly, but I believe Winston. I mean, he's got no reason to make stuff up, has he? And this is a bit too surreal, even for him.

I start to wonder what the naked guy and this Bunny were into, what with the gel and electrodes. Was it some sadomasochistic, nurse-patient thing?

I try to shake the thought away, but there are some images you just can't shift once they've attached themselves to your brain.

There's something else too. Where had Bunny hopped off to? Did she have a burrow out that way? Were there two of them wandering about, naked, in a state of frenzied arousal?

Suddenly 'Bunny' seems like an appropriate name.

I shudder and try to think of something else, something the complete opposite of frenzied arousal.

Liz.

Yeah, I think I'll talk to Liz. She's my editor, and, even on a good day, I'm terrified of her. She has this look, you see. She turns it on you and you feel like you've just been stapled to the wall, and you get this message which flashes like some weird code from her eyes. It has a kind of sequence. When you decode it, you find it goes like this:

I don't suffer fools gladly; you know that don't you, Philip?

Yes, Liz.

Are you a fool, Philip?

No, Liz.

You look like a fool from where I'm standing, Philip.

No, I'm not a fool, Liz.

Yes, you're a fool, Philip. Repeat after me, "I am a fool, Liz."

I'm not a fool, Liz. Really, I'm not.

I don't like you, Philip.

Okay.

She's about 50, five foot two, and made of carbon fibre. I mean, she's tougher than anyone I've ever met. But she's devoted to the paper, and she's a real professional. There are no typos in her paper, no grammatical errors, no mistaken names, dates, or locations, and no dodgy sources. Liz's news is so thoroughly researched and corroborated, it's as watertight as a nuclear warhead. And when she gets her teeth into something, it would take a six-foot crowbar and a team of brave men to prise her off it. Even the owners of the paper shudder at the thought of questioning her judgement. I've seen them standing outside her door, taking deep breaths before entering.

I mean, that woman is formidable.

And single.

She's married to her job, I think.

They're a devoted couple, inseparable, and God help anyone who gets between them.

Just now, I hear the door to her office open, and she's pacing between the desks. It's now or never. I need her advice about the best way to follow this up — the best people to see. There isn't much about Sefton-on-Sea that she doesn't know. I reckon she's been here since Caxton invented the printing press.

I need to find out about Westleigh Hall and anything else in that neighbourhood. My guy must have come from somewhere. He couldn't have walked far like that. According to Winston, his centre of gravity had shifted well forward.

'Liz?'

She stops and turns, and I feel staples flying towards me.

'Yes, Philip?'

'Have you got a minute? I might have a story.'

'In a newsroom? Surely not.' She pauses and glances at her watch. 'I'll give you five minutes — come through to the office.'

I don't sit down. I've not been here long enough. Fifteen years is the minimum, they tell me, before you can sit down.

'Well?'

Liz perches on the edge of the desk and pins me with that look.

'Well,' I begin, 'it may be nothing. I met this friend — more of an acquaintance, really — someone I knew in school — and he was telling me this story. I'm not sure...'

'Get to the point, Philip. I'm due to die in the next forty years.'

I take a deep breath.

'He was the driver for a guy burgling a house out near Westleigh.'

'Nice company you keep.'

'He was standing at the drive of this house. It was two in the morning. He hears this strange sound and then...'

And I tell her, and she listens, and she doesn't laugh. She doesn't even smile. I tell her everything, every detail, and then I tell her I checked the hospital and the police station.

'Nothing,' I tell her.

'Is your source reliable?'

'No.'

'But you believe him?'

'Yes.'

She stands up and checks her watch again.

'I've been summoned by the owners. I have to go. What are you working on at the moment? Never mind, I don't want to know. Give it to Alice. She'll be grateful. She's keen and very silly. I doubt there's anything in this story; someone will have found him and taken him home, and he'll be tucked up in bed somewhere but… gel and electrodes, you say?'

'That's what Winston told me.'

'Drive out there; do a bit of house to house. See what you can find out. Check out the new owners of Westleigh Hall. It changed hands about a year ago, and I believe they had some plans to create a hotel or a clinic or something.'

'It was for sale?'

'Don't you read your own newspaper, Mr Tyler? Never mind, don't depress me; I don't want to know. Westleigh Hall has an interesting history. You should look into it, get some background.' She pierces me with one of those stares. 'Educate yourself, Mr Tyler. My local history is a good starting point. I won't ask if you've read it, not if you don't even read your own paper.'

She pulls down a tome from her bookshelf and hands it to me.

'Now, is there anything else?'

'No, I don't think so.'

'Good.'

She brushes past me, breezing out of the door. Halfway down the press room, she pauses and turns back.

'Well done, Mr Tyler. We'll make a journalist of you yet.'

With that, she's gone, and I walk back to my desk, conscious of the uncomprehending stares of my colleagues. Words of praise from Liz are a rare commodity. People write diary entries about them.

Then I open Liz's history of the local area, and my momentary feeling of elation deserts me.

Chapter 3

I skim through the early history of Westleigh Hall, pausing briefly to read the compulsory, *every-old-house-has-got-one* ghost story. This one's about some young woman who was bricked up in a wall and left to die — for adultery, apparently. Try that in Sefton today and you'd empty half the streets; the walls would be bulging.

Anyway, that was way back in the sixteenth century when the Westleighs still lived there and ruled over the area — local, self-important, minor nobility.

I feel my socialist instincts stirring.

They do the usual side-swapping during the Civil War but end up on the wrong one, and that's the end of the Westleighs. The new owners are even more boring, and, eventually, they die out too, and then there's a couple of industrialists, and they die out until there's just some old lady. She lingers on through the war when the hall is turned into a hospital, and then it's her turn, and she dies. Shit, this is a depressing story — death, death, death... anyway, that's 1953. The hospital lingers for a while, and then it's bought out and becomes a sanatorium which doesn't make a profit. That closes in the seventies. The owners — relatives of the old lady, I think — stay on in one wing, but they can't keep up with the maintenance, and, eventually, in 1996, they pack up and leave. It's left to slowly decay.

Twenty years later and it's on the market; it's been taken over, and some redevelopment is underway. I wonder why it took twenty years? Sentimental attachment maybe? I feel like that about a handful of vinyl records from my teens and a book my first girlfriend gave me one Christmas. Melissa, yeah, that was her name. She broke my heart — the bitch.

I turn to the computer to find the agent — Mackenzie-Green — but they just put me on to the solicitor from London who dealt with the purchase. I get on the phone to them, only, they're as helpful as a hole in a sock. They tell me the hall was for sale (which I knew) and that it was sold (which I knew), but they won't divulge the name of the buyer (which I want to know) because the buyer doesn't want them to (I want to know why). They're very polite, like saccharine on a cyanide capsule. I say thank you through gritted teeth, check Land Registry, and find the name of the company which bought the place — Logrum Research — and I think I'm getting somewhere.

But I'm not.

I check out the directors and phone them and email them. The phone calls go to answerphone and the emails bounce. I'd have more luck sticking my head out of the window and shouting their names. I hope none of them are called Bunny.

So I go back to the computer and dig deeper. Logrum Research, it turns out, is a subsidiary of another company which is a subsidiary of a company that is based somewhere so obscure, you'd need to mount an expedition to find it. By now, it's late in the day, and all I've got from my hard work is a headache, backache, and repetitive strain injury in my hands and arms. The joints in my legs are locked.

To hell with this, I think.

Then I get stubborn, and I think, *I'll give it one last try*, and I go back to the solicitors Pettigrew and Slim, and, this time, I apply a bit of journalistic pressure.

'I've heard from a source that Logrum Research is planning to open a hotel or a clinic of some description. Do you have any comment?'

She doesn't. It seems she's unfamiliar with the concept of independent thought.

'Can I speak to Mr Pettigrew or Mr Slime?'

'It's Slim,' she tells me. 'S-L-I-M.'

'Can I speak to him, then?'

'It's Lorraine Slim,' she says, with a voice which could be used to poison wells. 'She's a woman.'

Ouch.

Okay, let's try something else.

'I'm writing an article about the future of the hall. I'd like something more definite than 'its future is shrouded in a mystery which its new owners, Logrum Research, are unwilling to reveal.' You know how people respond to uncertainty. I dread to think what they'll make of this. They'll start to imagine a prison, a young offenders' institute, a holiday camp, or something really awful like wind turbines.'

She hesitates. I can hear cogs beginning to turn. Maybe she's asking her computer for a decision.

Will she? Will she?

'If you'll give me fifteen minutes, I'll speak to Mr Pettigrew and get back to you.'

Yes!

'Thank you. I'll await your ca—'

She's already hung up.

Twenty minutes later, the phone rings, but it isn't Mr Pettigrew or even Ms Slime. It's some official guy with a voice which sounds like it's just escaped from a subterranean vault. He introduces himself as Clive Wigmore, agent for Logrum Research. He's American, I think — kind of mid-Atlantic. He has a message he wants to get across, and he doesn't want to be bothered by anything which doesn't relate to that message. His is the manner of the curt media man, the guy who represents a big organisation or a senior politician in the US — abrupt, verging on ignorant, and immediately annoying — a red rag to someone like me.

His message is simple:

'My clients plan to open a rehabilitation centre for a very select clientele, the sort of people who value their privacy and are willing to pay for it — television and movie stars and high-powered business people — the rich and famous. The location of Westleigh Hall is ideal for our purpose. It is close to road and rail networks but isolated enough to offer complete seclusion to our guests. My clients will make an appropriate disclosure of their plans in the near future. In the meantime, we would ask you to refrain from raising unnecessary speculation about our work. Its effect on the local population will, after all, be minimal.'

'Do you have any clients in the facility at present?'

'No. We're still at the stage of renovating and modernising the building. It'll be some time before our first clients take up residence.'

'Can I speak to one of the directors?'

'That won't be possible. They're very busy people.'

'Who are the owners?'

'Logrum Research.'

'They're just a subsidiary. I mean, who *really* owns the place?'

'The clinic is owned by Logrum Research, its shareholders, and its directors.'

'Who owns the company which owns Logrum Research?'

'It wouldn't be appropriate to disclose anything further at present. There's nothing sinister here, Mr Tyler. Everything relevant will be revealed at the correct time. I'm sure you understand the need to control the flow of information in order to prevent speculation and to avoid unhelpful publicity.'

'I usually find frankness prevents undue speculation.'

'We have a great deal of experience in this area, Mr Tyler. You must allow us to reveal our plans in a way that suits our purposes and the nature of our clientele. I hope I can rely on your discretion for the few weeks it will take for us to establish ourselves. I can assure you we will be as frank as possible at that time. Perhaps I could offer you a tour of the establishment in return for your cooperation, prior to our first clients arriving?'

'When is that likely to be?'

'I doubt we'll be ready before September.'

'Do you have other establishments in the UK?'

'That, Mr Tyler, I can't divulge. It can lead to unhelpful intrusion. There are too many people out there, and some of those who, alas, are on the fringes of your profession, would be only too eager to photograph a celebrity at a moment of weakness. The location of our clinics is no secret but we don't advertise their presence. I'm sure you understand.'

'What about elsewhere? The US, maybe?'

'As I said...'

'What about the old house a few hundred yards down from the hall? Did you buy that too?'

'Yes, we acquired that to provide accommodation for the medical director of the clinic.'

'Has she moved in yet?'

'I don't have that information, Mr Tyler.'

I decide it's time to mention Winston's naked man.

'There was a man covered in some sort of gel and he had electrodes fitted — the sort you might have in a hospital or clinic.'

There's a brief pause, but it isn't long enough to make anything of it.

'I can assure you, Mr Tyler, whoever that unfortunate man was, he had nothing to do with us. As I said, we are yet to open our doors to our first patients. Now, if there's nothing else...'

That's pretty much it. He asks again for my cooperation, but I hedge that. I tell him I have no plans to print anything at present, and if the situation changes, I'll let him know.

'If that unfortunate circumstance occurs, I'd appreciate a copy of your article prior to publication.'

'Of course.'

I take his email, and that's that.

When I sit back and think about what he's said, it's pretty clear I've heard only what he wants me to hear. Maybe that is just a sensible precaution on his part. There's nothing to link Westleigh Hall with Winston's story.

And I'm no nearer to finding the naked man.

It's late now, and there's not much else I can do, so I think maybe I'll take a drive out there tomorrow, call at a few houses, ask a few questions. Maybe someone will know something. I'll call at Westleigh Grange and see if the doctor has moved in. If nothing comes of that, I'll probably give up and go back to my day job.

I pack up and turn off the computer, and I'm about to head to my car when the door crashes open, and Liz storms towards her office. We all watch as she slams the door, and we hear her swear.

'Bastards,' she shouts. 'Weak-willed, spineless, money-grubbing, mercenary, worthless bastards — the only man amongst them was a woman!'

There's silence across the room — not a murmur.

When she doesn't emerge after ten minutes, I go home.

Chapter 4

Should I take Winston with me to Westleigh Hall?

The thought of Winston in a confined space like a car isn't a pleasant one, and he's not someone I want too close to me when I'm working. Winston is trouble. The biggest mistake you can make with Winston is to believe he's your friend and can trust him. He isn't, and you can't.

Remember Benny? Benny is the closest thing to a best friend Winston has, and Winston left him on a country lane at two in the morning, five miles out of town, with a quantity of stolen goods, a naked rambler, and a long walk home. At the first sign of trouble, Winston was out of there.

On the other hand, Winston can show me exactly where he saw the guy, where he was coming from, and where he was heading. He can show me the house Benny was burgling and where he was standing.

In the end, I decide to take him because it's better he's there if I need to ask him something. But there'll have to be rules; if he starts with that 'Bunny! Bunny!' voice, I'll pull up and leave him — swear to God.

I leave a message for Liz, then I drive out to collect Winston. It's ten o'clock. He's wearing a college scarf, a hat his gran knitted, a red shirt, and blue jeans.

'I see you're going for the subdued look.'

'Why be one of the crowd?' he grins. 'If you've got it, flaunt it.'

That's a really big *if*, Winston.'

We drive along the promenade to the bridge over the Sefton River, then turn down the main road inland. It's busy. There are queues at every roundabout and at all the traffic lights, but, eventually, we leave the town and turn first down one lane and then another until we reach the railway crossing.

The barriers are down.

'Have you heard from Benny?'

'Nah.'

'He's not come looking for you, maybe to have a chat about the other night?'

'What about the other night?'

It's like he's forgotten all about it, like it never happened, or, if it did, like it was something so trivial, it wasn't worth thinking about. I don't bother answering.

'I guess he split without finishing the job,' he says.

A train clatters by, three carriages heading inland, travelling seventeen miles to the next town. It looks crowded, and people are standing between the compartments.

'You pay a fortune and you don't even get a seat,' I comment.

'Bastards,' Winston says.

That's as profound as we get.

Ten minutes later, when I think the lane can't get any narrower, and hawthorn and blackthorn branches are scraping the windows, Winston tells me to pull over into a driveway on the left.

'This is the gaff.'

'Which way was your guy heading?'

'Back towards the railway... "Bunny...B..."'

'Winston!'

'Okay, okay.'

'There are just a couple of houses along here, and then there are the cottages by the railway line.'

'Yeah.'

'Where's the hall?'

'A mile down the lane.'

'Any other houses?'

'Nah. Hey, man, if he came down the lane from the hall,' he laughs, open mouthed, 'he'd have to have carried a caber like that for a mile. I mean, that must be some sort of record.'

It's not an image I want to linger over.

'Let's drive on down there before we start making house calls — just to take a look.'

The lane widens after half a mile, and then there's a private road which turns left. A hundred yards further, we're stopped by high, double gates. There's a sign which says "Westleigh Hall. No Entry." There's just sufficient space to pull off the road and park up.

'Shit, it looks like a prison,' Winston says.

He's right.

The trees on both sides of the walls have been cleared, and the wall itself has been raised to about ten feet and topped with a coil of razor wire. The gates, steel barred, are set in concrete pillars with cameras mounted on their tops. There's a push-button intercom beside the gate. Everything is new. Even the drive, which leads from the gates down to the hall, winding through trees and around wide lawns, is newly gravelled with sand-coloured stone.

'I'm going to have a look,' I tell Winston. 'Stay here.'

I'm talking to myself. Winston is already getting out of the car and sauntering towards the gate. He looks up at the cameras with an expert eye and then grins and waves at them.

'For goodness' sake, Winston!'

'Bunny! Bunny!' he simpers towards one of them. 'That should bring them,' he grins.

'If I want to bring them, I'll use the intercom. I want a couple of minutes to myself first.'

I stand by the gates and look along the drive. It's difficult to make out much of the hall, and I wish I'd brought binoculars, but even at this distance, it's evident a lot of work has taken place. The whole Georgian frontage has been restored, the ivy on the walls has been trimmed back, and new windows and doors have been installed.

'The solicitors told me there are no clients here yet,' I tell Winston. 'Should I believe them?'

'They're all liars,' Winston says without enthusiasm. 'Have you seen the cameras?'

He points along the drive.

In addition to those set on the columns at the gate, there are others fixed to trees, and Winston's expert eye can make out even more across the front of the building.

'They do take their security seriously,' he says.

'I'm going to take a walk round before someone comes out asking questions,' I tell him. 'If they do, it will be thanks to your song and dance act.'

Winston is bored now and goes back to the car, and I hear the blare of the radio. He's got the window open and he's smoking.

At least the window's open; I hate the smell of smoke in my car.

He's right, though. The security at this place is tighter than a prison. There are cameras at intervals along the entire perimeter. It doesn't take much imagination to picture guard dogs patrolling the space between the fence and the cluster of trees which protect the house from prying eyes. There's something of a prisoner-of-war camp about the place.

When I get back to the car, Winston's got company. The gates are open, and a dark four-by-four has pulled up beside him. He's leaning against the car smoking a cigarette and talking to a surly-looking guy in a dark suit and sunglasses, who's standing there, arms folded, impassive.

I walk across and flash a press card.

Big smile. Charm.

I hold out a hand, which he grasps suspiciously, like I might be trying to steal a limb.

'This is the git who nearly drove me off the road,' Winston's saying. 'Same stupid car, same stupid face.'

The guy turns towards me. 'What's he talking about?' He's courteous and smooth, but he doesn't look like a man to be messed with.

Not that Winston cares.

'Driving like an idiot...' he says. 'You could've killed me.'

I find all this righteous indignation pretty rich coming from someone who was an accessory to a burglary, but, at the moment, I just need Winston to shut up.

'Excuse my colleague,' I say. 'He's just getting back in the car,' I flash Winston a look, 'unless he wants to walk back to town.'

'Just saying, man,' he says. 'Guy should learn some courtesy.'

He's just closed the door when I hear a sound behind me, and three vans, white, 'Logrum Logistics' emblazoned on their sides, roll past, raising a cloud of dust.

'I'd heard you weren't open for business yet,' I say.

'That's right.'

'A very select alcohol and drugs rehabilitation centre, I heard.'

'Where'd you hear that?'

I give him the name of the company agent, Clive Wigmore, and he thaws a little — but only a little. The look he throws Winston's way is at best suspicious.

'Who's he?'

'My photographer.'

'You can't take photos here,' he says. 'Didn't you see the signs? This is private land.'

'I was hoping for an interview.'

'We're too busy. Mr Wigmore must've told you that. He must've told you we don't welcome visitors either.'

'Yeah, he did mention something like that. He promised me a tour before you open.'

'Well, then...'

'I just wanted to take a look.'

'There's nothing to see. You've had a wasted journey.'

'The new owners have spent a hell of a lot of money on the place.'

'It's a big company — big investments, big returns.'

He glances back down the drive towards the house, where I can see a couple of white-coats watching as crates are unloaded from the vans. He's impatient to be rid of us.

'Impressive security,' I say, 'but a bit excessive, maybe?'

'Our guests need privacy,' he says. 'It's what they pay for.'

'What's all the gear?' I ask, indicating the vans.

'Medical equipment, recreational equipment, furniture...'

I nod.

'Now, if that's everything...'

'Any medical staff here yet?'

'A few...'

'Is that what you are?'

'I'm security. Now, can I ask you to get back in your car, sir, and move on? You can see we're busy here. I'm sure Mr Wigmore will be in touch.'

'Okay.'

I head back to the car, and then I pause and turn back.

'You wouldn't know anything about a naked guy with electrodes attached to him, wandering around here in the early hours of Tuesday, would you?'

I hear Winston from inside the car. 'Bunny! Bunny!'

'He was heading away from here, towards the railway.'

I get the feeling this guy is pleased he's wearing shades. His body tenses ever so slightly — just enough to tell me he knows something.

'No,' he says. 'You should try the police and hospitals.'

'Yeah, you're probably right.'

He watches as I turn the car and drive away. Through the rear-view mirror, I see him clamber in the four-by-four and drive back towards the house. The gates close.

'Well, what do you make of that?'

'Dickhead nearly took me off the road,' Winston mutters.

Yeah,' I say. 'I was thinking about that. Was he heading towards the railway?'

'Yeah.'

'Towards the naked guy, then?'

'Yeah.'

'Let's go and make a few house calls, shall we?'

'Can't we go to the pub and get some food?'

'Work first, food later. I'm paying, remember?'

'Capitalist!'

Chapter 5

When I turn into the drive to Westleigh Grange, Winston sinks so low on the passenger seat, he looks like some slowly deflating doll.

'The naked guy,' he whispers, 'he might have seen me and told someone.'

'I think he had other things on his mind, don't you?'

'Bun... yeah, right. But I'll stay here, just in case, man.'

That's fine by me. I'm beginning to think this is a visit I should've made alone.

I pull up outside the house and climb out to look around. It's clear at once that no one's living here yet. The curtains are shut, and there's no answer when I ring the bell. I take a stroll round the back, checking windows and trying to peer inside, but there's not a chink through the lined curtains, except at the back where a window is broken and a small gap opens into an empty room. I walk on round the house till I reach the car, then I stand outside the entrance porch. It's an old building, probably Victorian, with five windows on the upper floor and six tall chimneys. Ivy is growing on either side of the door and round the four ground-floor windows. It's a solid-looking house made from local stone, and it looks a bit dark and gothic. There are a couple of circular, corner towers broken by small windows, and it's capped by a turret.

Behind me, I hear the car window slide open, and Winston's head appears.

'Let's get out of here, man,' he calls. Then I hear him swear, and the window closes. There's a car approaching between untidy trees. There's no sign of Winston now. I imagine him curled in the footwell with his thumb in his mouth and his eyes closed. A guy about my age clambers from the cab of a small van that is towing an open trailer. He walks over to me.

'Doctor Harris?' he asks, hand outstretched.

I take the hand and shake it.

'No, I'm looking for the owner,' I tell him. 'Phil Tyler from The Evening Post. Do you work here?'

'Not regularly — I've been hired to tidy the garden.'

'You're local?'

'Sefton,' he tells me. '"Gavin's Garden Maintenance". I advertise in your paper.'

'Does it do much good?'

'Some — are you writing about the hall?'

'Trying to; they're not very forthcoming. I wonder what the neighbours make of the changes.'

He laughs. 'They moan about the extra traffic. Cars and vans going up and down — builders, plumbers, electricians, tree surgeons, landscape gardeners, interior decorators, delivery vans, heavy plant — right through the night too. They're mainly elderly folk down by the railway. They like a good moan. I spend most of my time listening to them, and then they tell me their garden isn't how they want it.'

'You can't win. What do they want you to do here?'

'Tidy up the ivy, clear some of the undergrowth from the trees, cut off some of the branches over the drive, prepare some flowerbeds, prune the roses, get the lawn in shape — a bit of general gardening. It's a couple of months' work, I reckon, but I'm hoping they'll keep me on to stay on top of things.'

He opens the trailer and starts unloading equipment: a rotavator, a chainsaw, a strimmer.

'Who hired you?'

'Some agent for the owners — a guy called Wigmore; I think he's American.'

'Yeah, Clive Wigmore, I've spoken to him. Did he tell you what they're doing with the hall?'

'Some sort of clinic for the rich and famous, I think. Like you say, they're not giving much away.'

I take my wallet out and remove a card.

'Can you let me know when Doctor Harris arrives?'

'Yes, sure.' He takes the card and looks at it. 'I've read some of your stuff,' he says.

I wait for him to say he likes it, but he doesn't.

I hate it when people do that. What does that mean? He doesn't think much of it? What?

'Maybe I'll meet some celebrities,' he grins. 'I'll have to dig out my autograph book.' He glances over my shoulder. 'Is there someone in your car?'

'That's Winston,' I tell him.

'He's sitting in the footwell. Is he okay?'

'He's trying to be inconspicuous. He's not very good at it.'

'He should try a different hat.'

'His gran knitted it for him.'

'Right.'

It's time to go.

'Are you telling me Benny was burgling an empty house?' Winston says when I tell him what I've heard.

''Fraid so.'

'And he had me out there at two in the morning?'

'Yep.'

'Useless sod.'

'I think he got inside, though. There's a broken window at the back. Maybe we should find out find out if he saw anything — apart from a layer of dust.'

'Now? Do we have to?'

I see the look of despair on Winston's face, and I take pity on him.

'We'll get something to eat first. There's a nice pub a couple of miles the other side of the railway, down by the river. What do you think?'

Winston thinks it's a good idea, and he's brighter at once.

We sit in *The Dog and Feathers* for an hour, and I watch Winston eat and drink like he's been on a starvation diet. Then I look at my watch.

He fails to take the hint.

'We should go and see Benny.'

Still nothing.

I stand up.

'Come on, Winston. I can't sit here all day. I need to get back to the office later. My editor's not a patient woman.'

He shakes his head. 'You keep working like this and you'll get an ulcer, man.'

I look at the empty glasses and plates and wonder if this is what passes for irony in Winston's world. I decide it isn't. Winston doesn't really do *subtle*.

'Drink up. It's time to find Benny.'

Chapter 6

Benny lives in one of the old council blocks that was built in the sixties and hidden away from tourists. You know the type, six-storey-half-way-to-high-rise-heaven places with concrete stairwells, broken lifts, and front doors opening on drab walkways. It's owned by a housing association now. God, it used to be a rough place. Way back, they used to bring people here when the prisons ran out of options. In more recent, enlightened times, they tried moving in some ordinary, respectable people. The poor sods must have wondered what they'd done to deserve Wellington Towers. They didn't last. First chance they got, they were out of there. A tent in the park was better than The Towers.

The biggest problem is the gangs: there's the Wellington Tower Gang and the Nelson Tower Gang. They're the sort of people you just long to meet if you want a night out ruined. They hate everybody, especially each other.

If I wasn't such a left-wing, liberal do-gooder, I'd be thinking, *Napalm — yeah, that's a good idea,* but I have this socialist streak in me, and I feel kind of sorry for them if that is how they measure their lives. I mean, really, how painfully hopeless is that?

Benny lives in the corner flat on the top floor. It's the one with the English Defence League stuff and the Cross of St. George in the window. Yeah, it looks like he's a real sweetie. I bet he spends most of his days walking the streets hating people; then, at night, he burgles the homes of the elderly — for therapy.

We don't use the lift. Nobody who can walk uses the lift. I get the feeling people only summon it if they need the toilet. Even the stairs fill me with dread, and it's a relief when I reach the open space of the walkway. I glance over the rail. It's a long way down. People have been thrown off here.

Winston beats on the door with his palm.

Then he beats on the window.

Then he beats on the door again.

'Benny's probably asleep,' he says.

'It's half past two in the afternoon.'

'Maybe he was working last night.'

He beats on the door again and shouts, 'Benny! Benny!' Benny doesn't appear, but a shrivelled woman with eyes like a snake opens the door to the next flat. A cigarette is hanging from her lips, but it doesn't impede the flow of invectives she hurls in our direction. Apparently, the fucking baby has just gone to fucking sleep and she doesn't want the little fucker woken up by some fucking moron banging on the fucking door and fucking shouting so shut the fuck up, fucker.

Winston flashes her a big smile.

'You seen Benny?' he asks.

'Not for a couple of days.'

The door shuts. I hear a baby start to cry, a crash, and a few more oaths. I feel a surge of pity for the child inside that room. Between its mother and the street gangs, it hasn't got a hope. It makes me angry. I want to write about it, but where do you start?

Maybe one day...

Winston is rooting inside a space above the door, just below the roof. He emerges with a key and waves it at me.

'For a burglar, he hasn't much idea of security,' I say.

'Sod all to nick,' Winston grins. 'Nobody round here robs their neighbours — there's no point.'

When the door opens, and I recover from the blast of stale air and cigarette smoke which rushes past me, coughing, I step over the threshold and brace myself. I reckon I'm about to realise the true meaning of squalor.

But it's not like that. The door opens into a tiny hallway that has just enough room for there to be a door ahead of me, a door to the left, and a door to the right. They're all open and reveal a kitchen, a lounge, and a bathroom. Sure, nothing's especially tidy — there are unwashed pots in the sink and on the table, the floor could do with a quick vacuum, and there are items of clothing on the worn, faux leather sofa. But if you ignore the far-right posters, a two-foot swastika, and a poster which looks like it was left over from a Nuremberg rally, it's actually quite presentable. Through an open door in the lounge, I see the bedroom. Even the bed's made.

Benny's not there.

I pick up a photograph in a simple black frame. There are three people, a woman and two children, on the beach south of the Sefton Road Bridge. She's about 30, I guess, and the kids are about 7 or 8.

'Who's this?'

'That's Debs, his wife.'

'Not here now, I take it.'

'Nah, she left him.'

'And the kids?'

'Jason and Megan. Jason's dead — overdosed. That's when Debs left. She couldn't hack it... had to get away.'

'And Megan?'

'She's in London. He doesn't see her.'

There are other photos about the place of Debs and the kids. There's one of Jason as a teenager; he's about 15, and he's already got that pinched, suspicious look which marks the kids round here like an identity card.

'Sad,' I say. I don't like to admit it, but I feel kind of sorry for Benny. It's like I've just seen him for the first time.

'Yeah, dead right,' Winston says. 'Benny went to pieces. No job, no wife, no family, no friends...'

'Except you.'

'Yeah, well, we go back a long way.' He walks through to the kitchen and opens the fridge. 'He hasn't even stocked up on beers,' he mutters. 'Where the hell is he?'

We head out of the flat and back down to the car.

'I'll hang round here a while and see if I can find him,' Winston says.

I think it's time I head back to the office to check in with Liz. I've not much to report for a day's work, except for a handful of suspicions, so I guess I'll be back at my desk tomorrow.

She's in her office, and I can tell from the atmosphere in the press room that her mood hasn't improved. I catch a few warning looks and the odd gesture like throat-cutting. I steel myself and knock on the door. I imagine my colleagues ducking down behind their desks, and I glance back. They're watching me like you'd watch a mouse nearing a trap.

'YES!' Liz's voice breaks through the door like an exploding shell. I feel shock waves.

I open the door and step fearlessly inside.

'Oh, it's you, Philip. WELL?'

I figure it is best to be succinct, so I pare the story down to a few sentences, and Liz stops what she's doing and listens. When I finish, there's a silence as she continues to stare at me.

'SO?' she snaps.

When I don't answer after about two seconds, she takes a deep breath. I think she's fighting off the temptation to rip out my throat. She speaks slowly, like she's talking to a kid who's not very bright.

'So Westleigh Hall is to be a clinic for the rich and famous who've fallen on hard drugs, the house beside it is home to the medical supervisor, they're moving in all their equipment, they've put heavy security in place, no one knows anything about your naked man, and the burglar can't be found. Is that it? Have I missed anything?'

It doesn't sound much when she puts it like that. I swallow like a guilty child. My mouth is dry.

'Pretty much.'

'It hardly amounts to a successful day's work, does it?'

'No, I suppose not.'

'No, I suppose not...' she repeats slowly, and it's like she's steadily coiling a spring inside her, and, at any moment, she's going to release it. She breathes slowly.

'What will you do now?'

It feels like one of those teacher questions.

So what are you going to do now, Philip?

I'm going to say I'm sorry.

Yes, Philip, you are. And then what are you going to do?

I'm going to miss my playtime.

All *your playtimes, Philip.*

Yes, Mrs Goddard.

Mrs Goddard was my teacher when I was in year four — Jesus, there's a memory.

'I don't know if there's much I *can* do. Everything's a dead end. Maybe I should leave it and wait to see if Benny turns up.'

I can see the spring gradually unwinding. Liz is struggling to control the energy output. She walks over to the window, grips the sill like she wants to break it, and looks outside. Then she turns sharply back.

'What is your profession, Mr Tyler?'

'I'm a journalist.'

'Really? Tell me, do you have even a single gram of aptitude for your role?'

I'm getting a bit annoyed now.

'I think so. My writing's good. I research my stories well. I know what I'm doing.'

'My niece has those talents, Mr Tyler, and she's only 12. What I'm asking...' She pauses and runs a hand through her hair. 'What I'm asking is if you have that special aptitude which makes a mere hack into a proper journalist?'

'I'd like to think so.'

'You'd like to think so...'

The spring finally uncoils, and I feel something like whiplash.

'Then tell me something I don't bloody well know. Tell me what the journalist in you thinks. Tell me what you smell; tell me your suspicions. Do not bore me with bare facts which any schoolboy could discover. What do you think, Mr Tyler? Is there a story here or is there not?'

I've lost it now. I've got a spring of my own, you know.

Only, mine's more of a rubber band.

'Yes, there's a story. I don't know what it is, but there's something going on, and I want to get to the bottom of it. I want to know who this naked guy was and why he was out there. I think the answer lies in that clinic, and I think there's something not right about it — not right at all. Is that clear enough for you? What I don't need is you on my back with your sarcastic remarks. So tell me what to do. Do I go on with the story or go back to my desk? I don't give a shit.'

Suddenly, she smiles.

'But you do, Mr Tyler. You do give a shit. My God, there's a journalist in there after all. I'd all but given up hope. Now, stop telling me there's nothing you can do.' Her voice rises to a crescendo, her hands are flat on the desk, and her eyes are flashing. *'Tell me what you're going to do*!'

It's like I'd reached a dead end and there were walls ahead of me and around me, and they rose so high I couldn't see the sky — but now they're dissolving away; I can see ahead, and I know what I'm going to do. It's as clear as a sunny day.

'I'm going back to the clinic. Only, this time, I'm going to see if I can look inside. And I'm going to give social media a shot, just drop a hint, tell a story, see what comes back.'

'Dig a bit deeper into Logrum too. If there are other establishments, go and visit them.'

'That could be expensive.'

She flashes me a strange look. 'To hell with the expense,' she says. 'Now, if that's all...'

I walk towards the door, but she calls me back.

'Just one thing, Mr Tyler,' she says. 'Be careful. I too have a nose for a story, and, at the moment, it's twitching. I had a telephone call earlier this afternoon from a Mr Wigmore. He described himself as an agent for Logrum Enterprises, but I doubt he's any such thing. He was very smooth, quite charming, remarkably plausible — and a liar. He requested our cooperation. He would like to prevent any unhelpful publicity prior to the opening of his clinic and repeated his promise of an exclusive tour. No doubt it would be a well-sanitised, selective tour controlled by him. I asked him some questions which he parried like an Olympic fencing champion. I didn't get any answers, and he didn't get his promise. He was at pains to describe the influence and power of the company he represents and their willingness to go to any lengths to protect their interests. It felt very much like a threat. I don't respond well to threats, Mr Tyler, and neither, I suspect, do you. But be careful.'

Chapter 7

I wonder what makes Liz think I don't respond well to threats? I do. I really do. Threaten me and I'll say anything you want; I'll do what you tell me. But first I'll try and run away. I'm not like her, not one bit. She's got nerves of steel and a look that could freeze mercury. She makes me tremble just by opening a door. I like the sort of journalism that involves sitting in a chair and phoning people or going out to interview old ladies and people who win things or grow things.

Why the hell did I tell her I'd go back to the clinic and find a way in?

Macho bravado, was it? A foolish rush of blood in response to being shouted at?

Did I get angry because she said I was a crap journalist?

How pathetic is that? I am a crap journalist. I like being a crap journalist. I like keeping my head down and writing crap stories about boring people with ordinary lives. I don't want to be an investigative journalist; I don't want to go out there, exposing crimes and corruption, getting awards, and being admired and envied by my peers. I like the words "steady" and "boring". Do I want to face untold dangers in the name of truth and justice?

No thank you.

No.

Well, maybe justice — yeah, maybe justice. I can't stand injustice. It's the one thing that really angers me, not just as a journalist, but as me. I'm all for the little man — the victim — the little kid the big kids bully. It goes back a long way.

I think maybe Liz is like that too.

I still don't want to go out to the clinic. I think maybe I'll leave that till tomorrow or next month. For now, I'll turn what talents I have to Facebook,

Twitter, and all those other social media sites I don't trust but often use. I open my computer and get to work.

I don't specify where and I don't specify when, but I tell the story Winston told me, keeping it brief and light.

'Hey, guys. Just gotta share this story. Someone I know was out walking their dog (Winston? A dog? Well, it's better than telling the truth, I figure). *It was after midnight — last walk of the day down a country lane near their house. There's no one about — just them, the trees, and a clear, moonless sky.... or so they think. They hear a strange sound like someone calling a name, softly and weakly. Then, out of the darkness, a figure emerges, stark naked, with electrodes attached to his torso and gel glistening all over his body. My friend shrinks back into the hedgerow but the naked rambler just walks past, arms outstretched, and disappears into the darkness.*

What do you make of that?

Suggestions on a postcard.

The Twitter version is shorter. I hashtag it half to death and post it.

Will anyone read it, I wonder?

I have this theory that no one reads Facebook posts. They just look at the pictures. I should have found a naked model to pose for me... or maybe not; I'll get enough weird replies as it is. Anyway, that's done, and it's way after five, so I think I'll go home. There's no one here now anyway, except for Liz.

I don't know why, but I think I'll go and say goodnight.

She's standing by the window, her arms folded, and she seems to be deep in thought.

'I've posted something on a few social media sites. It may stir some memories, you never know. I'll head out to the clinic again tomorrow.'

She nods without turning.

'Goodnight, Liz.'

'Goodnight, Philip.'

I pause for a moment. There's something about the way she's standing — something about the tone of her voice.

'Are you okay, Liz?'

She brushes her eyes quickly and half turns towards me.

'I'm fine,' she says. 'I'll give it another half hour and then I'll head home too.'

'So long as you're sure.'

'Yes, Philip. Goodnight. And thank you.'

She turns back and looks out of the window again, but I get the feeling she's not seeing anything. I close the door and head down to the car park. As I'm getting in my car, I look up and she's still there, staring out over the emptying streets. I feel a surge of something like sadness. What is it I'm looking at? Is it loneliness? Tragedy? Regret? A part of me wants to go back and see if I can help.

But I don't.

I get in my car and drive home. But her image lingers until a couple of beers drive it away.

Chapter 8

The next morning, I get up early and convince myself I'm too busy to go to the clinic. I don't take much convincing. Like I say, I'm not heroic, macho-man material. Courage to me is cycling downhill with minimum brake application. Nothing more than that. I busy myself doing nothing in particular, and then I open my computer to see if there's been any response to my posts. It takes me a moment to realise that, while I've not exactly gone viral, I have been 'shared' and 'retweeted,' and I have 217 'likes' and 38 'comments' on Facebook. There are even more on Twitter. Most of them are predictable enough — bad puns, innuendos, and laborious and tedious attempts at wit, most of them horribly clumsy and rarely amusing, and all of them time consuming and irritating. I spend a few minutes discarding them. Then there are the pervy ones which make my flesh creep and the misspelled, ungrammatical ones which make my flesh creep even more. I discard those too. There are a few which seem more sincere; they are pretending to know the gent in question, to be his wife or his lover, or to be his sister or son, but when I've filtered out the serial offenders who will respond to anything, I'm left with just two.

The first is intriguing. It comes through as a private message and just says, "Contact me, please. I don't know who else to turn to." There's a phone number. The second is scary. "I'm a nurse; I used to work at L. Can we meet? I'm being watched." The email address is "anxious.nurse@yahoo.com". It looks like it might be a new email address that could have been set up just to contact me.

Suddenly, I don't feel too good.

I send "anxious.nurse" my email address. Then I pick up the phone and call the number from the private message. A young woman's voice answers.

At least I think she's young. Voices on the phone are deceptive — like on the radio.

'Hello?'

'Hi, this is Phil Tyler. You messaged me?'

'Yes. Can you wait a moment?'

I hear a door close, and the muffled radio in the background is silenced. In the distance, a dog barks.

'That's better.' Her voice is a low whisper, as if she's trying not to be heard.

'My husband says I shouldn't,' she begins. 'He says it's family business and that I shouldn't trust... well, you hear such things about journalists, don't you? But I don't know what to do, you see. No one wants to help us. The medical people, well, they try their best, I suppose, but they don't understand. I mean, they can't, can they? Not unless it's happened to them. And it's just not right, is it? I mean, it doesn't make sense... like your naked man...'

I have to stop her before my brain implodes.

'Slow down. Take your time.'

'It's your story, you see. It's like my sister — the gel, the electrodes, and... well, the state of undress... although at least she had a nightdress and a sheet round her shoulders. But it's not funny, is it? Not when it's someone close to you — someone you care for. Don't you agree?'

I agree. I try to control my breathing and my heart rate, but it's not easy.

'Are you telling me that something similar happened to your sister?'

'Yes, yes that's precisely it, and we can't get her back — not properly. It's like we've lost her, you see; it's like she's been taken away from us. She went away as one person and came back as another — not my sister at all. Do you see?'

No. Not at all. Not one single word.

But it's getting more intriguing by the minute, and this is the first real clue I've had. This has happened to someone else. What the hell is going on here?

'Was there a clinic involved?'

'It's complicated. Wendy was in a bad way. She didn't tell us just how bad. There was a clinic, yes... a retreat, she called it, but I only know the name we use locally — Westleigh.'

'Westleigh is owned by a company called Logrum Logistics.'

'Was that where your naked man...?'

'Yes. When did this happen to your sister?'

'She was transferred to Westleigh about six months ago. Then, eight weeks back, she was discovered walking down a lane beside the railway.'

So much for having no patients — liars.

'Is Wendy staying with you?'

'No, she's far too unwell. We found a nice place for her where she'll be looked after — if *they* leave her alone.'

'If *who* leave her alone?'

'They came to our house. My God, the threats...'

'Who?'

'People from Westleigh, but I don't want to talk about it, not on the phone. Such strange things have been happening — silent phone calls, cars parked on the road, people watching us. Tim says I'm paranoid, but he's out at work all day. He doesn't see.'

'You don't work?'

'I'm self-employed when I'm lucky enough to have clients. I work from home.'

'Do you think we could meet?'

'I don't know. Tim doesn't trust journalists. Maybe I shouldn't have...'

'It really is important, Mrs...?'

'Smart, Heather Smart.'

'It really is important, Heather. I want to find out what's happening. Maybe I can help you and Wendy. I'd like to try. I promise I won't write anything without your agreement.'

'Well... yes then... I suppose I must.'

She gives me an address in a place called Rigg, a small town about thirty miles away, which is commuter country for the cities, and we agree to meet the next day.

'Tim will be at work; it'll be easier.'

I book a couple of nights in a cheap hotel. It's better than driving back and forth, and I'll need to stay if I'm to check things out properly.

Well, Liz did say not to worry about the expense.

Still, I think I'll call in at the office and check.

It's better to be safe than sorry where Liz is concerned.

She's in her office when I get there, but the blinds are drawn, and there's a sign on the door which says "DON'T DISTURB". It's not a sign you ignore. People have been fed through the shredder for intruding when that sign is on her door.

I look around. There's only Alice and Jon in the place, and Jon is concentrating, his bald head down, in deadline mode. Alice is 24, a graduate, and learning her job the hard way under Liz's uncompromising tutelage. Looking at her makes me feel old. It's not so much the ten years; it's the vitality and freshness and the enthusiasm and energy. Yeah, she makes me feel old — and tired.

'What's going on?' I ask her, nodding towards the cloistered office.

'Men and women in suits,' she whispers. 'Lawyers and money men.'

'The spawn of Satan,' I murmur.

She sidles across and leans on my desk, and I'm suddenly aware that her not-unattractive body is encroaching into my personal space. I feel an urgent need to focus on her eyes to avoid the temptation to focus elsewhere.

'What have you been up to?' she asks.

'What do you mean?'

'Your name was mentioned. They didn't sound pleased with you.'

I feel the colour rising to my cheeks, and anxiety sets my stomach nerves jangling. I try to control my face and make light of things. I laugh drily.

'What did they say?'

'I didn't hear much — just your name and the words "invasive and inappropriate inquiries". Tut-tut — it sounds like you've been a naughty boy, Philip, a very naughty boy.'

I cringe a little. I hate that kind of banter. I hate the words "naughty boy". There's something rather ugly about them, like they're vaguely, perversely sexual. Maybe I'm just a bit sensitive to language. It's like when people use "your" for "you're" and "should of", "would of", "could of".

Bugger "of"! I usually think.

I think I'll "bugger of" before the door opens and I find out what's going on. Alice wanders back over to her desk, dragging a train of perfumed air behind her, and I type a quick email to Liz, explaining what I'm doing and where I'm going.

I press 'send' and then pick up my laptop and phone and head for the door before anyone stops me. Half an hour later, I'm out of Sefton, heading west towards the little market town of Rigg. I accelerate. I pretend I've got to get there before it disappears forever, like those places on the East Coast that have fallen into the sea — or Brigadoon.

Sometimes, I worry about myself.

Chapter 9

I spend most of the short journey thinking about Liz and her visitors, as well as Winston, Benny, and Clive Wigmore. As I get nearer Rigg, I clear my head by trying to imagine what Heather and Tim Smart look like. Silly, I know, but it's just something I do; I do it with radio presenters too. I listen to the voices on Radio 4 and try to picture the speakers. Then I Google them to find out if I'm right — it's often a disappointment. They turn out to be 60, grey, and wrinkled; the men are even worse.

Their names aren't auspicious. Heather and Tim sound like characters from a 1980's sitcom about a middle-class couple living in suburbia. They're ineffectual and rather twee, with friends who are pretty much the same. They have dinner parties where no one is allowed to speak about anything interesting in case it becomes controversial. They live in a recently built, smart semi which is identical to all the other houses in a two-mile radius. Tim works in an office, and Heather does voluntary work when she isn't doing part-time secretarial work for a local builder who's very working class and common. They have two children, a boy and a girl, and a dog with large, adorable eyes and a cute nature; it's of an indeterminate breed. Heather is a bit scatty and silly, and Tim shakes his head a lot in a condescending sort of way, as if to say he knows what she's like, but he loves her all the same.

Like I say, I worry about myself sometimes.

When I've checked into my hotel (a nice, ordinary little pub just off the marketplace), I make my way to the town centre and turn, after a few yards, into the narrow street where Heather lives. Terraced houses front the road, and it's all bay windows, flower boxes, and hanging baskets. I figure I've got that wrong at least. Then I meet Heather, and the whole edifice I've constructed tumbles like a tower of cards. It's the Radio 4 presenters all over again.

She's about 30, wears a paint-stained smock, and has hair which springs from her head like an overgrown flowerbed.

'Sorry, I was in the studio,' she says, brushing aside a couple of weedy strands. 'God knows I've got enough to think about, but thinking doesn't pay the mortgage, does it? And I've got a commission. I just had to get on with it.'

'You're an artist,' I say before I've had time to stop myself, and then I wince. 'Sorry, blame busy roads and a difficult day. That was a singularly stupid statement. I'm Phil Tyler. We spoke on the phone.'

'Yes, come in.'

'Now I'm anticipating the house of an artist, untidy with books and papers scattered everywhere, flamboyant ornaments, and strange sculptures. Only, it isn't like that either. There are pictures alright, but they're delicate watercolours of flowers, animals, and birds. There are ornaments too, and sculptures and tasteful items of pottery, but it's all extraordinarily ordinary, right down to the family photos, the television, the magazines, and the flowers on the table and windowsill.

I like it. But then I would. I like homely and ordinary. It's my favourite style.

She motions me to sit down in an armchair by the stove and pushes some papers into my hand.

'Read these,' she says, 'while I brew coffee and make some sandwiches. You'll come for dinner too, won't you, if you don't need to go back? I told Tim I'd invite you, and he was okay about it, although he'll probably give you a bit of a grilling. Might as well be grilled over a salmon which has suffered a similar fate, don't you think?'

I think I nod. There's not really much else I can do.

'Are you staying over? I'd offer you our spare room, but we haven't got one. In the absence of a garage, we've filled it with junk.'

'So long as you haven't tried to park a car in it,' I manage to say. 'I'm booked in at a little hotel in the town centre. It's very pleasant.'

'Excellent,' she says. 'Now, will it be cheese, ham, or tuna?'

'Tuna would be nice,' I say, and I sit back and start to read. Heather disappears into the kitchen. I listen closely. No dog. No children either, though they could be at school or visiting friends, I suppose.

I'm not very good at my game.

I look round the room and there's this photograph above the fireplace which catches my attention and holds it like I've been deep frozen. It's a fair-haired young woman with the bluest eyes. She must be in her mid-twenties. I walk across to look at it more closely, and I know at once that it's Wendy, and I don't even know how I know. She's looking straight at me, and I know if I look any longer, I'll start to weave a story. It's that kind of face, the kind that draws you in and weaves a web around you, trapping you. It's a face I could fall for. It's the face of someone I want to help.

Fortunately, Heather backs through the door before I start to drool or, worse still, cry. I replace the photo and clear a small table for her to set the tray on. Over sandwiches and coffee, we start to talk, but not until Heather puts the photograph of Wendy right in front of me.

'This is Wendy. She's 28, bright, funny, sensitive, and terribly vulnerable; I don't want you to forget that. She isn't just an article for your paper. Will you promise me?'

'I promise,' I tell her, and I mean it.

'I don't want you writing anything disrespectful about her.'

'I won't.'

'Only, you hear such stories...'

'I promise.'

'Have you read my notes?'

'Yes. It's one hell of a story. But there's something I don't understand — about her parents and how they died. I thought you said you and Wendy were sisters?'

'We're cousins, really; she came to live with us after her parents died. My mum and dad adopted her. I've always thought of her as my sister.'

'I see. And their death — the manner of their death — that was responsible for the state of her mental health?'

'Yes.'

'It's hardly surprising, is it? That's a hell of a weight to carry.'

'She's spent a lot of time in clinics. Nothing seemed to work. Maybe that's why Westleigh. A last resort.'

'Quite.' I look at the notes again. 'But she was found...'

'Like you wrote on Facebook, yes. It was just like the man you described.'

I skim through the notes.

'The only difference I can see is that she was rescued by a compassionate lady who saw her from the window of her cottage. The guy in Sefton hasn't been seen since.'

'We weren't allowed to visit her at Westleigh or even phone her. They said it was part of the treatment. I don't understand what happened, Mr Tyler. I mean, what were they doing to her? How did she end up walking a country lane at that time of night? I asked the clinic, but it was a waste of time. They kept talking about confidentiality agreements and gagging orders and all sorts of things we were supposed to have signed. They say we've got to send her back because she hasn't finished her treatment and that it could be very dangerous for her. They say we have no choice — that they'll take us to court and force us.'

'But you haven't sent her back?'

'I don't trust them. I don't like them. They said they could sue us and take our house away. Why would they threaten us like that if there was nothing to hide?'

'You sent her somewhere else, somewhere safe?'

'Yes, I won't be bullied, and I won't let them hurt her.'

'Did you contact the police?'

'The police aren't interested. I know this will sound silly, but I think they were *told* to back off.'

'And you think you're being watched?'

'More than watched — intimidated. Tim says I'm paranoid, but I know they're out there.'

I read the notes again. Her mother and stepfather and both her little brothers were murdered. Jesus, how do you get over something like that? Fourteen years ago — that's not a long time, is it? Not really, not for something like that.

'There's something I haven't written down,' Heather says. She pauses to take a deep breath. 'It was her biological father who killed them. He couldn't cope with the separation and divorce. He'd been stalking Lisa, Wendy's mother, for months. Then one evening — it was 21 October, a Thursday — he broke in and killed them. Then he killed himself. Wendy had no one left, so she moved in with us until she went to university.'

'It must've been difficult for all of you. I mean, that's one hell of an elephant to have in the room.'

'We tried really hard, but what she wanted — what she really wanted — we couldn't give her. Her whole life had changed, and she could never go back, and the future she'd always imagined had gone too. I think that was worse, imagining life without her family.' She pauses. Her hands are trembling, and she brushes away a tear. 'It was Wendy who found them,' she says.

I can't think of suitable words. I just stare. It's awful.

'She'd been staying with me that night. She'd often sleep over if we'd been out in those days. She found them when she got home from school the next day.'

'I can't begin to imagine...' I start to say, but then I stop because, yes, I can imagine it — only too clearly. I can feel an echo, a reverberation of the nightmare she faced when she opened the door and a normal homecoming was instantly and irredeemably transformed.

'Jesus,' I murmur.

And I feel an outflow of sympathy and sorrow coursing like a wave — a really big wave — a tidal bore.

'We thought she was getting over it, especially when she went to university. We hoped maybe she'd meet someone and live a happy life, you know? She did have one relationship with a guy called Adam, a third-year Physics student, but he couldn't cope with her insecurity and her changing moods. They were together for over a year, but, eventually, he left her. It hurt her a lot; it was another loss — another tragedy, you know.'

'When was that?'

'About a year and a half ago; a few months later, her doctor arranged for her to be admitted to a clinic. We visited whenever we could. It was nice — very caring. They tried hard to help her, but nothing seemed to work.'

'And she was transferred to Westleigh.'

Heather pauses as if to collect and sort her words like shells on a beach. 'Yes. Wendy said she was going away — going to get herself well and start a new life. She was excited and kept talking about this great opportunity she'd been given.'

'And when she turned up again, how was she?'

'It was like meeting a different person. She barely recognised us. There were days when she didn't seem to know us at all. She kept talking about people we didn't know: a friend, Sasha, and a man she'd met called Marcus. Sometimes, she looked straight at me but didn't see me. It was as if she was talking to someone who wasn't there.'

Heather wipes a tear away and busies herself with the tea tray. I think I'll leave now and give her a chance to recover before the ordeal of dinner and Tim. My brain is vibrating, and I have that dizzy, unfocused feeling you get on a long journey — only without the journey. I check what time Heather wants me back, and we agree on 7.30. That gives me time to do a write-up, take a quick nap, and check my emails. Maybe I'll hear back from "anxious.nurse". I need to contact Liz too.

Only, I sleep rather longer than I planned, and, by the time I phone the office, there's no one there. Liz must have called it a day and gone home. When I check my inbox, it's disappointingly empty — nothing from the nurse. Even the spam folder has nothing in it. I apply my technological skill and come up with the only solution I'm capable of: something somewhere must be 'down' — whatever that means.

I just have time to take a shower and put on something clean before I head out to meet Tim. I feel like a gladiator preparing for a fight to the death. I take a few deep breaths and then, armed with my laptop and my approachable, trustworthy manner, I'm ready to go.

Chapter 10

It's gone nine, dinner is over, and Tim is still looking at me like I'm there to steal the silver or kidnap the kids. While Heather chats away, telling me about her school days with Wendy, Tim eyes me suspiciously and says very little. It's as if there's a price tag attached to every word, and I'm not worth the expense. He's decided he doesn't like me enough to pay for complete sentences, and he doesn't trust me enough to tell me anything.

'What do you do, Tim?'

'Computer repairs and web design.'

'Is it interesting work?

'Not really.'

'Who do you work for?'

'Me.'

'Self-employed, eh? Have you been doing it long?'

'Yes.'

'Have you lived here long?'

'Since we got married.'

'It's a nice house.'

'It's okay.'

Eventually, I give up and talk to Heather.

'You have children?' I ask.

There are photos displayed around the room of two boys. I guess they must be about 3 in the most recent ones. Tim's eyes narrow. He's wondering if this is a ploy to get information so I can sneak back later when everyone's asleep...

'Yes, Ben and Aaron — they're twins. They're with their grandparents tonight. I thought it would be more peaceful without them here. They're both very fond of Wendy, especially Ben.'

'We're all fond of her,' says Tim.

It sounds like a warning, and the look he gives me should be accompanied by lightning.

I don't ask many questions about Wendy. I figure it's better not to give Tim the ammunition. Maybe if I don't say much, he'll relax — if he knows how — and see what a nice, trustworthy guy I am. Anyway, I don't need to ask anything. Heather tells me everything I want to know and a great deal more. By the time dessert arrives, I feel as if I've known Wendy for years. I feel as if I know all of them.

I like them.

Except Tim.

He's not the likeable sort. He's got the protective-brother-act down to a tee, even though he isn't her brother. I can't help but wonder if maybe there's something not altogether brotherly about his attitude to Wendy. Is Tim part of the solution or part of the problem? He tries to sound like he cares, but there's something I don't trust. As we sit with a couple of beers in the darkening room, the conversation moves to recent times.

'The people from Westleigh were scary,' Heather says. 'They tried everything to make us send her back. At first, it was all about poor Wendy, and how they wanted to meet her needs — about the radical new treatments they used and about how they just needed a few more weeks and then we'd see a difference. When that didn't work, they brought in a couple of solicitors brandishing agreements signed by Wendy. They said we had no rights — that they were representing Wendy's interests, and they had documents to prove it. They said they'd get a court order and take her by force if necessary. They said it was for her own safety.

'I told them I'd write to the radio and television and every newspaper I could think of. I said I'd splash Westleigh all over Twitter and Facebook. If they wanted to take Wendy away, I warned them, they'd better be ready for a fight. By the time they left, I was screaming at them, and our neighbours were watching from their windows.'

'They didn't like that,' Tim mumbles.

'The older man muttered something to his colleague, and they headed for their car, but the younger man wanted the last word. He smiled — not a nice smile at all. *Don't underestimate us, Mrs Smart,* he said. *This isn't over. You have no idea who you're dealing with.*

'The older man snapped something at him, then they got in their car and drove away.'

'Where was Wendy while this was happening?'

'She was up in her room, but we didn't tell them that. She spent a lot of time there, just staring at the ceiling. On bad days, it was like she was asleep with her eyes open.

'And on good days?' I ask.

'On good days, I had my friend back... or part of her. We'd talk about the past and she'd remember something we'd done or somewhere we'd been. Once, she remembered a holiday we had together — me, Wendy, Mum, and Dad — at Keswick in the Lake District. She remembered how we walked the lakeside and the hills, and how the weather was beautiful all week. But even then, she sounded like she was looking back at her life from far away — like it was dissolving into mist.'

She wipes away a tear, and Tim takes her hand and holds it; only, I get the feeling this timely show of affection is for my benefit. His eyes have that sneaky, dark look I associate with police mugshots.

'After those horrid lawyers,' Heather continues, 'we decided to find Wendy somewhere where they could really help her — somewhere she'd be safe.' She turns to Tim. 'You weren't sure it was the right decision, were you?'

Tim goes a funny shade of red. The look he flashes at Heather could shatter window glass.

'We needed to consider all the options, that's all,' he mutters.

'But I'd made my mind up,' Heather says.

'And the Westleigh people left you alone?'

'They've never been back, not to the house anyway. But...'

She glances at Tim as if for support.

'But...?' I ask.

'The Facebook Pages I started, the Tweets I sent, and the emails — everything — it was as if they never existed. I never got a reply... not once. That's right, isn't it, Tim?'

Tim looks irritable, like he's being forced to tell me things he doesn't want to.

'Nothing,' he mutters without looking up.

'You think maybe they hacked into your computer?'

'I don't know.'

'Blocked you somehow?'

Tim shrugs.

'There's something else,' Heather adds.

'Go on.'

'Tim says I'm paranoid, but I'm sure we're being watched. Sometimes, I catch a glimpse, but only a glimpse, of people walking behind me or sitting in cars. I daren't use the phone or the computer. They're everywhere, watching everything and listening all the time.'

'If that's the case, they'll know I'm here.'

'Yes, I'm sorry.'

'Don't be. But I don't know why they'd be watching. What do they expect to see?'

'That's what I said,' Tim tells me. 'There's no reason to.'

'Maybe they're worried Wendy told me something.'

'Like what?' Tim says. 'There's nothing to tell. It was a clinic, for God's sake.'

'Like what they're hiding,' I suggest, 'like what happened to her.'

'You're as bad as her,' he snaps. 'You're paranoid, the pair of you.'

We're silent for a moment.

'Can I meet Wendy?' I ask.

'No,' Tim says sharply.

'Yes,' says Heather, and she gives him one of those stares only women can give. She turns back to me. 'We have to trust you. We need help.'

Tim doesn't look too pleased, but Heather's word is final. I get this irresistible urge to smile.

'When?'

'Tomorrow morning - Come here at ten o'clock and I'll take you.'

'*We'll* take you,' Tim says. 'I'll take the morning off.'

When I get back to the hotel, it's past midnight.

Chapter 11

At about two o'clock, I wake up, and I hear someone at the door.

'Yes? Who is it?'

'I'm sorry to bother you, Mr Tyler. It's hotel security. Can I speak to you for a moment?'

I'm still half asleep, which probably accounts for the fact that I answer the door without allowing my brain to participate in the decision-making process. I mean, this is a ten-bedroom hotel in Rigg, not The Hilton. Security? The only security in this place is the lock on the front door and the landlord's poodle. Unfortunately, my power of rational decision making doesn't kick in in time to stop me granting admittance to a serious-looking guy wearing jeans, a t-shirt, swastika tattoos, and a really nasty look.

He doesn't introduce himself, and, five minutes later, I'm lying against the wall, curled in a ball. I can't breathe, I'm bleeding, and I think I'm going to die. There's a broken chair on the floor, broken ribs on me, and some moron in the next room banging on the wall, telling me to shut up because he's trying to sleep. If I had the power of speech, I'd answer.

I crawl into a seated position and reach for the phone to call the police. Then I change my mind and put it down again. I need to think. His words are still ringing in my ears, which are already doing a good job of ringing on their own account.

'Go home, Mr Tyler. Go home and don't come back. We won't tell you twice.'

With that, he'd left.

I crawl to my bed, curl like a foetus, and don't move. I'm pretending to think, but I'm actually waiting for the guy next door to tell me my heart's beating too loud and that he can hear me breathing. I can't think straight.

Who was he? Who was he working for? How did he know I was here?

Couldn't he have offered me money instead of wading in with his fists and feet?

It takes a while for me to sequence a few answers — long after I've moved painfully into a seated position on the bedside. Let's assume he didn't just pick me out on the street because he didn't like my face. Let's make a giant leap and imagine he planned to attack me and has a good reason for it. Let's say he works for Logrum and that he's paid to be a bastard. Let's also assume that his employers want me to back off. That must mean... yeah, I must be getting close enough to nip their ankles.

That should make me feel better, but it doesn't.

This is a warning. They're telling me they're losing patience and my prying has to stop.

Another thought lumbers through my brain, knocking things over to make room for itself.

What happens if I don't back off?

I don't even want to think about that.

I stand up, hobble over to the mini-bar, and pour myself a drink. Then I pour another and another. After the fourth, I throw up, go back to bed, and, despite the objections my brain raises, I fall asleep.

Over breakfast, I have to explain to an over-solicitous host that when I was out last night, I tripped over an uneven kerbstone and fell. Maybe I should add that I was then run over by a lorry while I was lying in the road. The look he's giving me says he knows the truth because he's seen it all before — a businessman on an away day who leaves the wife at home and goes out and drinks too much, then comes back and empties the mini-bar, falls over in the shower, and cracks his head. He pretends to be sympathetic, but I can see he's got me down as one of those losers trying to locate their lost youth. The broken chair doesn't help.

So I have to prove I'm not like that by eating a hearty breakfast and smiling a lot. Then I retire to my room, let the smile slip, throw up again, and phone Liz.

An unfamiliar male voice answers, and it sounds impatient, like it's got better things to do than answer phone calls, even in a newsroom.

'Yes?'

'Can I speak to Liz?'

There's a pause that is just long enough to make me nervous.

'Liz isn't here. Can I take a message?'

The accent is American, and, for a moment, I think I'm talking to Clive Wigmore. But the tone isn't as deep. It has that familiarity you get from watching too many gangster films. I always associate it with New York — or is it Chicago?

'Where is she?'

'Who's speaking?'

'It's important I contact her. Have you got a mobile number?'

That's just a ploy. I've got her number on my phone. All her journalists have it. Like I said, Liz exerts close control.

If this guy has her number, he's not inclined to say.

'Mr Tyler, is it?' he asks, and his tone sharpens like knapped flint.

'I need to speak to Liz.'

'That won't be possible. Liz is under suspension pending an inquiry into certain financial irregularities.'

My blood is pulsing, and I feel as if I'm swaying. This is plain crazy. Liz is the single most honest person I've ever met. She even signs for office pens. She's so careful with money, we joke that she rations toilet paper.

'Irregularities?'

'I can't divulge their precise nature.'

'No, I'll bet you can't. I bet someone's scurrying around right now, faking a paper trail.'

'I want you back in the office, Mr Tyler. We have things to discuss.'

'Like what?'

The voice slows to a drawl.

'Drive back today. Let's say 4 pm, shall we?'

'I'm in the middle of something. I can't just up and leave.'

He isn't listening. He drones his message, robot style.

'Your current investigation is at an end. You're to come back at once.'

'Who says so?'

'Your employers say so, Mr Tyler — the people who pay your wages.'

'Liz is my boss.'

He laughs. It's not a nice sound; it's a bit like a rattlesnake.

'Liz is just a very small cog in a very large set of wheels, Mr Tyler. Imagine how small that makes you.'

Suddenly, I'm out of control. It's like the anger I always feel when the big guy tramples on the little guy just because he can. It's like school bullies all over again. I hated it then, and I hate it now, and, suddenly, I don't care how big they think they are.

'It's about Westleigh, isn't it? Someone's pulling your strings.'

'Your inquiries in Rigg are over, Mr Tyler; be here at four o'clock.'

'The guy last night... did you know about that?'

'I don't know what you're talking about.'

'Some thug was sent to kick the shit out of me — to warn me off.'

'That's nothing to do with me, Mr Tyler. I'm just a newspaper man like you. People pay my wages, and I do what I'm asked.'

'You're nothing like me.'

There's a pause. I think he's measuring his words down to the nearest gram.

'No, perhaps I'm not. Four o'clock.'

'I have some unfinished business here. I'll be back tomorrow.'

'Then I'm afraid I must break some bad news to you, Mr Tyler. The newspaper has changed hands. Negotiations have been ongoing for some time, so don't try to turn it into a conspiracy. There has been some inevitable rationalisation in staffing. Your contract has been terminated. Given your attitude, I suggest you take one month's salary in lieu of notice. You can clear your desk when you get back.'

I suffer a momentary loss of control, and I tell him what he can do with his month's notice. It's not very literate, I admit, but it expresses my state of mind succinctly enough, especially when I conclude, *if you think you can stop me, then you really don't get it. I wouldn't stop now if you sent a whole army of thugs.*

The phone goes dead and my anger subsides; it is replaced firstly by doubt and then by fear. I wonder if that momentary bravado was quite the tone I was aiming for. It's a flaw in my character, I know it is, and I've regretted it on more than one occasion. Someone with a pathological fear of pain shouldn't lower their head, bellow like a bull, and then charge at the nearest wall. I mean, it doesn't make sense, nor is it sensible for me to make threats when my usual response to violence is to roll over like a puppy and whimper.

If you think you can stop me, then you really don't get it. I wouldn't stop now if you sent a whole army of thugs.

Did I really say that? I get the feeling these guys could squash me between a finger and thumb like a beetle. It's like I'm threatening a lightning bolt with a toy sword.

I need someone tough on my side so I can be aggressive by proxy. That's how I work best — by hiding behind someone strong and peering out. The toughest person I know is Liz, and she'll be feeling seriously pissed off if she thinks there's a conspiracy to silence her. These guys obviously haven't done their homework. If there's anything in this world guaranteed to put Liz into attack mode, it's someone telling her she's got to stop.

I mean, red rag to a bull or what?

I'm about to try her home number when I think better of it. Suddenly, I see conspiracies all around me. I don't trust my phone, I don't trust my laptop, and I don't trust Liz's phone or laptop either. In the modern age, that just about rules out any communication at all unless it's face to face. Even face to face might be problematic, though. They're probably watching us both.

My options are limited.

There doesn't seem to be much I can do, especially since I'm in Rigg, she's in Sefton, and neither of us has a job.

To hell with it, I think. I'll see Wendy tomorrow, and then I'll head home and work it out from there.

Chapter 12

It's eleven o'clock. We're at the entrance to the clinic where Wendy is being treated — me, Heather, and Terrible Tim. There aren't any locked gates here — no walls, no razor wire — just an entrance opening smoothly into a reception area, where a young woman behind a semi-circular desk stands up to welcome us. The whole place is bright and cool, and there are flowers with soft, sweet scents.

With my bruised face and unsteady walk, I feel like I'm bringing something into the place which would be better left outside. The smell of witch hazel doesn't help. Heather doused my bruises with it before we set out. Tim doused me with a look which said *you should've kept out of it; this serves you right.* No sympathy there.

I want to apologise to the young woman, but she stifles her initial reaction and produces a smile for me like a magician with a bunch of flowers. Then it fades like lukewarm applause and is replaced by something more sincere for Heather and Tim.

She's called Lorraine. I know that because she has a badge with her name on it pinned on her left breast. I read it quickly and turn away so as not to look as if I'm ogling.

Lorraine leads us down an immaculately white corridor (more flowers, photographs, and paintings, which are all bright and cheerful). I feel like the walls are smiling at me.

'Wendy is making good progress,' she beams. 'For the last two days, she hasn't left us at all. She's been talking about you, Heather, and about the past. She even spoke about her parents for a while. She's eating better too.'

Heather looks pleased; she's collecting straws of hope and this is a winter cornfield.

'She's in the sun lounge,' Lorraine says. 'She likes looking out over the lawns and flowerbeds, especially when the sun is shining like it is this morning. She was looking at a book earlier.'

'Really?' Heather reaches out and grasps another straw. 'Oh, that's good; that's really good. She used to read all the time.'

'She only looked at the pages for a few minutes, but it's a step forward,' Lorraine smiles, 'another small step.'

We pause outside a lounge where I count five people sitting in armchairs. I prepare a friendly smile, but no one pays us any attention, so we walk through double doors into a sun lounge. Sitting beside the window, in half profile, is a young woman, and, as we enter, she turns towards us, and her face brightens in a soft smile.

It's one of those moments.

Words just won't do it.

She rises from her chair as if gravity has no hold on her and flits across to Heather. Flits? Wendy is a butterfly. I mean, a shadow has more substance. A seed head is less fragile.

And that smile — I want it all to myself.

'This is our friend, Phil,' Heather says, and those pale blue eyes turn on me, and I feel like this is my moment in the sun.

And she smiles.

Oh Lord.

I've got to get a grip before I go weak at the knees or say something really foolish, so I just hold out a hand and enfold hers. I expect her to dissolve like mist under my touch. I think I just say 'Hi.'

'Shall we walk in the garden?' she says, and she opens the door and steps outside into the warm, summer air, drawing Heather behind her. I follow a few steps after. Tim is behind me, and I feel his eyes on me. I get the feeling he's just waiting for me to put one foot wrong.

Just one word, Tyler, just one word...

'Look at these flowers,' Wendy says, and she brushes her hand against them. 'I love flowers, don't you?' She turns and looks at me, but I only have time to smile before she turns away and starts talking to Heather. 'Do you remember...?'

And the two of them are on a journey into the past, and I feel as if I'm losing her in some strange way. Then she stops and reaches for a summer rose. She touches its petals and bends towards the scent.

'Marcus loved flowers,' she says softly.

'Marcus?' I ask.

Heather shakes her head, and Tim steps closer to my shoulder, going into protective, alpha-male mode.

'I miss him,' she says to Heather, and her eyes mist. 'I know... I know he's part of my past now. I have to move forward, but it's hard... so hard. When I lost him... when I had to choose... it was the hardest thing I've ever done. Sometimes, I wonder if I was right...'

'You were right,' Heather says, and she slips her arm around her waist. 'You know you were right.'

'Yes, yes, I know... but we were happy, you know — happier than I've ever been since Mum and Dad, and...'

'You're here with us, and we can look forward to the future together, can't we?'

The look of pain on her face is so sudden and deep, it sends shock waves through me.

'Do you know,' she suddenly smiles, 'during all the weeks we were together, I don't think it rained once — perhaps in the evening, though I'm not sure — yes, perhaps in the evening... but never in the daytime.'

I can't help it. I have to speak.

'What happened?'

Behind me, I feel Tim grow tense, and he steps so close, I can feel his breath on my ear.

'I woke one morning and he was gone. He left because I sent him away. I couldn't go with him, you see. I thought I could, but I couldn't. I thought I could give up everything for him... but I couldn't...'

The sun dips behind a cloud, and the air ripples with a chill that makes me shiver. It only lasts a moment, but it's like a spell has broken. We wander on across the lawns and between the flowerbeds, and we sit for a while on a bench beneath an oak tree. Then we head back to sit in the sun lounge, and, all the time, it's like I can't take my eyes off her.

Heather doesn't talk about the future. She talks about the past and about the present. Tim rarely says anything, and when he does speak, he follows Heather's lead and grunts supportive monosyllables. It's like he's treading through a colony of birds, watching every step so as not to step on eggs or young.

Wendy doesn't look at him — not once.

I don't think she likes him... or trusts him.

Or maybe I just want to believe that.

'The future makes her sad,' Heather tells me later when we're driving back. 'It's like a long straight road which goes on and on forever, and she knows that every step takes her further away from Marcus. She can't face that prospect — not yet.'

'So you lead her a few faltering steps each day and hope that time...'

'Gradually, she'll leave the past behind. She's come a long way already.'

I'm struggling with some pretty powerful emotions at the moment, and I feel as if I need to dig my nails into my palm so the pain can keep me on track. I want to wrestle with cable ties until my wrists bleed like in spy films.

'What do you know about Marcus?'

'He's an executive in some media business — that's what Wendy told us. He's American and quite wealthy, I think. He wanted her to move with him back to The States. I think he really cared for her, you know. He paid for her treatment.'

'She didn't want to go with him?'

'She couldn't go through with it. It was like he was asking her to turn her back on the past — on her mum, her family, and her memories — the good and bad. She couldn't do it.'

'Is that what she said?'

'It's how we've pieced things together.'

'We can't just wade in asking questions,' Tim says.

'No, I guess not. She'll tell you in her own time, I suppose.'

Tim frowns, and his hands tighten on the wheel.

I'm trying really hard not to say too much because I like Heather, and I don't want to worry her. But doesn't she know how phoney this sounds? I mean, let's take it one step at a time. How does someone moving in Wendy's circle meet someone like Marcus — a senior executive? I picture him with a yacht and a million-dollar lifestyle. And why would he fall for her? I'm willing to admit that Wendy could have someone like me crawling on their knees, but I'm a mug for a story like hers when it's told by someone like her. I've got a track record of emotional entanglements and romantic failures.

But this Marcus guy? No. No way.

He has to be a con man, doesn't he?

But why would a con man target Wendy? And what sort of a con man would pay for her to attend an exclusive clinic and then leave, never to be seen again?

Was he just some sexual predator with a big smile and an all-too-plausible tale to tell? Maybe, but it just doesn't feel right.

And then there's Tim; where does he fit into all this? He's hiding something, I'm sure of it.

There's a whole battalion of questions about Westleigh forming ranks in front of me. I mean, people must come and go in a place like that — they sign in then sign out, start a treatment then give it up, and climb on the wagon then fall off again. You don't see security staff scouring the countryside trying to force them back, do you? So why did they go after Wendy? Why the lawyers and why the threats? What's the great mystery that makes them send out some gangster to beat up a small-town journalist and frame his editor because they've asked a few questions?

A thought stomps, heavy footed, through my mind. Was Marcus hired to find a vulnerable young woman for some nefarious purpose?

I shake the thought away.

'For God's sake,' I mutter.

'What's the matter?' Tim asks.

'I'm trying to make sense of it. I can't.'

'If we leave her alone, she'll be alright.'

'You think the Westleigh people will leave her alone?'

'They can't get to her anymore. She's safe.'

'I wish I shared your optimism.'

His attitude is really starting to get to me. I decide silence is probably best, especially since he's driving, and I don't want to walk. Heather turns to face me.

'What will you do now?' she asks.

I glance at Tim. I think the answer he's looking for is, *go home and do nothing*. But the look he gives me makes me reckless.

'I'll take a closer look at Westleigh. And I'll find out what I can about this Marcus guy. I mean, how many media executives called Marcus can there be? Don't worry, I'll tread lightly.'

'Make sure you do,' says Tim.

When we get back to their house, he doesn't invite me in, and I think I'll save Heather the embarrassment of fumbling for an excuse, so I tell her I need to get back to the hotel and phone the office. I leave before I'm tempted to plant something that isn't a kiss on Tim's suspicious face.

By the time I get back to my room, I've got this idea swimming round my head like a shark, and there are lots of little fish swimming round it like question marks, circling and darting everywhere. To begin with, I need to see Wendy again, and this time I need to be on my own.

I figure I'll ask Heather since I don't want to go behind her back. I reckon she'll trust me. I want to call her now, while I'm feeling persuasive, but I think I'll wait until tomorrow — when Tim's at work.

Chapter 13

Heather is easily convinced. I think I'm the basket to which she's trusting all her eggs.

'I won't tell Tim,' she says, 'until later. It's nothing personal. He's just...'

'He's very protective of Wendy,' I suggest. 'I understand.'

I keep my real thoughts to myself.

'She's a little distant this morning,' Lorraine says when I arrive at the clinic. 'She might not have much to say.'

Wendy is in the sun lounge again. She seems pleased when the nurse tells her she's got a visitor, but it's pretty clear she has no idea who I am and that yesterday might as well be last year. I feel a moment of despondency, but what did I expect? I'm just not that memorable, even to women who haven't got Wendy's problems. Christ, even my mum forgets my name. She calls me Brian — that's her brother. He's 50, fat, bald, and boring.

Anyway, I settle down in a wicker chair close to Wendy, and we stay like that for an hour. Occasionally, she looks at me, and that sad smile flickers, but then her eyes drift away into some private world. Another half hour passes. The nurse appears with tea and biscuits. She persuades Wendy to try something. She lifts a biscuit obediently and raises it to her lips. When the nurse leaves, she replaces it on the plate. Then she looks up at me and it's different, like she's seeing me for the first time.

'Thank you, Mr Tyler,' she says softly.

'For what?' I ask.

'For the silence; I was in the garden, listening to the birds and the insects. People don't always understand. They try to fetch me back. But it was so nice out there and so warm, watching the bees with their little nectar sacks. You came before, didn't you, with Heather?'

'Yesterday,' I remind her.

'Was that only yesterday? I thought... but never mind. It's good of you to come and see me.'

She stands up, glides to the French windows, and opens them wide. The warm air flies in like it's been waiting for just this moment. When she sits down again, she breathes deeply and sighs, and then she falls away into silence.

Five minutes pass.

'I was very unhappy, you know,' she says. 'Heather was very kind. Everyone was very kind, but after my family... after they all died... I was so empty. It was as if there was a crack in me, and all the love they poured in just leaked away. I had no reason to live.'

'Was that when you met Marcus?'

'Marcus, yes — he gave me back my life, I think.'

She shivers as if the breeze has stroked the surface of her bare flesh. There's a shawl on the table beside her, and, for want of anything else to do or say, I pick it up and lay it over her shoulders.

'Thank you,' she smiles.

'I feel kind of helpless,' I say at last. 'I want to help you. I want to talk to you, but I don't know what to say.' I gesture hopelessly. 'I just want to understand.'

Shit, that's so useless. Why can't I tell her I don't want to spend precious hours hopping around subjects like I'm trying to avoid ants? Why can't I say that if I'm to really, truly understand, I need her to talk to me?

I guess I know the answer. It takes time to build that sort of trust. She won't just open her heart to some guy she's met once, no matter how much he wishes she would — no matter how little time he's got before he's got to leave. It's too much to expect. I wonder what I hoped for when I came here this morning. Did I think that when we were alone, without Heather and Tim, she'd look into my eyes, read my soul, and tell me everything?

That's Mills and Boon.

It's pathetic.

'Tim found the clinic for me,' she says suddenly. 'I'd forgotten. Yes, it was Tim. We didn't tell Heather, though.'

'I thought Marcus paid for your treatment.'

'Yes, he did. I remember that too.'

'Did Tim ever meet Marcus?'

'Of course not,' she laughs lightly. 'What a strange idea. Tim would have spoiled everything.'

'When did you meet Marcus?'

'I think perhaps I was in the clinic... but no, it must have been earlier. I don't know; everything's such a jumble. I sometimes think my mind is like a cluttered drawer that I've emptied onto the floor. Everything is there — Heather, Tim, the Clinic, Marcus, doctors, nurses, and you — but it needs sorting. I need to gather things together and put them in the right place.'

'Why did Tim find you a clinic?'

She frowns, thinking hard.

'I can't remember. I was unhappy — very unhappy. I think the shadow I cast over all their lives — Tim, Heather, and the children — became too much for them. I was glad to go away. I wanted so much to get better and to go back to how I was before.'

'But Marcus paid for everything.'

'Yes, I'm sure of that. I wish you could have met Marcus. You would have liked him. He was like you in many ways — kind and thoughtful. *He* knew the importance of silence too.'

There are tears on her cheeks, and I think I've asked enough.

'I'll have to leave soon,' I say. 'Shall we walk in the garden for a while?'

She wipes away a tear and smiles, and we spend half an hour just talking about flowers, birds, insects, and old memories.

Then it's time to go.

'You will come again,' she says.

'Of course,' I tell her, 'if you'd like me to.' I fumble in my wallet and pull out a card. Then I root for a pen. I cross out the work number on the front and scribble my mobile on the back. I give her the card, and, as I do, I'm thinking, *what the hell are you doing? Why would she want that? She'll just put it aside and forget about it the moment you leave. You're hopeless, Phil Tyler, you know that?*

But I press it in her hand anyway.

'If you need anything, or if you want to talk to me, just call. I'll be there to help you. Okay?'

'Okay.'

Then I'm leaving, and when I take a last look, it's like I'm watching mist evaporate in the sun.

I spend the journey back trying not to think, but it's like telling a burst pipe not to spill water. I think I'd better call in on Heather and let her know the morning went okay, but she's not in, and I'm kind of relieved because that means I can go back to the hotel and lie down. I need to organise the jumble of thoughts and feelings that make up this mush inside my head. What was it Wendy said? *Like a cluttered drawer emptied on the carpet.* Yeah, that's pretty much how I feel.

An hour later, I've just got a grip on reality when the phone rings, and it all goes to hell again.

It's Winston.

Chapter 14

'Where the hell are you, man? You've got to get back here. I've found Benny. You've got to see what those bastards have done to him.'

'Slow down, Winston. What do you mean you found Benny?'

'He's got God, man,' he says, like God is an illness or something. 'I mean, it's totally unreal.'

'You're making no sense. Start at the beginning.'

'I call at his flat, yeah? I call at his flat every day, but there's no one there. I go around the pubs and clubs, the snooker hall, the betting shops — nothing. He's vanished; it's like he doesn't exist. No one's seen him, no one's heard from him, no one knows anyone who's seen him. I leave messages — still nothing. Then I'm walking past that church in the town centre, the one with the tower where we went at Christmas back in Primary School and sung carols. Do you remember that? Top-class kids used to read stuff out — I never understood it.'

'Get to the point, Winston. My battery will run out.'

'Well, I'm walking past those big, wooden doors when one opens, and this guy walks out wearing a shirt and tie and these neat trousers. He's carrying a jacket over his arm, and he's with this other guy who looks like he shops at the same store. They look like those Moron guys — you know what I'm saying?'

'I think you mean Mormons, Winston.'

'Yeah, Morons, like I said. Only, one of them looks kind of familiar, so I stop and watch. It's Benny, man.'

'Benny was wearing a suit?'

'Yeah, that's what I thought — mysterious. It gets worse, man. He's had a haircut; it's short and neat like it's been done at a hairdresser's, and he's shaved. I mean, shit, Benny only shaves on Friday nights, and only if we're going out on the town. Anyway, he sees me and he steps across, and he's got these black, shiny shoes — polished. I mean, who the hell polishes shoes? Benny sure doesn't. And he takes hold of my hand, and he shakes it like I'm a long-lost friend.

'"Winston," he says, "I've so much to tell you. So much has happened."

'"You don't need to tell me that," I tell him. "Shit, man, what's happened to you? What the hell is going on?"

'He winces like I've breathed something nasty on him.

'"You should try not to swear, Winston," he says.

'"What the hell…?" I say.

'He draws back like I've hit him.

'"People might hear you. It makes you sound common, Winston."

'"Get the hell out of here," I say to him. "You've got a mouth like a drain. You're like one of those fucking fat-balls that clog the sewers. What are you talking about?"

'And each time I swear, it's like I've jabbed his face, and he has this pained look.

'"You're outside the House of God, Winston," he says.

'"I don't care if I'm driving the Popemobile," I tell him. "Come on, Benny. Let's ditch this stiff and go get a drink."

'"I don't drink — not any more. I've got a new life, Winston, and new friends. I've found God."

'"We'll call at the Police Station and hand him in — on our way to the pub. Come on, Benny, I want to know what happened."

'"I've found God; that's what's happened."

'"What about the job out at Westleigh?" I don't want to say much in front of the other guy. He doesn't look like he'd understand burglary.

'Benny just shakes his head.

'"That was in a different life, Winston," he says. "I'm a changed man."

'Well, that sure is some understatement.

'"I've got to go, Winston. We have things to do — God's work, you know."

'The other guy looks at his watch, then he looks at me like I've crawled out of a drain.

'"What are you looking at, dickhead?" I say to him. "What've you done to my friend?" He just looks away.

'"I've got to go," Benny says.

'"I'll call at the flat later," I tell him, "when you're on your own."

'"I don't live there now," he says. "I live with my new friends — with Daniel and Sarah and the others. Here." He slips a card from his pocket and hands it to me. "Come and join us."

'Then he shakes my hand, and, a minute later, he's gone. I look at the card. It's some mission near the River Bridge, down those streets near the new industrial estate.

'I tell you, Phil, they did something to him out at that hall. I know they did. He broke into that house and someone found him, and they did something to him.'

'Did you go and see him at this mission?'

'They wouldn't let me in. It was just this terraced house, down one of those streets they haven't demolished yet. This big guy stopped me at the door and made it really clear I wasn't wanted.'

'Did you ask him if it was a race thing?'

'This isn't funny, man. They've changed him. They've made him clean and... they've made him happy. You've got to get back and help me put this straight.'

I tell him I'll get back as soon as I can; then the inevitable happens.

My battery dies.

Chapter 15

After dinner that evening, I spend an hour in the bar. I'm reading the newspaper I used to work for, but it's difficult to muster interest, and I soon give up. Eventually, I give up on thinking too. Then I give up on the bar and head for my room. The trouble is I know what I need to do. I just don't want to do it. My knees are trembling just thinking about it, and I reckon a panic attack is imminent.

I can't put it off forever, though. It's got to be done.

Maybe tomorrow.

But that doesn't work anymore. It's got to be tonight. I have to get back to Sefton tomorrow afternoon to see Winston and Benny, and I can't afford to spend any longer in Rigg. I doubt I'll get any of this on expenses, and my bank account is so red, it stops traffic. Tomorrow morning, I'll see what I can find out about Terrible Tim, check out his work address, and get a feel for his business dealings. It's an itch I've got to scratch. Then I'll go and see the new Benny.

But that's tomorrow. I've got to survive tonight first. My stomach heads for my throat. Exit strategy: fight or flight without the fight.

It's about ten when I slip out of the hotel and head for my car. The roads are quiet, and, half an hour later, I cross the railway and head down the narrow lane. There are lights in a downstairs room at Westleigh Lodge. Doctor Harris must have arrived. That's a job for later in the week, assuming there is a later in the week.

I park some distance short of the steel-barred gate, and then, keeping to the cover of trees, I creep forward. I don't want those cameras picking me up, so I move really slowly, watching all the time. I know there are two on the gates and others along the wall, so I keep to the edge of the trees, beyond their reach, and make my way round the perimeter, looking for a weak spot. Only, it's like trying to break into a prison.

There's something else worrying me too. I mean, say I find a way to get in; how the hell will I get out again?

By the time I get to the final corner, I'm thinking it's time to give up and go home. I can't say I'm disappointed. I feel that relief you get when you've done your best without having to do anything at all — a kind of self-deluding virtuousness.

Then I come across a narrow, ivy-covered doorway in the wall. There's a path which leads away from it towards the Grange. Through the trees, a couple of hundred yards away, I see a single outside light flickering like a beacon, drawing me away — telling me to go home because I'm not cut out for this kind of thing.

But there's a tree at the corner, beyond the doorway, and when I look closely, I realise,

I might be able to get in after all.

And I think,

Shit.

Then I see a camera fixed above the doorway; it is peering through the ivy like a hostile face. I think,

No, there's no way in. I've given it my best shot.

And I think,

It's time to go home.

And I say,

Yeah, let's get out of here.

Only, I can't take my eyes from that tree. It's out of camera range, you see, and so is the branch that reaches tantalisingly close to the corner where the wall broadens. There's enough room either side of the razor wire to stand. And I tell myself,

Maybe, just maybe, I can do it.

Then I think,

No, you can't; it's impossible.

Before I know it, I'm having this weird conversation deep inside my head.

If I could reach that branch and crawl along it...

You'd fall off. Look at it. It won't take your weight. By the time you reach the end — if you reach the end — it'll be sagging like an old woman's tits.

But if I do reach the end, I can let myself down onto the wall...

You'll get torn to shreds by the razor wire. They'll find you tomorrow morning, wrapped up like you got caught by a huge metal spider.

I think I could step over it... I really think I...

You'll bleed to death. Besides, how the hell will you get down the other side? You forgot to pack your hang glider.

If I let myself down as far as I can and then drop...

And break a leg...

I reckon it's possible.

I reckon you're insane.

I've got to try.

Let's go home. You've given it a shot. You've done your best. Besides...

What?

How will you get out?

What?

Once you get in, how will you get out? You can't climb back onto the wall — no tree.

Maybe the door...

You got to be kidding me! You think you'll just open the door and walk out? Give me a break.

I'm going to try.

You're a stupid sod. You know that, right?

Yeah, I know.

Well, if we're going, let's go now before we change our minds. But hang on just a second — I need to pee.

For God's sake...

Ten minutes later, I'm lying bruised and bloodied inside the clinic compound. I'm covered in moss and tree bark, and it's mixing with the blood from a gash in my leg — I got caught on the razor wire. I think I've got a groin strain, and I've got a bruised back from when I fell back on the uneven ground.

That's the good news.

The bad news is there's no way out. The door has a push-button code.

Told you.

I hate it when you're smug.

I set off at a run down a narrow path which leads towards the house. I've got a head torch, but I don't use it any more than I have to. There's enough light from the building, and the path is covered in tree bark, and it's quite level. There's only one camera, and I bypass that by detouring through the trees.

I come to a vast, open lawn. Away to my left is the gravel drive. It leads round to the front of a large house which makes me think of Jane Austen for no real reason. It's symmetrical with balustrades and wings. It's the sort of house my mum and dad bored me with when I was a kid — a theme park for the over sixties.

There are cars parked outside — I count seven — and there are lights coming from windows across the front. There are more cameras at intervals along the building, but I reckon I can evade them if I keep to the shadows and then make a run across the shortest patch of lawn away to my right. There are walls, a kitchen garden, and a clutter of greenhouses and outbuildings, which should mask my approach.

It's time to take another deep breath and go for it. I can't back out now. Besides, I'm trapped here, aren't I? No way out.

Shit, blast, damn...

So I run, bent low like some agent in a spy film. I hop over a couple of walls and clamber over others until I'm standing with my back against the wall at the corner, and there's a window next to me. It's in darkness when I get there, but it suddenly belches light as someone goes in the room. I feel like I've just been caught in a spotlight on a stage. I drop down and freeze while I wait to see if I'm going to survive the upsurge in my heart rate. Then I inch upwards and take a look inside.

Only, there's nothing to see — not really. Inside, I see a room that is partitioned into separate alcoves like side chapels in a cathedral. There's a bed in each of them, three on one side and three on the other. There's a corridor down the middle like the nave of some weird church and a door at the end which looks like something from the eighteenth century; plaster chains are sculpted above it and urns and leaves — white on pale blue. I can only see one alcove clearly, and there's a guy lying there, wired up to these machines. I can't see his face, but the mattress is moving very slightly beneath him, following a strange pattern; it's like it's suspended above the floor of some moving vehicle. It takes me a minute to realise the whole thing is moving because he's making it move. It's like he's on a water bed which responds to his every twitch and turn. His body is moving like he's in a dream. It makes me think of how my parents' dog chases things in her sleep, moving her paws, twitching her nose, and whimpering.

I press my face closer to the glass. There's someone in one of the other beds, but I can't make out any details — just legs and a white bed sheet. I'm pretty sure the rest are empty. I've got to get in there and take a closer look. I try the window but the catch is tightly fastened, so I slip round the side of the building towards an entrance. I figure it leads down into the kitchen and the rooms 'below stairs.' I've been in enough old houses to know the signs.

I try the door. It opens with barely a sound, so I slip inside a long, pale, whitewashed corridor. There are no windows — just doors opening into pantries, larders, a boiler room, and a kitchen. There are stairs at the far end and, at the top of them, a door.

I don't get that far. As I pass the kitchen, I see a tough-looking woman standing there like a guard in a prison camp; more to the point, she sees me. It takes her about a millisecond to realise I really shouldn't be there and another to step across to the wall and press an alarm. The sound that emerges is enough to stun cattle, and it's more than enough to scare the hell out of me. When the woman walks towards me, I reckon it's time to go. She doesn't look like she's going to offer me a coffee — more like a blood transfusion. Before she has a chance to sink her nails into my arms and her fangs into my neck, I'm out of there, and I'm running, and I've absolutely no idea where I'm running to because I don't know how to get out of this bloody place.

There are floodlights panning across the lawns, and it doesn't take them long to pick me out, so I dive into the cover of the trees. I can hear voices behind me and people running, and then — shit — I can hear dogs barking, and I'm thinking about all those escape films where everything goes horribly wrong.

For want of anything sensible to do, I head through the trees and onto the drive, and then I accelerate, and I think — when I have the power to think — that my heart and my lungs are going to seize up like a piece of old machinery — everything will stop, and I'll grind to a halt and die. I can see the gate ahead of me. It's only fifty yards, but it looks like half a mile, and I don't think I'll make it. It's closed anyway, and there's a car approaching fast.

Then something surreal starts to happen.

Someone opens the gate for the car.

Then someone's starts to shout *shut the gate!* over and over.

But they're too late.

I reach the gate just before the car screeches to a stop behind me, and I duck beneath and between conifers and weave a path as far from the road as I can manage. I'm getting torn to shreds but I don't care. I barely feel it. I've got other things to worry about. There'll be time for pain when I get out of here.

At first, I can hear people swearing and branches breaking, but, slowly, they fade away until all I can hear is my own rasping breath and my heavy footsteps through the undergrowth.

When I can't run any further, I walk. Then I slow down, and I fall against a tree. My lungs are on fire like I've got a boiler burning inside me.

I think it's going to burst.

Spontaneous combustion.

I recover slowly, breath by breath, and listen, but all I hear are the usual woodland sounds and, behind them, a deep silence. I sit there for a few minutes, just listening, but, eventually, I clamber to my feet and convince my legs it's in their best interests to walk. They're not easily persuaded, but after a few steps they grow in confidence and we head back to the car, and I'm really glad I hid it down a track beneath trees.

That was a really good idea of mine.

Yeah, it's the only thing you got right tonight.

We're alive, aren't we?

Do you really want to call this living?

Let's get out of here.

Yeah.

Let's go home.

Yeah, but one thing...

Yeah?

Promise me you'll never ever do anything like this again.

I promise.

Right, let's get in the car and get out of here.

The car is just where I left it, and there's no one about; soon, I'm inside and driving back down the lane. I only relax when I've left the countryside behind me and I'm on the main road back to Rigg.

No, that's not true.

I only really relax when I park the car, slip through the back entrance to the hotel, and lock the door of my room.

Yeah, then I feel safe.

Sort of.

Only, according to the dreams that scare me senseless for the next few hours, I'm not really relaxed at all, and, when daylight comes, I'm really happy to slip downstairs and join the few other guests over breakfast.

I check out soon after. I want to put as many miles as I can between my thoughts and that clinic with its security guards and its dogs. And I don't want to do any more investigating — not today. Tim can wait. I want to get back on home turf. I want to go and have a cup of tea with my mum and dad. I want a big, reassuring hug.

But I reckon I should walk down to see Heather before I leave, so I drop my overnight bag in the hotel foyer and head down to see her; only, when I get there, she isn't in, and I've just wasted forty minutes. Now I'm telling myself I should've phoned. I head back to the hotel, my car, and the road out of this place.

I've walked about 300 yards when a car pulls up and a window slides open.

'Where the hell have you been? Get in, for Christ's sake. I haven't got all day.'

I clear away some chocolate wrappers and the remains of a few sandwiches and clamber into the front seat.

'Hello, Liz,' I say.

Chapter 16

Liz isn't alone. Jon, my old colleague, is squeezed into the narrow back-seat. We barely get the chance to nod and exchange greetings before Liz is exploding like Chinese firecrackers.

'I'm being followed,' she says. 'Can you believe those bastards? I'm also being hacked, bugged, and framed. Who do they think they are?'

We're in Rigg town centre, and a sharp right-hand bend is approaching more rapidly than it ought to. I brace myself for impact.

'It's the sheer impertinence — the sheer effrontery! Where's your car?' she snaps as we take the corner. We're on two wheels, I swear. I hear a gasp coming from Jon behind me. Even his cushioned frame can't take a pummelling like this.

'Next left,' I tell her as I grip the armrest and press my foot hard on an imaginary brake.

The car screams a protest, and I want to look back to see if my stomach is on the road. It must be out there somewhere.

'Next right... there. The car park's round the...'

But Liz manoeuvres into the car park before I can finish directing her. She pulls up sharply, and I feel the seat belt kick in as I head towards the windscreen. Jon hits the back of my seat and grunts.

'Have you travelled all the way here with Liz?' I ask him.

He nods. 'Yeah, every inch.'

'Brave man.'

'Go and get your stuff,' says Liz. She glances in the mirror. 'I'm going to have a word with the couple in that silver Peugeot. They've been following me since Sefton. It's time we were introduced.' She opens the door and steps out. 'Jon, get Philip's keys; you can drive his car back. I need to talk to him. Come on, what are you waiting for?'

'Thank you, God,' Jon says, and he raises his eyes heavenwards. 'I've never met anyone who drives like Liz. I don't know how she's lived so long.'

'So long as she lives long enough to get me home,' I say.

'I'll pray for you.'

As I run into the hotel and Jon heads for my car, I see her pacing towards the Peugeot as it turns hurriedly and heads away. Liz stands and watches, and I'm pretty sure that number plate will be fixed in her memory as clearly as if someone wrote it in indelible ink. I've never known anyone absorb information like Liz. Tell her something once, and, if she thinks it's important enough, it's there for life. Trivia like your name, a fatal illness, or a personal tragedy — anything you say that isn't immediately relevant — is discarded to make room. There's no wasted space with Liz.

When I emerge from the hotel, dragging my overnight bag, she's back in the car, drumming her fingers on the steering wheel. I just have time to fling everything on the backseat and clamber in the front before she's accelerating out of the car park and scaring pedestrians again. A car horn sounds as she spins to the left and heads towards the bypass. I've barely got my seat belt fastened when she slides onto the main road, accelerates so quickly my back is pressed against the seat, and I'm subjected to forces usually experienced by astronauts on take-off.

She glances in the mirror.

'I think I've lost them,' she says.

'You nearly lost me at that last bend.'

'I've barely started,' she snaps. 'Man up!'

'Where are we heading?' I ask. 'South?'

We reach a roundabout and circle a full 360 degrees to head back to where we've come from.

'North,' she says. 'We're going home. If they think they can drive me out of my own town, they've got another thing coming. Now, tell me what I need to know. And be brief, Philip; I'm in no mood for wasted words.'

Liz is never in a mood for wasted words.

Ever.

I take a deep breath, gather my thoughts, which, at the moment, are flying round the car like butterflies, and tell her everything. As I finish, I realise that's the first time I've spoken to Liz for more than thirty seconds without feeling like she's got better things to do than listen to me and that I'm one of those fools she doesn't suffer.

When I fall silent, she doesn't speak for a moment.

'You haven't heard from the nurse who contacted you?'

'No.'

'This Tim,' she asks, 'do you trust him?'

'I can't decide if he's overprotective or if he's got something to hide. But at the moment... no, I don't.'

'He's self-employed, you say?'

'He runs a web design, computer sales, and computer repair business.'

The silence falls again.

'Marcus, this rich Lothario, do we know anything about him?'

'Nothing; we don't even know his surname, though I doubt he'd use his real name. He's got to be a con man, hasn't he?'

'Hmm.'

'Though I can't see what'd be in it for him. I mean, Wendy is hardly a typical target for a con, is she? What's she got to offer? She's not rich, and she doesn't have a big house; she's just —' The qualities I see in her run through my mind like a scurrying of rodent feet on a wooden floor, '— she's just ordinary like you and me.'

'And that's why she needs us?'

'Yes.'

'You think Heather is genuine? We can trust her?'

'Totally.'

'Does she have any suspicions about Tim?'

'No, I'm sure she doesn't.'

We drive on for a few minutes as Liz works the information through her processing system. Then, without warning, she brakes and pulls into a small parking area with a picnic table, trees, and flowers in wooden planters.

'We're out of work, Philip. We have no newspaper, no outlet, and no influence. They've seen to that. They've attacked you, and they're trying to ruin my reputation and make me untouchable. They've hacked our computers, bugged our phones, and followed us. The newspaper has been sold. Did you know that?'

'Yeah, I heard.'

'They sold us out, Philip. We were bought out and sold on. I suspect our newspaper is now a minor part of a subsidiary of Logrum Research and its parent company. No, that is incorrect. I don't suspect; I *know*. Have you heard of Mark Van-Doren?'

'No, should I have?'

She turns one of her stares on me. 'Sometimes, Mr Tyler, I despair for the new generation of journalists. Do you actually read any newspapers? No, don't answer me. I feel bad enough already. Mr Van-Doren is an American businessman who runs a multi-billion-dollar internet marketing empire. I know little about these things, but I know he made his money during those early silicon-rush years when fortunes were there for the taking — or losing. I always think of it like the Wild West with its frontier settlements, but I doubt it was that civilised, and I doubt the simile is supported by reality. Most of Mr Van-Doren's riches were obtained by backing young, enthusiastic entrepreneurs, tying them into cast-iron contracts, forcing them to sell cheaply when the market was about to turn in their favour, and leaving them with nothing. He's a real charmer. He made his money, bought himself several big houses, a couple of private islands, a few large boats, and an aircraft, and then disappeared from sight. He's a very reclusive individual nowadays. I've tried in vain to locate him or even to find recent press coverage. He does no interviews, he's never seen in public, and there hasn't been a decent photograph taken of him for twenty years or more.'

'And this Van-Doren guy is an investor in Logrum?'

'He owns the parent company which owns the parent company. Mr Van-Doren owns Logrum.'

'And he's the rich shit who got me sacked?'

'I doubt he was personally involved. He deals with bigger fish. You and I aren't even minnows in his particular ocean.'

'Plankton,' I mutter, 'that's me — plankton. And this man is responsible for what happened to Wendy?'

'I believe so.'

'Bastard.'

'Indeed.'

'So what are we going to do? We've no paper, no jobs, and we've agreed we're just plankton to these whales.'

'What would you like to do?'

'Go home, lock myself in my bedroom, lie down in a foetal position, and suck my thumb.'

'Not an option.'

'Then I'd like to find some secret place where I'm safe from acts of violence, and I'd like to hunt these people down, find out what they're doing, and tell the world all about them. I want to ruin them.'

'Well said — a bit melodramatic and rather tabloid for my tastes, especially the last bit — but well said. The reality, of course, is that we're doomed to failure. They're too big, and we're too small — like you said, we're plankton.'

'Okay, wrong metaphor,' I say. 'Let's think of ourselves as bacteria.'

'I like that better. Let's be a contagious and potentially fatal bacteria, immune to antibiotics. Very good, Philip. I feel better already.'

'But first, I want somewhere to hide,' I add, and she gives me a disappointed look.

Then,

'I know just the place,' she says, and she presses her foot on the accelerator and hits the outside lane. I close my eyes. I think we've entered a time warp.

When we reach Sefton, she drives down to the promenade and takes a left towards the quiet end of town, over the river bridge. A mile further on, she turns right into a holiday caravan park and weaves between vans until she pulls up outside a particularly large chalet, which is tucked behind some dunes and close to a long beach. It's got a veranda and flower tubs and a barbecue.

'It's my sister's,' Liz says.

'Funny,' I say before I've taken full control of my mouth, 'I never thought of you having a family.'

She gives me one of those looks.

'Did you think I'd been beamed down here solely to edit a newspaper?'

I'm not sure how to read her. Is she making light of my remark or is this a trap she's about to spring?

'Well,' I say after a moment's lack of thought. 'Yeah, I suppose I did really.'

I'm relieved when she laughs.

'This is our new control centre, the hub of our operations — our press room. It's also where I live at the moment since I don't like people watching me. Let me show you to your room.'

'My room?'

'You didn't think it was safe to go home, did you? Don't be silly.'

'I did imagine I'd be sleeping in my own bed tonight.'

'Think of it as a holiday. It'll make you feel better.'

It doesn't. I don't want to go on holiday with Liz. I certainly don't want to share a chalet with her. I mean, she terrifies me. I won't be able to sleep — not in there, separated from her by a flimsy partition wall. What if she gets hungry? What if she wanders round in a nightdress? Liz is my boss. I don't want that level of intimacy. I want to think of her as this ogre who controls my days. My nights are a kind of sanctuary.

Shit, I'd rather stay with Winston.

'We've got to accept they're probably watching our homes,' she says. 'Believe me when I tell you that the thought of spending my days under the same roof as you doesn't fill me with unbridled joy. You look like the sort of person who watches sport on the television and snores. Both of those habits are banned, by the way, as are smoking and drinking unless I initiate it.'

'Can I bring my girlfriend back?'

'You haven't got a girlfriend.'

'How do you know?'

'A woman knows,' she says with an irritating smile.

I hate it when people say things like that. What makes her think I haven't got a girlfriend? Is there something about me? Do I give off strange, 'single man' vibes? Do I transmit the word, 'loser' over and over? What the hell...?

'Don't think about it too much,' she says.

Which doesn't help.

She opens the door and I follow her inside. The chalet is huge; it has a king-sized lounge, a kitchen with all the facilities, a shower room, and two substantial bedrooms.

Next to each other.

Shit.

I don't snore, not ever, but I'm certain to now, aren't I? Either that or I'll lie awake all night, just in case I wake Liz.

'What does your sister do?' I ask.

'She's an accountant; my brother-in-law is a banker.'

'Oh dear. Ah well, never mind — rich, no doubt?'

'Very. You disapprove of money?'

'I don't trust it. It goes against my instincts. I was brought up in a well-off family with strong socialist leanings. I spent my teens feeling guilty about it. Besides, I distrust the modern preoccupation with 'stuff' and the relentless anticipation of the next sensation. Money encourages both.'

'You'd rather not have any?'

'I like having enough, but I don't want to spend my life touring the world taking selfies just to show what a great time I'm having.'

'My, I can see we're going to have some interesting conversations during the long evenings ahead. I can hardly wait.'

Long evenings ahead? A dark cloud descends, bringing with it a feeling of doom.

I focus on the lounge to dispel grim forebodings. There's a table with two computers and a printer on it, and there are recording devices and all the usual tools of our trade, even paper and pens. There's some other gear too — stuff I don't recognise, and there are cameras and lenses.

'What are we going to do?' I ask. 'What's the plan?'

'We're going to create our own newspaper, Philip. We're going to open an online news site, and we're going to devote it in the first instance to exposing Logrum and Marc Van-Doren. I have plenty of links in the media and a number of contacts that I have built up over the years; I know people with just the expertise we'll need. When we're ready, we'll have the means to tell the world. I plan to go viral.'

'They'll try to stop us.'

'They won't know what's hit them. By the time they try to close us down, it'll be too late. It'll be out there in every newspaper, on every news channel, and on every outlet I can think of — and I can think of plenty.'

For a moment, I'm carried along by her enthusiasm. There's not much self-doubt in Liz. She sees what she wants to do, and she does it. That's Liz's way. I'm more the wavering, fearful, paranoid type who sees problems at every turn. Between me and what I want to do, I see swamps, wild animals, minefields, and no footpaths. I have this permanent feeling of dread, as if something awful is about to happen.

It usually is.

'Can we keep something like this secret?'

'We have to.'

'Maybe they'll be looking for us, if they think we're investigating them.'

'Let them look.'

'We'll have to work quickly. Sooner or later, they'll trace us back here.'

'Then there's no time to waste. Now, Philip, what are we going to do?'

It sounds like another one of those teacher questions where she knows the answer and I don't.

'I'll find Winston and talk to Benny. I want to see whether this is just the usual Winston bullshit or if something really has happened to Benny. And I want to check out Tim. I want to dig a bit and see what I can find out about him. And if I can't go back to my apartment, I need to buy some underwear. What are you going to do?'

There's a gleam in her eyes like I'm a fly, and I've just flown needlessly into her web.

'No, Philip, the question is: what are we going to do right now, before I let you go out to play?'

'I don't understand. What do you mean?'

'As fully signed-up members of the journalist profession, what is our immediate course of action?'

'I thought I just said... Winston... Benny...'

'Sometimes, I'm driven to despair. That's for tomorrow. This evening — nay, most of the night — we have more pressing matters.'

'I'm sorry... I don't...'

She sighs a long, deep sigh like her disappointment is about to overflow, swim around the room, and drag her down into a swamp of despondency.

'Firstly, we're going to sit at our respective computers, and we're going to write. Do you remember that — writing? We're going to write down every damned thing that has happened — everything we know, everything we think, everything we want to know, and everything we ought to know but don't, and then we'll top it all by writing down all the things we're going to find out.'

'Of course.'

'Of course.'

God, she does a good line in withering, and I'm just too tired to be withered. Time for a diversionary question.

'What are you going to do tomorrow while I search out Winston and Benny?'

'I'll take a closer look at our Mr Van-Doren. I'll phone some people — discrete people — fellow professionals who might have information or the means to acquire it, and I'll start to prepare our news outlet. But first...'

'We write.'

'Don't be silly.'

'What?'

'Coffee,' she says, 'the journalist's best friend. I can't work without it.'

It's past two when I finally drag myself to my bed, and I don't care if I snore. I don't care if I wake screaming after some nightmare about clinics and security guards. I don't even care if I spend my night making love to Wendy right next door to Liz. I just want to close my eyes and slip away to somewhere which isn't here.

When I wake, it's morning, and I can hear Liz beating a pan to death in the kitchen. I throw on some clothes and stumble through.

'Scrambled eggs,' she says.

'To match my brain,' I mumble.

'Get a coffee; it'll be ready in five minutes. And in case you think I'm one of those old-fashioned women who do the catering, be assured I'm not.'

'It never crossed my mind, Liz, not for a single second.'

'Good. You can make dinner.'

'Pizza, then?'

'Perfect.'

Chapter 17

I'm actually looking forward to seeing Winston. That's not something I'd normally admit. It's not a feeling I'm familiar with, but, after the last few days, Winston is the closest thing to normality I can think of. I know where I stand with Winston — even if it's on the edge of a precipice. I know I can trust him as far as I can lob a camel, but I can read him too, and I know how to ferret out the grain of truth in the whole heap of bullshit he shovels.

Besides, in a stupid sort of way that I can't explain, I like Winston.

Not many people can say that.

He's just heading out of his house when I see him. He lives with his mum. She's got MS or something, and she can't get around as much as she wants to, so Winston lives in and looks after her. It's been like that for years — since school days. He arrived late nearly every morning. No one knew, not even the teachers; I doubt they cared back in the day.

He stops in the doorway and shouts, 'Bye, Mum! I'll be back for lunch.' Then he closes the door. When he sees me, he walks across, grabs my arm, and leads me back to my car.

'They can't stop me,' he mutters. 'Come on.'

'Where are we going?'

'To see Benny. I'll break the door down if I have to. Let's see what the bleeding do-gooders do about that!'

'We need a better plan,' I say once we're in the car. 'They'll call the police.'

'Not if I break their fingers,' he says. 'Let's see them press the numbers with their fingers broken.'

He pauses for a moment, and then he throws back his head and laughs.

'Come on,' he says. 'You're the one with brains. How do we see him?'

I start the engine while I'm thinking.

'Yeah,' I say. 'Let's break their fingers.'

We set off down the street, and we're both laughing and saying stupid things. Then Winston directs me down a particularly grimy terraced street and tells me to pull up. He points towards a double-fronted terraced house which has been converted into something that looks like a shop or an office — or some dodgy business which keeps its transactions hidden behind smeared glass and curtains. There's a board hanging above the door like a sign for a Medieval tavern. It says "Marsh Street Mission" in lettering that must've been gold once. There are two hands drawn above it that are reaching towards each other as if in friendship. They look like they need a good wash. You could catch something shaking hands like those.

'Ready?' Winston says.

'As I'll ever be,' I tell him.

We get out of the car like we're the good guys in some film and walk across. I beat on the door. It's not a timid beat either; I give it a heavy thump like I mean business. Like I said, I get all my courage by proxy. With Winston next to me, I feel almost brave.

Then I brace myself and prepare for trouble.

The guy who opens the door is wearing a suit and tie and, for no identifiable reason, I find myself wondering if he sleeps like that. Then I see the neat creases, the clean haircut, and the newly shaved cheeks, and I know he doesn't. He stands with his hands clasped in front of him and this sickly-sweet smile on his face.

'Welcome to our mission,' he says. 'How can I help you?'

When he sees Winston, a flicker of recognition passes across his face, the eyes glaze just a little, and the smile freezes.

I flash a press card.

'I'm here to see Benny,' I tell him with a really lovely smile of my own.

'I'm afraid Benny can't see you at the moment.'

'Oh. Why's that?'

'He's at prayer.'

Winston snorts, but the battle of the smiles continues.

'Could you ask him?' I say.

'I'm afraid that isn't possible.'

'Why not?'

'He doesn't want to be disturbed.'

'Then perhaps *you* can help me.'

My smile slips away as if I've wiped it with a cloth. I can see his anxieties fluttering round his head like moths. He even raises his hand as if to brush them away.

'I'm really not sure I...'

'Who brought Benny here?'

'I really can't...'

Do the names "Logrum" or "Westleigh" mean anything to you? What about "Wigmore" — "Clive Wigmore?"'

'I don't know what you're talking about.'

'Was Benny brought here willingly or did he have people in white coats holding his arms?'

'This is a mission. People choose to come here.'

'Tell me about Benny's conversion. I mean, it must've been a rapid process — very road to Damascus because he had no interest in religion a week ago.'

'I'm sorry, I really can't...'

He's trying to close the door now, but I've applied the journalist's foot, and he can't — not without letting his mask slip and slamming it against me.

'I don't know what you've done to Benny, but I don't believe in all this conversion bullshit, and I'd like to bet that a significant amount of money has changed hands. I mean, look around. You need cash, right?'

'If you don't leave now, I'll call the police.'

There's another voice behind him now, and footsteps are approaching.

'What's happening, Julian?'

That's too much for Winston.

'Julian? The dickhead's called Julian?' he snorts. 'That settles it.'

Suddenly, the door is kicked open, Julian is sent flying, and Winston has brushed aside his brother missionary and is heading towards the back rooms.

'The other dough-brain is probably called Nigel,' he says.

There's no one in the ground floor rooms, so Winston heads for the stairs. I stay with Julian and Nigel. They're trying to clamber to their feet.

'Better not,' I say, shaking my head. 'You're safer down there.' They slip back down against the wall.

'We'll call the police,' Nigel threatens.

I reckon he's bluffing, so I ignore him.

'We know people,' Julian says. 'You'll not get away with this.'

That's a better threat, but it still doesn't work. Winston and I are feeling kind of empowered just now.

Winston has found Benny, and he's dragging him down the stairs. Benny is shouting, 'Leave me alone,' and then, reverting momentarily to type, he shouts, 'Get lost, Winston, you moronic bastard; leave me alone and piss off.'

'It's for your own good, Benny, man. Why the hell would you want to live with a couple of stiffs like these?'

'I'm happy!' Benny half screams.

'Don't talk shite, Benny.' Winston heaves him through the door. 'Morning, gents,' he says, and he grins at Julian and Nigel.

I start to back towards the door.

'They'll find you.' Julian clambers to his feet. 'They'll find you, and they'll make you pay for this.'

I stand in the doorway for a moment, shaking my head.

'And you're a couple of good Christians,' I say. 'You should be ashamed.'

I follow Winston towards the car. He's gathered quite a crowd of onlookers if you include the thin, grey faces at windows all along the street. It's not surprising. Benny is shouting and swearing, Winston is swearing back, and he's sporting this big grin like he's just won on a scratch card.

'This is seriously cool, man,' he says, 'like some TV film. We're the good guys, right?'

It's a novel thought, Winston being a good guy, but I don't have time to frame a reply. I'm too busy forcing Benny into the backseat of the car. All the way back to Winston's flat, I listen for sirens, and I wait for police cars to hurtle round corners and block the road.

They never appear. I guess the grey faces have decided it's all in a day's entertainment and none of their business. Better to keep a low profile and not get involved. Off the radar is a good place to be. Someone else will call the police if they want to. No one really cares.

Back in the flat, with a multipack of beers we buy from the Co-op, Winston clears a seat and drops Benny on half a sofa. He disappears into the kitchen, and I hear him opening cans. He appears a moment later and hands a beer to Benny, who is quiet now and compliant.

'Drink that, you stupid git,' he says.

He disappears again, this time into the bedroom, and he comes back with a pile of clothing.

'Get these on,' he says. 'It's like talking to a solicitor.'

Benny looks up at him, then he looks at me, and there's a kind of sad, distant, puppy-dog look in his eyes.

'I was happy,' he says.

'No, you weren't,' Winston snaps. 'I don't know what the hell that was, but it wasn't happiness.'

Benny looks at him, and there's a momentary flicker of recognition, which moves across his eyes like someone's removed a film.

'Winston, you're a son of a f...' The rant continues for several minutes with a range of expletives I don't often say and some I can't even spell. 'You know that?' he concludes.

Winston gives him this huge grin.

'Yeah,' he says.

Chapter 18

'What do you remember about Westleigh Grange?' I ask.

It's after midday now, and Benny's on his fifth beer. It seems to be having the desired effect. He's back in his old clothes, and he's got a cigarette hanging from his lips. It's about his tenth that morning, and the air in the flat is starting to catch my throat. Another hour and we'll have our own private climate crisis.

'When you came out of Westleigh Grange...' I continue.

'Oh yeah,' he says as if I've just reminded him of something from way back. He turns to Winston. 'Where the hell were *you*?'

'Had to split, man... *Bunny, Bunny*! You catch me?'

We've been subjected to the story twice this morning already. Maybe that's why Benny needs the beer and fags.

'I start to walk back to town, but I don't get far. This four-by-four pulls up, and a suspicious-looking guy leans out of the window. He doesn't speak — just looks. "What are you doing here?" he asks.

'"I'm looking for a strip joint. What do you think?" I tell him sarcastic like, but this guy has got as much sense of humour as a fish. Then I see someone lying on the backseat, covered in a blanket, and I start to wonder what I've stumbled on. I mean, the guy looks dead. His eyes are shut, and he's not moving. I'm scared, and I think the guy driving notices because he reaches out and grabs me, and he jabs this syringe into my arm. The next thing I know, I'm on the front seat looking out at the sky, and everything's swimming and swirling. It's like an acid trip — all colours and movements — only, I'm getting really tired, and my eyes are closing. I remember the car slowed and then stopped, and then...'

'And then what?'

'Not a thing.'

'Come on, Benny, there must be something.'

'Not a thing. The next thing I know, I'm in this house with Julian and Nigel, and we're big buddies; it's like we've been friends forever, and I'm meeting their friends. I'm in a suit, I'm shaved, I've had a haircut, and it all feels normal like I've always been like that. And I've got God — like big time. It's all I think about.'

'They must've taken you to the clinic at Westleigh,' I say. 'There's no other explanation. Are you sure you can't remember anything that happened once you got inside?'

'Maybe it'll come back to me. But at the moment,' he shrugs, 'nothing. It's a complete blank. All I know is that I lost four days somewhere. It was Friday and then it was Wednesday, and I've no idea where I was or what happened.'

'They tried to brainwash you,' says Winston.

'Yeah.'

'Didn't know your brain was already mush.'

'Yeah.'

'No brain to wash.'

'Yeah.'

I don't think I can listen to any more of this, and it's clear I'll get no more out of Benny, so I make to leave.

'It's good you've got a friend like me,' Winston's saying.

'Yeah.'

'The way I waded into those guys — superhero heroic.'

I've got to interrupt before Winston recreates history before my eyes. I figure I'm going to hear this story a lot over the next few weeks anyway.

'I've got to go. Let me know if you remember anything,' I say to Benny.

'Where are you going?' Winston asks.

'Back to the control room.'

'What's that?'

'It's where the fightback begins.'

'Yeah?'

It's a fist bump moment, and Winston takes full advantage of it.

I'm at the door when I turn back to extend a word of caution. It'll slip off Winston like water off grease, but I've got to say it.

'Be careful, Winston. These guys don't mess about. When you go out, check no one's following, yeah?'

'Bastards aren't going to make *me* happy,' he grins. 'I like how I am.'

I give up and follow a circular route to the chalet. No one follows me.

Liz is sitting before the computer. She looks like she hasn't moved all morning. Without taking her eyes from the screen, she indicates some freshly printed sheets of paper. On top of them, there's a photograph of a youngish guy who must be in his late twenties. He has a round face which looks like it's been French polished, and he's smiling from big, naïve eyes like he's just been born into the world and thinks it's all really cool. Only, it's not a convincing look. Maybe it's the casual t-shirt, the expensive watch, or the huge office desk he's sitting on. It makes me think of the days when they draped good-looking girls over cars to persuade gullible fools to buy them.

I was probably a gullible fool, but I had no money, so I could pretend to be virtuous.

'Who's he?'

'That's Mark Van-Doren.'

'Somehow I imagined him older.'

'It was taken over thirty years ago. Like I said, he's a very private person.'

'No recent photo?'

I thumb through the papers. There are a couple of distant shots of a man sitting by a swimming pool or on a golf course, but, even without the sunglasses and the beard, they wouldn't give much away.

'Van-Doren?' I ask.

'Yes.'

'You could walk past this guy on the street and not recognise him.'

'The beard will come and go — the hair too, and if anyone gets too close, he just buys them off. He can afford it.'

'And this guy's worth more than most third-world countries?'

'And he's more powerful.'

'And he's behind whatever is behind Logrum?'

'Yes.'

'What else do we know about him?'

'He wants to change the world. He wants to cure everything, produce new body parts on a commercial basis, offer annual rejuvenation, and postpone death forever.'

'But only if you're rich enough...'

'Indeed.'

'So if you're fabulously wealthy, eternity can be yours; unless you're unlucky enough to die in an accident, of course.'

'I suppose so.'

'I guess that means his customers would lock themselves away in a padded room. They wouldn't dare go out in case death caught up with them.'

'It's a reassuring thought.'

'And they'd die slowly of boredom.'

'Very slowly.'

'Good.'

I pick up another piece of paper which looks like an extract from a bank statement.

'What's this?'

'Study it and tell me what you think.'

'I think whoever this belongs to has some serious debt problems. Is it a business account?'

'Now look at this.'

She hands me a second sheet.

'That's close to miraculous if it's the same account.'

'It might surprise you to learn that both these statements are for a business called *Smart: Internet and Web Design Services.*'

'Catchy.'

'Timothy Smart was on the edge of bankruptcy — no, he was leaning over the edge and peering into the abyss — now, suddenly, he has money. The debts have gone. How do you explain that?'

I look at the dates and a number of payments.

'Maybe some overdue bills started to come through. Maybe it was just a cash flow problem. The amounts are all different — £750.45, £1274.38, and £96.73 — and they're from different accounts.'

'Yes; perhaps you're right. But...'

'But his change of fortunes coincides with Wendy and Westleigh Clinic.'

'Precisely, and I don't like coincidences. I think Mr Smart has a few questions to answer, don't you?'

I can hear machinery grinding inside my head and something falling into place. I just wish I knew what it was.

'You think maybe Tim was paid to encourage Wendy to go there?'

'I could speculate... but I'd rather not.'

'If that's true, Heather will rip his balls off and choke him with them.'

'It could be a coincidence, of course. Bills do get paid. A cash flow problem does occasionally right itself. Businesses do go through bad spells. Maybe it's completely innocent.'

'Yeah,' I say, but something deep inside me is screaming out that he's guilty. I'm telling myself that I knew there was something dodgy about him — that I didn't trust him from minute one.

But I don't like him, so I would, wouldn't I?

'What's for dinner?' Liz asks.

'Oh shit,' I say, and I head to the door.

Chapter 19

Something weird happened today.

I think it's called *nothing.*

It's the first time that's happened in a while. *Nothing* is something that hasn't happened much recently.

After I've written up Benny's story and it's been checked, questioned, and corrected by Liz (I tell you, that woman is seriously obsessed with accuracy — classic OCD — like my mum used to be about brushed teeth, combed hair, and a healthy diet), I spend a couple of hours reading about Mark Van-Doren.

I keep asking myself the same questions.

How come he'd made billions by the time he was my age and I haven't?

How come he's got more mansions than I've got socks?

How come he's gone through girlfriends faster than I can eat French fries?

How come he's rich and successful and I'm just me?

I try to pretend that it's because I'm virtuous and I've got principles, that I wouldn't want to be like him, and that I'm not envious. No, definitely not. He must have something wrong with him, mustn't he? I mean, you can't be that rich *and* normal *and* nice, can you? He must've been an obnoxious nerd when he was younger — not a normal kid like the rest of us were — not cool.

I wouldn't want to be like that. Rich, famous, a success story by the age of 30, yachts, houses, women... No, not for me.

Bastard.

As it turns out, it's easy to feel contempt for this guy. His practice is as sharp as a cut-throat razor. He's the worst sort of bully — a rich one. I'm starting to steam and snort by lunchtime, so Liz slips my leash and lets me go out to play.

'Make sure you aren't followed,' she says. 'Go and see if Benny has remembered anything. Take your notebook. And make sure you're back for dinner. It's my turn, and it'll be on the table at seven, whether you're here or not. I've no time to be wandering around after you.'

'Yes, Mum,' I say.

'Cheeky sod,' she says.

'My mum never spoke like that,' I tell her.

'Maybe that's the problem,' she says and closes the door, and I'm left wondering what she means by that. What problem?

Benny's remembered something. He says he remembers a face looking down at him and bright lights.

'Was it a smiling face with white hair and a beard? Was he wearing a long, white gown?'

'He was wearing round glasses and a mask.'

'Well, we can rule out a near-death experience, then.'

Winston was thinking about the nude guy he'd seen.

'Maybe they were testing some super-strength Viagra?' he says.

'And then watching a video about mating rabbits?' I suggest.

'*Bunny! Bunny!*'

Time to go.

I wander into the town and lose myself in the crowds in the town centre. I slip in and out of a few shops just to feel normal, and then I start to get claustrophobic and head to the promenade. Sefton does that to me. I like the place: it's homely and ordinary. You can spend hours people-watching. You get all sorts here. I like the old people and families best. I can live without the swaggering drunks and the shallow, 'anything for a good time' morons that gravitate here at weekends. I hate the stag and hen parties. There's something about that sort of mindless jollity that repels me.

Or maybe it's just another item on the list of things that I envy.

It's becoming a really long list.

By the time I'm 60, I'll need a bigger notebook to write them in.

There's a breeze blowing and a chill in the air, so the beach is almost deserted. Not like in the old days when I was a kid. There wasn't room to lick an ice cream back then. There were so many people, I reckon you could walk along the beach from body to body without touching the sand.

The promenade is quiet, occupied mainly by older people in couples, walking slowly, and the odd cyclist using them for slalom practice. I stroll along as if I'm a tourist with nowhere particular to go except for up and down, and I listen to the hush of the waves as they gradually encroach on the sand — it'll be high tide in a couple of hours. The sea eats the sand then rolls against the defences, digesting slowly, like my dad after Christmas dinner.

My phone rings. It's the gardener from Westleigh Grange to tell me the doctor has moved in; I haven't the heart to tell him I already know.

'American,' he tells me, 'or Canadian... or maybe from Norfolk,' he adds. 'I'm not good at accents.'

I thank him.

Should I go out there? Maybe not today. Being chased by dogs and security guards once a week is enough.

I put it out of my head and wander about for a few hours, grab a beer in my favourite bar, treat myself to a burger, which tastes as appetising as the leather seat on my gran's sofa, and head back to the chalet.

All in all, it's been a pretty good day. Even Liz is tolerably chilled, and, over dinner — a nice, old-fashioned shepherd's pie — we drink a few bottled beers, and we chat about things which aren't work. Liz tells me about places she's worked, people she's hated, and holidays. Funny, I never thought of her as a person before. She was always an editor — a boss. I find myself smiling.

'What's so funny?' she asks.

'Nothing. I was just wondering what Jon and Alice would think if they knew you had a soft side.'

'You tell them and I'll throttle you with your own intestines.'

I believe her.

'The doctor's moved into Westleigh Grange,' I tell her. 'Shall I go out to see him?'

'Not yet; let's gather more ammunition before we go into battle.'

'I feel like I'm parrying cruise missiles with a wooden sword.'

'We're still here and still fighting — David against Goliath.'

'I always figured Goliath nailed David before he had a chance to pick up a stone,' I say.

'We're still in the fight,' Liz says. 'I like the feeling.'

'Yeah, it feels good when it doesn't feel bad. Trouble is, most of the time it feels bad — like I'm about to put my foot on a landmine.'

'When you see this story in print and you watch other journalists pick it up and it starts to spread... I tell you, there's no finer feeling.'

'You've experienced it before?'

'Once or twice... but nothing like this. I've got this feeling, you see, deep down in my gut, that this is the biggest story I'll ever get the chance to report — a once in a lifetime opportunity — my personal Watergate.'

'It might turn out to be nothing.'

'There's always that risk.'

'But you don't think so.'

'No.'

'Me neither.'

'Then let's drink to the biggest story in a decade. Open another bottle.'

'Here's hoping we live to see it in print. Haven't you had enough to drink?'

'I'll drink you under the table any day of the week, Mr Tyler.'

I can only laugh. I'm sure she could.

The next morning, she's up early and already at the computer when I stumble through and start making breakfast. It's my turn.

'Toast and jam?' I ask.

'Scrambled egg, I think, and cereal and fresh coffee.'

'Your risk.'

I'm beginning to think that I might have another good day. Two in a row — wow, that'd be something. Then my phone rings. It's Heather, and she sounds like the world's coming to an end, and it's starting in Rigg.

'Slow down, Heather; take your time, and tell me what's happened.'

As she speaks, a chill spreads through me, as if it's emerging from the phone, freezing my fingers, my hands, and my arms. I feel the blood leave my face. Liz has stopped typing, and she's looking at me. I sit down heavily on the box seat. I'm forcing myself to think fast, to ask the right questions, and say the right things.

'Last night? Tell me what happened. Tell me exactly what happened.'

I listen as she explains.

'Did they take her?'

'Have you heard from her? Has she phoned?'

'So you don't know... they could have... yes, yes, I understand. And Tim?'

'Yes, yes, I see. When is he back?'

'Listen, Heather, I'm sure she'll contact you when she can. Maybe she heard them and got out, you know... maybe... yeah, I know. Let me know if you hear from her... okay, yes. In the meantime, I'll...'

I'm lost for words. I'll what? There's nothing I can do except break down the walls of Westleigh Clinic, beat people to a pulp, and make them tell me where she is. And, right now, that's what I want to do.

'What's happened?' Liz asks when I close the phone.

'It's Wendy,' I tell her. 'She's gone; some guys turned up at her clinic with warrants, court orders, and an army of doctors and solicitors. There was nothing anyone could do. They had to let them through to take her. Only, when they reached her room, Wendy's bed was empty.'

'You mean she got away?'

'Her coat and some clothes were missing. Maybe she heard them, grabbed her clothes, and skipped.'

'So either they caught up with her outside or they're still looking for her.'

'I've got to find her, Liz. I've got to. I'm going back to Rigg and Westleigh.'

Liz is shaking her head. 'If they've got her, the security will be as tight as an asthmatic lung. If they haven't, she'll make her way to Heather. Either way, there's nothing you can do.'

'I can't just sit here.'

'You can do your job, Philip. We've got to find out what these bastards are up to so we can stop them.'

'But they might have her now. God knows what they're doing to her. I've got to go, Liz... I have to...'

And I'm out of the door and stumbling to my car, and all I can see is Wendy sitting in the chair in that sun lounge, a breeze moving frail wisps of hair, and she's turning her head towards me and smiling, and I know I've got to find her, and I don't know how. I don't even know where to begin.

I stand by the car. I want to get in it and ride down there like Sir Galahad, but I'd just be passing the time, pretending I was doing something. No, I've got to think... *think*.

I turn away from the car and retrace my steps to the chalet. Liz is standing at the table, her hands grasping it tightly and a look of intense concentration on her face like she's in pain.

And I know how she feels. I know just how she feels.

Helpless.

I try to speak slowly and carefully.

'There's someone I know — an ex-Detective Inspector. He retired last year. He's old school and a bit unorthodox, but he knows his way around. He's called Slattery. I'm going to see him. It's time to bring out our secret weapon.'

Chapter 20

If ever there was a last resort, it's Slattery. Even the temporary celebrity status his final case brought him hasn't improved him. When I walk into the dull, brown interior of The Wheatsheaf, with its station clock above the bar, its mahogany tables, its opaque half windows, and its rounded, wooden chairs, it's like entering a time warp. And there's Slattery, same as ever, talking to a woman at the bar.

She's got red lipstick, a grey complexion, leopard-skin boots, and a shiny silver handbag — need I say more? No, I didn't think so. She's inhaling one of those vaping devices and exhaling it over Slattery, who's pretending it's a pleasure. She laughs like she's just invented humour and she's giving it a test drive, revving it up and letting it go.

Slattery is wearing a jumper and jeans, which makes a change from the suit he used to wear. I think he inherited that suit from his grandparents and formed a nostalgic attachment to it. The jeans are doing him no favours. As he leans forward, an extensive cleavage appears.

'For God's sake, Slattery. Cover yourself up. You're enough to make me stop drinking.'

At the mention of drinking, he empties his glass. The woman flashes a wide-mouthed smile and a close-up view of chewing gum.

'Mine's a pint. What about you, Cheryl?'

'G and T — double,' she says, and she gives that laugh an extra rev.

She takes her drink and heads down the bar. 'See you about, Slattery,' she says with a wink.

'You can believe it,' he says.

We head to a round table in a corner, which is under a particularly grimy slice of window. Two men crash pool balls together and a couple pick their way through breaded haddock and fries.

'I think I'll have some of those,' Slattery says. He raises a hand towards the barman. 'Two,' he mouths. 'You'll join me?'

'Why not? I guess I'm paying.'

'That's very generous. I wouldn't have presumed...'

He'll never change.

'How's retirement?' I ask. Small talk.

'Really boring, to tell the truth; you get no respect, not without the badge of office — not even from her...' He flashes a look towards the skirt and heels at the bar. She's moved on to a bearded guy with a football tattooed on his cheek. Her glass is full again. 'Even to Cheryl I'm just an old fart who's only worth a drink or two... no respect, Phil. Years of public service, and look at me.'

I see a face like the wrinkled bark of an old tree, grey skin, a balding scalp, and a paunch you could rest a kettle on.

'You haven't changed a bit,' I tell him.

He taps the place where some people house a heart and then indicates his head.

'It's here, Phil; it's here I feel the difference. There's no passion — no excitement. Every day's the same. It's like sailing on a flat sea, Phil. I want *waves*. And I want respect.'

'If it's any consolation, I didn't respect you even with the badge.'

'That's reassuring. If that's the pleasantries over, how can I help you and what's it worth to me?'

I tell him the whole story over a couple of drinks and a surprisingly edible lunch. It's amazing what you can do with a freezer and a microwave nowadays. When I conclude, he turns that cynical look on me.

'Winston?' he says, drawing the syllables apart as if he's trying to stick his tongue between them. 'Win-ston?' It's like I've just mentioned him for the first time. 'That thieving git.'

'Yeah.'

'And Benny?'

'Yeah.'

He's quiet for a moment, as if he's chewing some profound idea and extracting its juices.

'Rigg,' he says at last; then he turns it into a question. 'Rigg?'

'Yeah.'

'And you had to go there?'

'Yeah.'

'Shit.'

He's frowning now, but I don't know if it's the thought of Rigg or something deeper, so I say nothing.

'And the girl's gone?'

'Yeah.'

'And you think this rich prick is behind it?'

'Mark Van-Doren? Maybe; his minions are at least.'

'And you've heard nothing from this nurse who emailed you?'

'Nothing.'

And he goes on like that, repeating things I've told him like he's finding the right drawer to file them in and tidying them away. Only, before he can close the drawer, he's got to cross-reference everything. It's painful to watch.

'Liz,' he says. 'She's one tough bitch. She'd make Margaret Thatcher look like a Christmas tree fairy.'

I don't allow the image access to my brain. Thatcher was the evil queen of my childhood. My parents had her marked down as the daughter of Satan.

Eventually, after another round of the repetitions game, he drains his glass.

'Come on,' he says. 'It's time for a ride in the country. You'd better drive.'

He's outside the door by the time I've paid the bill, and he's got that impatient, man-of-action, bull-at-a-gate look. I feel as if I've just launched a warhead.

'Where are we going?' I ask once we're in the car, heading nowhere.

'Westleigh Grange to see the doctor.'

'Why?' I ask foolishly.

'I've got an enlarged prostate. Why do you think?' he says. 'Which reminds me... pull over there, will you? I need to take a leak.'

'Where?' I almost howl. 'We're on a busy road. There are people everywhere. There's nowhere...'

'By those bins.'

I pull up where three bins await collection, and he climbs out, leaving the door open. He turns towards me and begins to open his zip to urinate in the gutter, his back to the bins.

This isn't a sight I want to see on a full stomach, so I stick my fingers in my ears, close my eyes tight, and try to think of something — anything. I only open them when I hear the door slam shut, and Slattery eases himself back on the seat like a dog making a bed.

'I tell you, Phil, there's nothing good about growing old. Bloody prostate — you get no notice; you've just got to go.'

'Not really compatible with a beer-drinking lifestyle, then?'

'Ain't that the truth.'

We pull up outside the Grange, and it's clear at once that the gardener has been doing his work. The lawns are freshly cut, their edges trimmed. There are plants in the newly turned soil, and there are more in hanging baskets and tubs along the front of the house. He's even started work cutting back the trees and bushes along the drive.

There's a builder's van too and some scaffolding at the gable where a couple of guys are working on the chimney, and it looks like someone's started on the paintwork.

Slattery climbs out and stands at the front of the car. He leans against the hood and lights a cigarette. I see a face appear at the sash window beside the door; then the door opens and someone comes out. He's not a big guy, but I get the feeling there are substantial muscles underneath that blue suit, and I think I hear the ground reverberate under his polished tread. I want to swallow and whimper, but Slattery is unmoved.

'Are you sure that's safe?' he says to the guy, casual-like, and he nods towards the scaffolding, blowing smoke like an indicator.

The man stops in his tracks.

'What?'

'The scaffolding was moving. There! See it?'

The man looks bemused. Slattery eases himself off the hood and steps past him towards the house.

'Is the doc at home?' he asks.

The man runs to block his way.

'Have you got an appointment?'

Slattery laughs. 'What sort of a dickhead would turn up without an appointment?' he says.

'What's your name?'

'Slattery — Detective Inspector Slattery, Sefton CID. We're investigating a missing person.'

'And him?'

He looks at me as if I've just crawled out from under the car.

'Mr Tyler,' Slattery says, as if the guy should know who I am just by looking at me. He lays this emphasis on Mr — *Mr* Tyler — like I'm a surgeon or something. 'Chop-chop; we haven't got all day.'

The guy disappears only to return a moment later. Behind the muscles and the expensive suit, a scarcely adequate brain is slowly revealing itself.

'She says to go through.'

'That's evolution for you,' Slattery mutters. 'Put an ape in a suit and you don't get Einstein.'

'Maybe Frank Einstein?' I suggest, but Slattery ignores me.

She's waiting for us at the door to a sizeable office; it's big enough to hold my entire apartment. I'm expecting someone about 50, power dressed, who looks like a cabinet minister out to impress, so I wouldn't be exaggerating to say I'm shocked to find I'm looking at someone my own age — shocked and depressed. She's dressed, managerial style, in a suit, scarf, and efficient shoes, and her hair is brushed back so it won't hinder her penetrating and incisive stare. Suddenly, I want to go home to scour Facebook for someone I used to know who is doing worse than me. *Schadenfreude* — it's my guilty secret.

The shock and depression get worse when I see a look of recognition light up her face. She reaches out a hand, and says, 'Philip? Philip Tyler?'

I nod like one of those stupid dog toys people put in the back of their cars. Then I recognise her, and I want to go away into a corner and hide my head. I struggle to dredge a weak smile from somewhere, but it's half-hearted at best. At worst, it looks like I've eaten something nasty and I'm about to throw up on the carpet.

'Melissa,' I manage to stutter. 'Melissa Barr...'

She leans across to plant a kiss on my cheek. I try to reciprocate and manage to kiss nothing.

'It must be eighteen or nineteen years,' she says.

We were 15, I think; it was my first real romance — followed by my first real heartbreak. I thought the world was going to end when we finished. I vowed never to love anyone else. I played the same stupid song over and over. I wept buckets. Every time I saw her at school or on the streets, I wanted to sink through the cracks in the paving. Either that or I wanted someone to attack her just so I could heroically rescue her. Then I got all bitter and reckoned I'd leave them to it — I'd just watch and then walk past with a 'to hell with you' look.

Then I met Tanya. She dumped me too.

Your teens are the happiest days of your life, they say; that doesn't leave me with much hope for the rest of them.

'I didn't realise you were...' I wave my hand airily to indicate the house and the clinic beyond. 'You work for Logrum?'

'Yes.'

'As a doctor?'

She laughs. 'I'm their administrative assistant,' she says. 'I deal with the office side of things. I'm also a private secretary for Doctor Harris. She manages the clinic.'

'You're doing well for yourself,' I say through half-gritted teeth. God, I wish I could be sincere.

'Yes, I suppose I am. I've been lucky.' Then comes the question I hate. 'What about you?'

I hear this snort from Slattery who's taken himself off to look at some of the photos on the wall and to skim through a few items on a table. Melissa is keeping a close eye on him.

'I'm a journalist for The Evening Post.'

'How exciting!' There's another subdued snort from Slattery's direction. 'Are you working on anything at the moment?'

I can feel my skin prickling and my face turning an unnatural shade of red.

'He wants to interview your Doctor Harris,' Slattery says, 'about the work at the clinic — a background piece.'

'And you?' Melissa turns to him, and her face sharpens. I start to think of scalpels. 'What's your interest?'

'Missing persons, a kidnapping, and unreported burglaries... just routine inquiries. Is the doc in?'

'Please sit down,' Melissa says, and it's clear she's pressed a switch marked "business mode".

'Is there anyone here called Bunny?' Slattery asks.

'What?'

'Never mind. Have you a broken window round the back?'

'Yes, but I don't see...'

'You were burgled. The silly sod didn't know the place was empty.'

'Well, there's no harm done. I can assure you that security is very tight now. There'll be no more opportunities for a thief.'

'The thief didn't turn up for a few days after he came here. He'd been born again — truly miraculous — got God and everything. We can't figure it out.'

'I don't see what that has to do with us. As you said, the place was empty.'

'Maybe. Maybe not; we're trying to find out what happened to him.'

'If he's just some common thief...'

'Have you seen a naked man wandering about? No, don't answer. Your private life is your own. Only, we've lost a naked man, you see, and he was last seen wandering down the lane at night, calling out for the love of his life...'

'I have no idea what you're talking about. I...'

'No, nobody does. Forget it; like I said, it's just routine inquiries.'

'Inspector...?'

'Slattery.'

'Could I see your identification?'

Slattery ignores her.

'What's going on in this clinic, then?' he asks; it's a change of subject that could cause whiplash. 'Rich druggies, is it?'

Melissa stands up, and, suddenly, the security guy is there, standing with his feet apart, flexing his muscles, and looking serious.

'What do you want, Philip?' she asks, turning to me.

I take the photo of Wendy from my pocket. It's a bit creased now so I press it smooth and lay it on the table.

'Pretty,' she says. Her eyes add, "out of your league," but I ignore them. What does she know?

'She's missing.'

'And you're looking for her?'

'Yes.'

'That's just like you — always looking out for the underdog. How does it concern us?'

'We think she could be here,' I tell her. 'Some guys with suits and court orders tried to abduct her. They said they worked for Logrum.'

Now she's laughing, and it sounds genuine, like she isn't scornful or defensive — just bemused.

'There's no one here yet. We haven't opened. You must be mistaken.'

'She was in this clinic some months back too, but she managed to escape.'

'That's impossible. Like I said, we don't have any patients; besides, you don't "escape" from places like this. Unless you've been sectioned, you just walk out of the door.'

It's my turn to laugh.

'I think she might be back here. Maybe she was brought back here yesterday, but no one told you.'

'I can assure you, there are no patients here.'

Either she really believes what she's saying or she's mastered the art of perfect lying. She nods to the guy at the door, and he opens it without taking his eyes off us. He stands waiting like a menacing concierge at a dodgy hotel.

'Are you from the States?' Slattery asks the guy. His voice takes on a characteristic sharpness, like he's pinning an idea to the door.

'Washington,' the guy says, 'DC.'

'And the doctor?' he asks, turning to Melissa. 'I bet next week's pension she's from the States.'

'We're an American company,' Melissa says. 'It's hardly surprising.'

'Is that where you were hired, love?'

'I was headhunted from another establishment since you ask.' There's more than a hint of anger in her voice now. I don't think she likes being addressed as "love" by someone who looks like Slattery.

'Someone tried to do that to me once,' he says, 'but I fought them off. My head's my own. Who owns your head, sweetie? Do they own your thoughts too?'

'These gentlemen are leaving,' she says, rising to her feet, and the guy at the door steps forward as if he's about to take Slattery by the elbow. The words "red rag to a bull" flit through my mind, and I wince, expecting the worst, but Slattery just steps away and lifts a paper from the table top.

'You seem like a sensible girl,' he says. 'Take a look around.'

That's "love," "sweetie," and "girl". I think he's doing it on purpose, riling her and throwing down a challenge. I can see a tic developing in her cheek. 'You're either a sweet, naïve little thing or you're complicit; unless of course you've just been seduced and silenced by a large paycheck.'

'Leave now!' she snaps, and she clicks her fingers towards the guard.

Two seconds later, the security guard is doubled up on the floor, Slattery is nursing his hand, and he's swearing. He's not lost the element of surprise, and his penchant for brutality seems undiminished.

'There's something going on, Mel,' I say. Then, before I have time to control it, out comes a string of clichés the size of tenement blocks. 'You don't know what you're getting involved in. These people are dangerous. You've got to get out while you can.'

Shit, that sounds so pathetic.

'And while you're mulling over that good advice, can you call the organ grinder, dear?' Slattery says. 'I've some questions to ask. Shit, I think I've broken my hand; I need to see a doctor.'

Melissa looks like she's about to tear at his face. I can already see claws emerging at the ends of her fingers: mee-ow! Only, less cat and more tiger.

Then doors open simultaneously at each side of the room. Two security guards appear at one, and a dark-skinned woman in a floral robe appears at the other. She's about 50 I'd guess and definitely on her day off. She raises a hand, and it's clear where the power lies in this place because, at a flick of the wrist, she dismisses the security guards. They pick up their colleague and slink away.

'You may go too, Melissa,' she says. Melissa hesitates. 'Go!' She turns to me and flashes a smile. 'Mr Tyler, I assume.' She holds out an elegant hand. 'And your colleague?'

'D.S. Slattery, Sefton CID,' he says.

'Retired,' she says with half a smile. 'Last year, wasn't it? Are you enjoying your retirement?' She doesn't give him a chance to answer. 'Now, what's all this nonsense about a naked man and a missing woman?'

I glance round the room. She doesn't look like someone who'd listen at doors, but she's obviously heard everything. There must be a camera or a microphone here somewhere, only, I can't see it.

'It's not nonsense, I can assure you. She was brought here. I got a visit from a vicious thug the other night too; he made it very clear I should stop asking questions about this clinic. What are you hiding?'

'That's no secret, Mr Tyler. You've spoken to Mr Wigmore, so you understand our reasons for secrecy. However, I can assure you that, whoever your mystery assailant might be, he wasn't sent by us. We have nothing to hide and no reason to threaten people. Our work is entirely above board, and it will be open to inspection by the relevant authorities.'

'Who *are* the relevant authorities?'

She sighs.

'You're searching for a conspiracy where none exists, Mr Tyler.' She moves — or floats rather — towards a table by the window, unlocks a drawer, and removes a business card. 'Our work has received clearance at the highest level. We'll be caring for patients who've chosen to come here and who have paid for our services. They'll receive the very highest standard of care and the most innovative approaches to therapy.'

The card carries the name of an official at the Home Office.

'Why is the Home Office involved?'

'Speak to them, Mr Tyler.'

'Can you not tell me?'

'I'm afraid not. I can assure you, however, that if this young lady was admitted to any establishment like Westleigh, she would have gone there voluntarily. But wherever she is, she's not here.'

Slattery is getting impatient, but he barely has time to start his sniffing-the-air routine before the door opens and a handful of burly police constables surround us. Even Slattery knows better than to fight back. One or two of them nod at him — hesitant old friends.

'Hi, guys,' he grins, wide mouthed. 'You're just in time. Arrest them.'

Five minutes later, we're handcuffed and in a police car heading back to Sefton.

'Well, this is fun,' Slattery laughs.

I doubt Liz will think so.

Chapter 21

We're out within a couple of hours but not without written warnings. Slattery only escapes the deepest of deep shit piles by denying that he was impersonating a police officer on the grounds that he was one — not now, admittedly — but he definitely was one once. I back up his assertion that he misled no one intentionally. Anyway, we get a high-order bollocking from the new DCI and leave.

'Think yourselves lucky they don't want to press charges.'

Slattery slips him an unwelcomed wink. 'I consider myself truly honoured,' he says.

'Come on; let's get out of here.' I risk giving him a dig in the ribs with my elbow. The last thing we need is a pissed off DCI on our case. This is a moment for a bit of humility. If I had a forelock to tug, I'd be pulling at it right now.

Yes, sir, I'll stay out of trouble. No, sir, I'll never do it again. I'm sorry for the trouble I've caused, sir.

Not Slattery, though; he still sees himself as the rebel. It takes an effort to prise him out of the door, and I add a few extra grovelling apologies on his behalf. Even then, he has to have the final word.

'They daren't prosecute us,' he calls. 'They're scared of what we might say. You remember that.'

When I manage to drag him out, we head for a coffee at Maggie's just to settle my nerves. Slattery wants a whisky at The Wheatsheaf, but my stomach is in no shape for alcohol, and, for once, I win. We sit near the window while Slattery shows his resilience by ordering a plate of cakes.

'Your treat,' he says. 'You owe me.'

'For what? Getting me arrested?'

'You'd have got nothing without me.'

'I got nothing anyway. What do we do now?'

'Get rid of the guy from the police station who's been following you and go back to the chalet. I'll phone a few old friends and see what I can find out. Only, I don't see there's much you can do unless the nervous nurse gives you a new lead or the girl turns up. I mean, you know they're up to something, and it's not all that squeaky clean, doing-their-bit-for-society shit. But unless we turn up something new...'

He shrugs.

'But you'll help us?'

'I don't like them,' he says, 'and I'm bored, so yeah, count me in.'

It's good to have Slattery on side. He adds a whole new dimension to the phrase "loose cannon"; he's more like a loose warhead — our very own nuclear umbrella. It makes me feel just a little bit safer in a dangerous, unpredictable sort of way.

Then it hits me — what he just said.

'What guy who's following me?'

'He's sitting over there by the flowerbed, pretending to read a newspaper.'

Slattery raises a hand and waves, like he's saying hello to a little kid. The guy buries himself deeper in the news sheet.

'He's reading The Evening Post,' I say.

'Well, that's alright, then. For a minute, I thought we should be worried.'

He can be a sarcastic bastard sometimes.

'He's only holding it in front of his face,' I tell him. 'He's not reading it.'

'That must be a disappointment for you. Why don't you head off and lose him somewhere? You're making me tired.'

I manage to lose my pursuer by taking a route through the snooker hall, The Botanical Gardens, two pubs, and Marks and Spencer, and I'm feeling pretty pleased with myself by the time I reach the chalet. I take a deep breath before I explain to Liz, but she's really cool about everything. She says it's better to do something rather than nothing, even if you do make a complete bollocks of it and learn nothing.

'We've got to keep nipping at their heels and show them we're not going away. We've rattled them, and we'll keep rattling them. That's all we can hope to do at the moment.'

She's cool about Slattery too.

'That man gave me good copy over the years,' she says, 'but keep a tight hold. He's like a hand grenade with a loose pin.'

Dinner nowadays is microwaved ready meals. We've given up on home cooking. We've given up on the washing up too, so we don't use plates; we just scoop the lukewarm mush from the packaging it's delivered in. Then we have yoghurt or ice cream or packaged syrup puddings, which we finish off with chocolate digestives and bottled beer.

It's a diet to die for — or be killed by.

'There's something troubling me,' I say as I bite into my third biscuit. I take the business card the doctor gave me and set it in front of Liz. 'The doctor said "our work has received clearance at the highest level" — those were her exact words. What does that mean, Liz? Why would they need clearance for work which involves nothing more than catering to the emotional whims of the certifiable rich in rehab?'

'It means we're right. Something's going on in that clinic — something secret.'

'What is "the highest level?"'

'Good question — we should ask.'

'Shall I give this guy a ring?'

'No,' Liz says with a crocodile smile. 'Leave him to me. I eat self-important civil servants. It's my favourite dish.'

The next day, I get a phone call telling me Logrum has taken out an injunction. I have to keep well clear of its clinic and its employees or I'll be transported to the Colonies or something.

When I show it to Liz, her face widens into a smile.

'It feels like a victory, doesn't it?' she says.

'Not really; I feel like I've been clamped, ready to be towed away.'

'Don't be so negative,' she says. 'I can almost smell their fear.'

'That could be me,' I tell her.

'Richard Cross, Home Office,' she says, reading the business card for about the fifteenth time. 'I've never heard of him. I think *you* should call him.'

'I thought you planned to eat him all by yourself?'

'I'll hold myself in reserve,' she says. 'Phase two: the heavy guns...'

I head to the bedroom to make the call.

'No listening at the door,' I warn her. I don't want Liz hovering just behind me, telling me what to ask and what to say. 'I'm doing this my way.'

She puts her fingers in her ears and starts to sing.

'Regrets, I've had a few, but then again, too few to mention...'

It's too much. I can't cope with this frivolous version of Liz. I preferred it when I was petrified. At least I knew my place back then. I quicken my pace and close the door.

'I did it my way...'

Mr Cross is just what I expected — Eton, Oxbridge, the City, then a comfortable job with like-minded people in the higher reaches of the Civil Service. He has an accent which could be used to polish tables and a textbook diplomatic manner. As soon as he starts to speak, I hear a metronome in the background, ticking away the syllables.

I don't like him.

I've never met him, but I know I don't like him.

I think it's a class thing.

I have this weird response to people like Cross. I think maybe I'm compensating for a deep-rooted feeling of inadequacy. I try to be everything he isn't, and a careless, free-flowing application of local dialect is the weapon of choice. And I don't waste words either; I'm abrupt, to the point, and sharp to the point of rudeness. I want to be a stereotypical, call-a-spade-a-fucking-shovel northerner — which isn't like me at all.

It's great fun, especially since he talks like he's reading from a script.

When I emerge from the bedroom ten minutes later, the grin on my face must be wide enough to block streets. They'd need detours in place just to get past it.

'A successful call, I take it,' Liz says.

'Yeah, that was fun. Apparently, Logrum and its parent company are engaged in some research which could be of enormous benefit to the people of this country — nay, the entire world. Mr Cross was cautious enough to tell me as little as possible but enthusiastic enough to verge on hyperbole. "It's work of a sensitive nature and has significant economic and social potential" — quote. Apparently, it's a joint US/UK enterprise which could be a target for industrial espionage by other companies, hostile countries, and even, perhaps, the inhabitants of distant planets. He was close to suggesting that evil forces would think nothing of lining the streets with bodies in order to lay their hands on the data the clinics are producing. Clinics — plural, you note.

'I asked if he could be more specific about the research project, but he couldn't, so I asked whether the projects involved experimental procedures on human patients. "The research undertaken by Logrum complies with all the relevant regulations and is closely monitored by the Home Office" — another quote.

'I asked how patients were chosen to take part in the research. He assured me they were volunteers who matched the required medical criteria. When I asked whether people with serious mental impairments were in a fit state to volunteer, he said that their families were closely involved in the decision-making process.'

'Tim, perhaps,' Liz says, 'but maybe not Heather. I hope you asked him whether money ever changed hands as part of this decision-making process.'

'He was adamant it didn't.'

'I'll bet he was. What about the bullshit they told us about the purpose of the clinics?'

"The two aspects of Logrum's work aren't incompatible. The money raised by dependency treatments helps fund research work" — that's another quote; I wrote it down. The research work is secret. He's only telling us now to ensure there'll be no further intrusion or inquiry.'

'And he believes that? My goodness! How delightfully naïve of him!'

'He quoted the Official Secrets Act, several minor pieces of legislation, "D" notices, the likelihood of financial penalty, and incarceration.'

'I hope you laughed at him.'

'No, but I asked him about Wendy.'

'And?'

'He couldn't comment.'

'What about harassing her family?'

'Nonsense — it never happened — couldn't possibly have happened. They don't need to, since they have the law on their side.'

'Trying to kidnap her?'

'Any legal action would only be taken if it was in the patient's interests or if a law had been broken.'

'What about the frenzied bunny hunter?'

'He had no information about any such incident.'

'Why did they tell us there were no patients?'

'Understandable concerns about security.'

'Does the Home Secretary have any comments? Have there been any enquiries from our honourable member? Has he been made aware of what's happening in his constituency?'

'I didn't ask.'

'Are the relevant permissions available for public scrutiny? Can we go and have a look round and speak to a few patients? Is anyone from Logrum available for an interview? Who owns Logrum? Why is there so much secrecy about its parent companies? Why are the usual protocols regarding clinical research not being followed? How can there be a financial return on a clinical procedure unless it involves the use of new drugs or high-tech, specialised equipment? Isn't it usual for new techniques to be shared in order to benefit similar research elsewhere? What aspect of the research is of particular interest to our government?'

I was feeling pretty good about the phone call until now. Suddenly, I see the gulf between me and Liz. Where I finish the interview, she's just warming up. I get the feeling she could have asked questions for the rest of the day. I thought I'd finished after the opening salvo.

My moment of self-satisfaction melts like butter in a microwave.

Liz sees the look of pleasure disappear from my face as the grim reality of my inadequacy drops on me like a cowpat.

'You did very well,' she says. She even pats my shoulder and offers to make a coffee.

It's funny how it's often the words people *don't* say which cause the most distress.

What did you think of my article?

It was okay.

Or,

I love you.

Yes, you do, don't you?

Shit.

Chapter 22

I phone Heather, and we talk for half an hour or more. She's making a nuisance of herself at the police station, she tells me, but there's still no news of Wendy. The officer at the desk says he's contacted the clinic, but she's not there, and he has no reason to doubt whether they're telling the truth. It's a clinic, after all — a hospital. Why would they lie about a patient? The police have circulated Wendy's description, but there's not much else they can do. She'll turn up, the officer tells her.

'What about Tim? What does he say?'

'He says we should never have moved her out of Westleigh in the first place. He says no wonder she's so disorientated when she's only partway through her treatment. And he says...' She hesitates.

'Yes?'

'He says it's no coincidence that she ran away from the Westleigh people after *you* visited her. He thinks you tried to get a story out of her, scared her, or put silly ideas in her head. It's my fault for getting you involved, of course.'

Bastard, I think.

I also think there's something very suspicious about Tim.

'How are *you* coping?' I ask.

'I get through the days by keeping busy, but the evenings are bad. Don't worry about Tim. He'll come around; he's just worried about Wendy, that's all. He doesn't mean half of what he says.'

Bastard, I repeat, just to myself. 'I understand,' I tell Heather — diplomatic mode.

I tell Heather what little I can, mutter a few inadequate words of sympathy and support, then I hang up and make another coffee. For the next few minutes, I sit on the bed and let images of Wendy drift by like smoke, and

I get all melancholic and sentimental. I wish I had my CD collection here. There's something I really want to play just now — something depressingly sad...

The phone rings and it's Mel, the one-time love of my life, now Westleigh administrator, and I hit suspicious mode. Whatever she's after, she can't have it. No way. I'm cleverer than that. If it's a ploy, a trick, or a honey trap, I'm ready.

'Hi Phil,' she says. 'It was great seeing you again after all these years. It brought back so many good memories. I'm sorry I wasn't too welcoming — work, you know, and you took me by surprise... and your friend... well, that man has a real attitude problem; he's so aggressive.'

'Slattery, yeah,' I manage to stutter. 'He isn't famed for his social graces.'

'There was so much I wanted to talk to you about. I've spent the last couple of days thinking about nothing else.'

'Me too,' I lie.

'Maybe we could meet and have a drink or a meal just for old time's sake.'

'That'd be good.'

I'm so pathetic.

'Have you been to that new restaurant, The Silver Spoon, down by the river?' she asks. 'People tell me it's really good.'

'Yeah, I've been there a couple of times.'

I hope she can't hear my palpitations. The first time I went there, I was out to impress a girl, but the biggest impression was on my bank account. Jesus, I swear my debit card started to smoulder when I paid the bill. The second time, I got the cheapest item on the menu, and I still needed an overdraft.

'I love seafood,' Mel says.

I don't like shellfish, I can't stand crab, and I won't touch lobster because things that have been boiled alive aren't appetising, but I don't tell her that. It's not suave, is it? I mean, everyone who's anyone loves that stuff. They have some other dishes at The Silver Spoon, but they kind of look down on you if your food hasn't got an exoskeleton and isn't radioactive.

'Me too,' I lie again.

Really doubly pathetic.

'What about tonight? There's no time like the present.'

'Yeah, that'd be good.'

'7.30? I'll book us a table.'

'7.30 — that's fine with me.'

'I'll see you there, then?'

'Yeah, I look forward to it.'

'But no shop talk; let's make that a rule. Let's just talk about us.'

'Agreed — no shop talk.'

And that's that.

Like I said, I'm no fool. Does she think I'll just roll over and do whatever she wants? I'm no mug. Besides, there's no room in my life for romance — not at the moment — even if her motives are as pure as the proverbial. That space is taken by an impossible dream. For a fleeting moment, I feel guilty, as if I've betrayed Wendy, and I have to remind myself that we've only met twice, and, while I may be characteristically besotted, I'm about as interesting to her as a stale loaf of bread.

It's time for me to face up to reality about both of them, especially Melissa.

She's after something, isn't she? I'd lay a bet that she's out to prise information from me. I apply a cynical handbrake to my emotions, and I remind myself that Melissa hasn't given me a thought in years. She dumped me for Roy Pettigrew, who had acne and all the charm of a nosebleed. He was two years older than me, and he had a car, and, God, I hated him. If I'd had superpowers back then, I swear he'd have felt the full force of them. His atoms would have been scattered throughout the universe.

'Roy Pettigrew,' I mutter. 'I mean, dumping me for that pimply prick. What was she thinking?'

'Who are you talking to?' Liz calls from the lounge.

'My love life's getting complicated,' I call back.

'That's nice,' she says. 'It'll make a pleasant change.'

I decide it's easier to go for a walk than to think of a suitably sharp reply, so I grab my coat and head out.

Chapter 23

I arrive at The Silver Spoon far too early, and I sit with a bottle of beer in my hand, feeling uncomfortable. £6.50 for a bottle of beer! I think you pay a premium in this place if you don't drink expensive wines; the owners must be trying to discourage the habit. I'm wearing my best casual wear so I can pretend I'm feeling good about myself.

Then Melissa arrives, and every head in the place turns, and I feel about as stylish as a cobweb. I get the feeling people are looking at her, then at me, and it's *Beauty and the Beast* all over again. I have this irresistible urge to wipe my nose on my sleeve and grunt, just to show how little I care about what they think.

Ten seconds later, I don't give a shit about anything.

'You look fantastic,' I tell her.

'Thank you,' she smiles. 'I don't go out as often as I used to — there's always too much to do at that place we're not going to talk about. But it's been years since we last met, so I thought the occasion deserved a special effort.'

She doesn't mention how good I look after my special effort.

See what I mean? It's the words people *don't* say...

'So tell me about yourself,' she says. 'What have you been up to? My mum mentions you sometimes. She gets the Evening Post. You used to work for that local free sheet, didn't you?'

'Until someone threw petrol over it and burned it down.'

'Mum told me about that. It's awful.'

'It's amazing how bitter people get when they don't win "Letter of the Week."'

'Something to do with corruption and murder, wasn't it?'

'Look on the bright side: it got me the job at The Post.'

'It must be interesting to work on a regional paper.'

'It was until the company got taken over and I was made redundant.'

'Oh God, Phil, that's dreadful. What are you going to do?'

I shrug. I can't tell her the truth. That'd be like heading into deep water when you can't swim. No, it's time to head back to dry ground; I won't risk drowning.

'Something will turn up. What about you? Did you marry Pettigrew and have a family?'

She laughs like a tinkling bell, and her eyes shine almost as much as her hair. 'Oh my God,' she says. 'Don't remind me! What a mistake. What was I thinking?'

'You were thinking he had a car. Besides, he was two years older, mature, and sophisticated... and spotty.'

'The mistakes we make,' she laughs. 'Do you remember...?' and then we're off, and we only break from talking to order food, to watch it being served, and to eat it. The evening races by, we drink more beer and wine than we ought to, and we say more than we planned. She tells me about her time at Westleigh, the fantastic work they're doing, the clientele they're hoping to attract, and the people who work there. It's clear she has no idea about their little sideline — their mysterious, government-backed research project. As far as she's concerned, they're just a clinic offering a caring service to the rich and famous.

'I'll probably meet pop stars and actors,' she says. 'Maybe I'll marry an old, frail businessman and he'll die, and I'll become a rich widow. What do you think?'

'I think you'd make an outstanding rich widow.'

'You could be my secret lover,' she says.

'I'd make an outstanding secret lover,' I tell her.

Eventually, the restaurant empties. There's just me and Mel and a handful of disconsolate-looking waiters who want to go home. We grow quiet and look around.

'Time to go,' I suggest. 'That guy over there is falling asleep.'

I brace myself and pick up the bill.

'Halves,' she says, 'no arguments.'

It's a relief, I can tell you. The last time I saw an amount like that, it was on a mortgage statement.

It's dark outside, and there's a soft rain falling. Streetlights shimmer in pools. There are still people about — mostly couples heading home, a few families, and a few drunks.

'Listen, Mel, I've had a really great evening. I wasn't sure how it'd be, you know, after all this time, but it's as if the years have just faded away.'

'Me too,' she says. 'It's a shame it has to end.'

Then she looks at me, and, a moment later, we're kissing and then I'm taking her home. When we reach her apartment, we can barely wait for the door to open before we're all over each other. Buttons are ricocheting off the walls and there are items of clothing forming an untidy trail towards her bedroom. Then we're on the bed and...

And then...

And...

Well, I'll spare you the details. Words won't do it.

And in that warm, post-coital haze, as the occasional car slips by on the wet roads, and distant voices call, we lie in the glow of a bedside lamp. She rests her head on my chest, and we sleep.

I expect to wake up in the morning to find she's gone and left a note on my pillow that says "thanks but no thanks," but she hasn't, and there isn't. We lie there for half an hour, then we dress and go through to the kitchen for coffee and bagels.

'Can we meet again?' I ask.

She nods and smiles.

'What time is it?' she asks. 'Shit, it's half eight. I'm late for work.'

'And I'm late for Liz!' I add. 'She'll be wondering where the hell I am.'

Back to reality, I guess.

Chapter 24

Back to reality, eh? Only, reality isn't that good — not today. Liz is in a filthy mood, and she isn't holding back.

'Why the hell didn't you phone? Don't you understand how important it is that we don't take risks? You could have been mugged, kidnapped, or killed for all I knew. They could've been on their way here, and our work wouldn't have meant anything.'

'That's just melodramatic, Liz.'

'No, it isn't. It bloody well isn't!'

I guess she's right. I should have phoned. Only, I don't get a chance to apologise because she's turned her attention to Melissa. It's clear she trusts her about as far as she can throw the chalet, and she thinks I'm stupid enough to give away everything we decided to keep secret. I'm well past apologising by the time she says, 'No offence, Philip, but it only has to be female and feign vulnerability and you're on your knees in a state of total subjection. What did you tell her?'

I try that counting-to-ten strategy but it's not working, so I try breathing deeply. That doesn't work either. My heart's beating like a war drum.

'We didn't talk about work. It wasn't that sort of evening.'

'For goodness' sake, you *were* her work. Can't you see that?'

'Go to hell, Liz. It's possible for someone to like me, you know. They don't have to be paid to sleep with me.'

'I'm sure that's true — but not her. It was a piece of good luck for them that you and Mel turned out to have a history. They must've been rubbing their hands together. Think carefully; what did you tell her?'

'Nothing. I'm not a fool so stop treating me like one.'

'Did you talk about Wendy?'

'Well, yeah, but I only said that she was missing and I was trying to find her.'

'Winston and Benny?'

'She knew them from the old days. We talked about the past and only the past. Give me some credit, Liz.'

'You'd sell your soul for the right sort of smile.'

'You know nothing about me. You know even less about Mel.'

'I know enough. Did she tell you anything of interest?'

'She doesn't know anything. She has no idea about the research at Westleigh; she thinks the clinic is exactly what it seems to be — a very select dependency unit for the rich and famous. I swear she knows no more than we do.'

'And I swear she knows a hell of a lot more.'

'You're such a cynic, Liz, you know that?'

'Did you tell her where you're staying?'

'She didn't ask.'

'Did you say anything about what we're doing?'

'No.'

'Well, we can be grateful for that. Are you seeing her again?'

'Yes.'

'You're an idiot.'

'Go to hell.'

That's about as good as it got. I knew the chalet was a bad idea. Suddenly, the whole site is too small; I need to get out and go for a walk. *Again.*

'It's your turn to make dinner,' Liz yells after me. 'And I don't want another bloody takeaway.'

I'm on the promenade by the time I calm down. I think I'll walk around for an hour and then go back, pretending nothing's happened. There'll be no apology from Liz, that's for sure. She doesn't do apologies.

I'm about halfway through my meditative wander, and I'm not feeling good. Liz has sown a seed of suspicion, and I can't stop from it growing into a nasty weed in my cosy, romantic garden. What if she's right? What if Mel is just playing me? What if...?

Stop! Stop right there!

What?

Trust your own judgement for once. You were there. Liz wasn't. Did Mel try and get any information out of you?

No, not once.

Did she know anything about the research programme?

No, I'm sure she didn't.

Does she like you?

Yeah, I think so.

And you like her?

Yeah, I guess so. She makes me feel...

Okay, okay, spare me the details. Do you trust her?

Yes.

So you just have to be careful not to say anything and it'll be okay?

Yes. I just have to be sensible.

You can do that, right?

Yeah.

Okay then. Liz can sod off.

I suppose so.

This is as far as I've got with my internal dialogue when a police car passes me and pulls up just ahead. The window slides open, and a face I half recognise looks out. It's a guy who worked with Slattery — one of the trusted few.

'Get in,' he says. 'There's not much time.'

'Why? What's going on?'

'Just get in, will you? Slattery says I'm to use force if it's required.'

When we approach the police station, there's a black limousine parked outside, right across the entrance — apparently, its owner is too important to use the parking bays. It's sleek, with shining chrome, and has dark windows.

'I've never seen a car as clean as that,' I say.

PC Jim Davey — I remember his name now — doesn't look pleased to see it. He swears under his breath, slows down, and turns the car towards the side of the building.

'We'll need to go in through the back. Stan will stall them for as long as he can. You remember Stan, our desk sergeant?'

'Yeah. What's this all about, Jim?'

'Slattery's waiting in the cells.'

'What?'

He doesn't have time to say anything else before we pull up by a rear door. He climbs out and punches in the code. Slattery is inside, pacing a corridor. From beyond a closed door, I can hear impatient voices. Stan is repeating something in a relentless monotone; it sounds like the buzzing of a drone.

'Here, sign this,' Slattery says, 'and make it illegible.'

'What am I supposed to sign?'

'How should I know? Just scribble something. Make it look medical. Hurry up.'

I scribble "Doc Holliday". Slattery grabs the paper and hands it to Jim.

'Thanks, Jim,' he says. 'Tell Stan I owe him one.'

'What's this about?' I ask, but I don't need an answer because he pushes a cell door open and the answer is standing there looking at me.

'I lost your card,' she says. 'But I remembered you were called Phil.'

'She turned up at the desk, asking for a journalist called Phil. She was confused and distressed, and it looked like she'd been sleeping rough,' Slattery murmurs. 'Luckily, Stan was on duty. He recognised her, and he called me before he spoke to Jennings, the new DCI — good job too, because DCI Jennings called Westleigh as soon as he heard. We've got to get her out of here, Phil. Stan won't be able to bluff for much longer. There are three lawyers and two doctors out there. They're really pulling out all the stops. They're desperate to get her back.'

We slip out the back door and into Slattery's grey Escort. Then we take the rear exit to the car park and drive away with Wendy sitting silently in the back seat.

'God knows how Stan will explain this,' he grins. 'Still, your signature should buy us a bit of time.'

'You think so?'

'Nah, not really, but it might keep Stan out of the shit pile for a few hours.'

'Where are we going?'

'Around in circles at the moment,' he says. 'I have no idea. Your place isn't safe and nor is mine. Any ideas?'

Desperate situations, right? I fall back on a seriously desperate measure and give Slattery directions. He looks at me as if I just fell out of a cloud.

'You've got to be joking,' he says.

'I wish I was,' I tell him.

We pull up outside a neat terraced house on a quiet estate near the park. The garden wall has gone, and there's a paved area for a car. It's empty, so Slattery pulls into it.

'I hope you know what you're doing,' he says.

We help Wendy out of the car, and I ring the bell. It plays some reggae chime deep in the interior. Then we wait.

Nothing.

I ring it again as Slattery looks up and down the street and eases a protective arm around Wendy's shoulder.

'Maybe there's no one in.'

Then I hear someone approach and fumble with the latch. The door opens, and a wizened, dark face appears. There's a smile of recognition, and the door opens wider to reveal an old woman with a walking frame.

'Hi, Patience,' I say. 'Is Winston about?'

Chapter 25

Slattery has taken over the kitchen. He's pretending to make coffee, but, mainly, he's keeping out of the way. He's left the doors open, though, so he can hear Patience and Wendy in the lounge. If he can hear half of what I can hear as I climb the stairs behind Winston, he'll have a grin on his face the size of a crescent moon.

Lord, when you hear Patience talk, you know where Winston gets it from. She might not find it easy to get around anymore, but that hasn't stopped her mind from travelling or her conversation from following where it leads. Within five minutes, she and Wendy are talking like sisters. I wouldn't have believed it if I hadn't seen it. When I left the room, she'd already got the photo album out.

'He's such a good boy, my Winston — always was. Look at him here...'

Winston shuts the door of his bedroom behind us, and their voices are gone.

'What the hell, man?' he says. He's got a look on his face like I've just told him I'm carrying a contagious disease. 'I mean, he's with the police, and she's...she's...'

'A woman, yeah,' I help him.

'Yeah. I mean, shit, man, why'd you bring them here?'

'I was desperate, Winston. Why else? I need somewhere for her to stay for a few days, until I can sort things out.'

'No way, man. No way.' I've never seen Winston look startled before. It's like I've plugged him into a socket. 'I mean, this just ain't the place.'

'We got her away just in time. If it wasn't for Slattery, she'd be banged up in that clinic — like Benny.'

'I'd like to help, man, truly. But here? In my house? You've got to be kidding me. There's my mam to think of...'

'Sounds to me like they're getting on okay; it's like they've known each other forever. It'd be good for both of them.'

'Yeah, well, that may be so, but what if they come looking?'

'It's just for a couple of days. Besides, your mum's more than a match for a couple of lawyers.'

'Yeah, man, but...'

'Wendy will help out and give you a break. You need a break, Winston. You look tired.'

'Don't try and play me, Tyler...'

'What do you say? Forty-eight hours? That's all I need.'

Winston opens the door and listens. Patience's voice rises up the stairs, and then she bursts into a laugh which seems to shower bright sparks like a firework.

'The old lady does seem to be enjoying herself,' he says, 'and she does like company.' Then he turns sharply. 'How much?'

'What?'

'I'm not a homeless charity. Fifty a night for bed and board sounds good to me.'

'It would sound good, wouldn't it? A hundred quid? Have a heart; I've just been made redundant, Winston.'

He shrugs. 'It's a seller's market,' he says. 'Business is business.'

It looks like we're back to normal.

I part unwillingly with the cash, and we head for the stairs.

'She's a nice-looking girl,' he says as we pause on the bannister. 'Do you think we...?'

'No, definitely no, Winston.'

'Spoken for, yeah?'

'Yeah, something like that. Besides, she's been ill.'

'So it's hands off.'

'Most definitely.'

'That's a pity, you know; we could be made for each other — kindred spirits.'

'Like a dog turd in the virgin snow,' I tell him.

'Whereas you...?'

'I'm a willow bending in her gentle breeze.'

'Shit, man, that's truly pathetic, you know.'

'Yeah, I know.'

He changes the subject so quickly, I get whiplash.

'Can you hear them in the lounge? I haven't heard Mum laugh that much in years.'

Slattery meets us at the kitchen door. He's carrying a tray of coffees and some biscuits on a plate. 'I found them in a cupboard,' he says. He nods towards the lounge. 'It sounds like they're getting on in there.'

'Yeah, but I've got to get that album off my mum,' Winston mutters. 'Some of the pictures... embarrassing shit, you know. You've got to help me, Phil, before she shows Wendy. I mean, some pictures are for family eyes only, right?'

'Whatever you say, Winston.'

We're a little late to save Winston. As we push the door open, Patience turns a page and points to a photo.

'And here's one of my Winston in his bath. He must be 5 or 6. Isn't he adorable? Look at his little...'

Wendy moves to one side as Slattery and I add to the embarrassment and Winston starts to sweat.

'For fuck's sake, Mum...'

She looks up sharply.

'I'll have none of that language in this house,' she says. 'God only knows where he gets it from; he has a mouth like a sewer — and with ladies present too. You should be ashamed, boy.'

'Sorry, Mum,' he says.

'It *is* little, isn't it?' Slattery says, deadly serious.

I want to laugh. I want to laugh so much. I daren't look at Slattery. I can't look at Winston. Even Wendy has a smile flickering like a candle flame.

Over coffee, I explain to Wendy that she'll be staying with Winston and Patience and that she'll be safe here because Winston will look after her when I'm not around.

'No one will bother you here, honey,' Patience says.

Wendy turns to me, and one of those smiles flows from her eyes. It's like a glowing mist. I think I need to sit down. But there's no time for that; I have to share a few things with Patience, just so she understands, and I need her to keep Winston in check. It won't take him five minutes to tell the world he's got a cute girl staying with him.

'You want to show Wendy her room?' I suggest to Winston.

'Yeah, sure,' he says with a stupid smile. He looks like a kid who's been given a huge ice cream all to himself. While he's out, I explain as much as I can about Wendy's state of mind, about what she's suffered, and about what she needs from Patience and Winston.

'Why, the poor dear,' Patience says, and there are tears in her eyes. 'That's a lot for a young soul to deal with.' She reaches out and takes my hands in hers. 'I'll look after her. You can be sure of that.'

'There's just one thing, Patience. No one can know she's here. If word gets out, it could be dangerous for her, and it could be dangerous for you and Winston too.'

'He won't say nothing to nobody,' she says, reading my mind. 'I'll see to that.'

I believe her.

Another formidable woman — where are they all coming from?

Slattery glances at his watch, and I figure it's time for us to leave. We catch a quick word with Winston, say goodbye to Wendy, and head for the car.

'I see your dilemma,' Slattery says as we drive out of the street and head towards the promenade.

'What dilemma?'

He just laughs.

'What dilemma?' I ask again.

'I would fall for her myself if I were younger,' he says.

'I'm with Mel, remember.'

'Yeah,' he grins, '*that's* your dilemma.' Then he grins even wider. 'It's like buses, isn't it? You wait for ages and then two come along at once.'

I don't even swear at him.

'Come on,' he says. 'It's time we consulted the organ grinder. No offence.'

'It'll be a change to watch her grind someone else's organs,' I tell him.

When we reach the chalet, Liz isn't there, but she's left a message which has been hastily scribbled on a post-it note and stuck on the computer screen.

Gone digging; I'll tell you what I find when I get back.

Don't use all the milk.

The chocolate biscuits are mine.

'It's like a home from home for you, isn't it?' Slattery grins. Then he adds, 'You and Liz, what a team! How can we lose?'

I don't bother trying to argue.

'We'll have a coffee while we wait,' I tell him. To show my independence, I tear up the note and drop it in the bin. 'And biscuits — chocolate ones.'

Chapter 26

Liz hasn't come back and Slattery is looking at his watch and tapping his foot like a man who has somewhere to go. Eventually, the strain is too much for him; he swears and heads for the door.

'Give me a ring,' he says, 'and keep an eye on Winston. That fool couldn't keep a secret if it was nailed to him. I'll get a couple of friends on the force to drive round there when they can, but it won't be often.'

'Patience will keep Winston on a choke chain.'

'I hope you're right, Phil, I really do.'

Then he's gone, and I'm on my own with too many worries to deal with. I've clambered out on so many limbs, one is sure to break. I mean, think about it: I've levelled threats towards people who have the power to hospitalise me. They've already shown their capacity for gratuitous violence at the least provocation, and they have all the resources of the Home Office and a multi-national corporation at their disposal. I've got no job; all I've got is a laptop and Liz — and Winston. Yeah, Winston. Slattery thinks he's as stable as feathers in the wind. And Liz thinks Mel is playing me for a fool. If either of them is right, I'm in the deepest of deep — and so is Wendy.

I hope I'm right about them.

I'm not the sort of person who likes perching on a high wire. I like the comfort of solid ground. I like to share really nasty decisions, or, better still, I like someone else to take them. I didn't even like being the library monitor at primary school. I used to have sleepless nights over missing books. Eventually, Mum tendered my resignation, which was reluctantly accepted.

No! I am not Prince Hamlet, nor was meant to be...

What is that from, T.S. Eliot? How does it go?

Am an attendant Lord, one that will do

To swell a progress, start a scene or two,

Advise the prince...

I studied that at school. Yeah, that's me alright — an attendant Lord on the sidelines, keeping my head down and keeping out of trouble.

So why am I overruling Slattery and Liz and telling them I know best? And why am I telling people who can break my legs that I'm going to investigate them? Why am I clambering onto a tightrope?

I'm just asking for trouble.

I phone Mel in the hope that talking to her will reassure me, and, for once, luck goes my way. We agree to meet and go see a film. It's one of those superhero things they churn out nowadays, and it's about as interesting as three-day-old gum, but that's what you get in Sefton during the summer. There's a cultural exclusion zone which starts about five miles out. The town's motto is "if it isn't mindless, we don't want it."

So I spend the evening with Mel, and everything's okay. I can watch sweat drip into a bucket so long as I'm with her. After the film, we go to a bar and try to talk above the din, and then we go back to her place and drink coffee.

I check my phone for the first time in hours, and there are two messages from Liz.

'What does she say?' Mel asks.

The first was sent at 14.37. It says, "I need to talk to you. Things are happening. There's no time to lose."

That's a bit enigmatic for Liz. Maybe she doesn't trust her phone.

I decide not to share it with Mel.

'Nothing much; we had a bit of a row this morning. She's just clearing the air.'

The second message is timed at 15.16.

"Make sure you're back tonight. I'll wait up. Don't phone."

'You look worried. Is everything alright?'

'Yeah, yeah, it's nothing that won't wait.'

I check my watch. It's after two. And Mel is changing into flimsy lingerie. And I can see through it. Liz will be tucked up in bed now anyway, whatever she said about waiting up. It's hardly my fault I couldn't hear my phone and didn't get her message until it was too late. If I'd got it earlier, I'd have gone back, I swear to God.

Mel is heading towards the bedroom. She's left the door open, and she's lying on the bed and...

I clamber to my feet and stumble after her.

Liz can swear at me tomorrow.

It's half eight when my phone rings and jars me out of sleep like my head's been stabbed.

It's Jon, my colleague from the paper, and the news is bad.

'When?' I ask. 'Jesus Christ, Jon, it can't be true.'

'What's the matter? What's happened?' That's Mel, who's breaking from sleep like she's pulling herself out of a web.

'It's Liz. There was a road traffic accident yesterday afternoon at about four. Jon says she ran out in front of a car — didn't even look — just stepped out as if it weren't there. The driver was this old guy taking his wife home from the doctor's; they weren't even going that fast.'

'How is she? Will she be okay?'

'I don't know. I've got to get down to the hospital. She's in an artificially induced coma. They're going to operate. Jesus, Mel, if I'd got that text... if I'd gone back...'

'It wouldn't have changed anything.'

She's right, but it doesn't make me feel any better. The last time Liz and I spoke, we had a row. When I think of that, I get this deep, burning pain, and I've got to work hard to drive it away. But there's no point in feeling like that now.

'I've got to go.'

'Phone me later,' Mel says. 'Let me know.'

'Yeah, of course.'

There's time for a warm, just-waking-up hug, and then I'm out of there and hurrying to the hospital, though why I'm hurrying I can't rightly say. Do I think I might not get there before she dies? Is that it? Or do I want to sit there and murmur words of encouragement and support into ears that won't even hear me?

Maybe I just want to know — to understand.

I mean, what happened?

Then it strikes me like a hammer blow, my stomach lurches, and I think I'm going to throw up. The accident was only a few streets away from Winston's house.

Chapter 27

'What was she doing down there?'

I'm with Jon, sitting in a waiting area in the hospital. Another couple are sitting opposite us with the same haggard, anxious looks on their faces. They're waiting for news, maybe of a mother or father, or of a sister, brother, son, or daughter. Like us, they're hoping for the best and fearing the worst while the seconds on the clock move like minutes, and the minutes move like hours. We exchange the occasional look and even a weak smile — mutual support that's worth nothing.

'I don't know. The old man, the driver, said she was running. She wasn't looking where she was going. She just ran into the road. They kept him in overnight — shock, they said. His wife stayed with him. She wouldn't go home without him.'

'How long before we know?'

'She's in surgery now. It'll be a few hours.'

'You should go home, Jon. You look done in.'

'Yes, I think I will. I've been here all night, but she has no one else, you know — just a sister who lives in London, and we've worked together for years.'

'I'll stay awhile,' I said. 'I'll call if there's any change.'

'Thanks. I'll get my head down for a few hours then come back.'

I sit for half an hour, drinking flavour-free coffee and reading a magazine about cars, which is as interesting as an insect bite. The doctor comes in once, and we all turn. He speaks in a whisper to the couple, and the three of them go out. There are no tears. Maybe it's good news. Or maybe he's taking them somewhere quiet to be alone.

Birth and death — the bookends of existence.

I wander through to find a nurse and ask about the old guy — the driver who ploughed into Liz. She says he's getting ready to leave. I think maybe I'll slip along and see if he can give me any more information. He's standing just outside the ward. His wife is adjusting his coat, and they're talking in low voices. They look like a nice, ordinary couple — the sort of people I like. They're growing old together and are somehow mellow, like they've worn out all their passions and are basking in a weird contentment only the old can understand.

I introduce myself, they ask about Liz, and we drift into a small waiting room to sit down. A flicker of sunlight breaks through the slats of grey blinds, and it patterns the table and walls.

'She just ran out.'

He's called Thomas, she's Helen, and they live out near the park, not far from my mum and dad. We call it the Retirement Zone locally. It's all bungalows, neat gardens, and "For Sale" signs from where people have either died or moved into care homes.

'I didn't even have time to touch the brake.'

'Where was she coming from — the coast side or inland?'

'She was heading towards the town centre and the promenade.'

Away from Winston's.

'I don't suppose you saw the street she came out of?'

'It was opposite the little Co-op on Hudson Road.'

She must've been coming from Winston's. What was she doing there?

I think back to the urgency of her message.

She must've spoken to Wendy. She must've... I've got to phone Winston.

I reassure Thomas and Helen, and I promise I'll phone them as soon as there's any news. Then I go back to the waiting room. Liz isn't back from surgery yet, so I head outside.

'Winston? Yeah, it's me.' I tell him about Liz.

'Shit, she was only here yesterday,' he says. 'She played rummy in the lounge with Mum and Wendy. You could hear them halfway down the street.'

'Played rummy?'

I'm having difficulty with this image — Liz playing cards with Patience and Wendy? Liz doesn't do frivolity — ever. Pure Calvinist, that's Liz, apart from the drinking, swearing, and atheism.

'Yeah, playing cards, and they were gossiping like a bunch of schoolgirls.'

'What were they talking about?'

'Damned if I know; I stayed upstairs and played music just to drown the sound. I tell you, man, if the old lady wasn't so happy...'

'You didn't hear anything?'

'As soon as they started talking girl-talk, I was out of there. Wendy was telling them about this guy, Marcus. I hate that guy, and I haven't even met him. You believe that?'

'Oh yeah, I understand alright. Did she mention Heather and Tim?'

'Yeah, though Tim didn't score high on the popularity scale. 'Tim: nil points; he sounds a dick.'

'Did she say why?'

'I didn't stay. Got a coffee from the kitchen and headed off upstairs. She was telling them about Marcus and this other friend when I left.'

'Did the friend have a name?'

'I can't remember. The next thing, Mum picks a king, and that's her with a full house. She's shrieking with laughter, and I've just got to go. Sometimes, I think it's better when she's miserable, I tell you, man.'

'Was the name "Sasha?"'

'I don't know, man. Maybe. Yeah, maybe it was. You know her?'

'She was Wendy's friend while she was with Marcus.'

'The rich prick?'

'Yeah.'

'Dick.'

'Yeah.'

'Yeah.'

'When did Liz leave?'

'Dunno, I didn't hear — I was deep into the blues by then. Wait, I'll ask Mum.'

I wait while he heads downstairs to the lounge, and then I hear him talking. I hear Patience's voice, and I figure he's telling her about Liz. Then he mentions my name.

'What? Philip? Why didn't you say? Hand me that phone... hi, Philip.'

'Hi, Patience.'

'I just heard about Liz. That's awful. How is she?'

'Hanging in there.'

'She's tough. She'll put up a fight.'

'Yeah, I know.'

'You want to know about yesterday?'

'Yes, please, Patience — anything you can remember.'

'I had to leave them in the lounge, Philip, but it was just for a few minutes. Call of nature, you know. Did I tell you how my Winston put in the downstairs for me? He's so good to me, you know. I don't know what I'd do without him. Anyway, when I come back, Liz was heading for the door, and she looked like something had just slapped her face, she was that flushed. She tried to smile and said something like, "I've been enjoying myself so much, I lost track of time," and then she left. That was at about two or thereabouts.'

'Did Wendy say what happened?'

'She didn't know, Philip. You know what she's like, poor soul. I think all the talk about this Marcus fella and her friend had tired her spirit. She's still a little distant today. She's up in her room, listening to music my Winston loaned her.'

'I'll call and see her later if that's okay.'

'She'd like that. She talks about you, you know.'

'Yeah?'

'She talks like you're her guardian angel — her big brother.'

I feel good about that, and then not so good; conflicting emotions battle it out inside me, kicking the hell out of each other. For a while, the good feelings — the brotherly, guardian angel feelings — are winning, and I'm really glad. Then I let my guard down just for a moment and WHAM — knockout — and I really don't feel good at all.

'Bye, Patience.'

'Bye, honey.'

I slip the phone into my pocket and head back into the hospital. As I arrive, there's a doctor coming out of the intensive care unit.

'Mr Tyler?' he asks, and he has this reassuring smile on his face.

'Yes, how is she?'

'She's come through the operation,' he says. Now the smile slips away, and there's a more serious expression. I wonder if they learn the whole routine in medical school and practise in front of a mirror until they've got it just right. Does someone test them at the end of the year?

Well done, doctor. Now you can go out and deal with worried friends and grieving relatives. Congratulations; you've passed with a Grade A in compassion.

'We'll keep her in an induced coma until the swelling on her brain goes down. The next forty-eight hours will be critical. We'll do everything we can.'

'Will she be okay? Will she come back as Liz... or someone I don't know?'

'Only time will tell, Mr Tyler. We were lucky that her other injuries were light. We can be cautiously optimistic.'

'Can I see her?'

'Of course.'

He leads me through a couple of doors and down a corridor to a ward that is divided into individual rooms.

'The first door,' he says.

I wish his qualification in compassion had taught him to prepare me for what I see inside. I guess that was a different course, and maybe he thought he was good enough without it.

She's lying on her back, supported by a couple of pillows, and she's got tubes everywhere, and the tubes are linked to machines, and the machines are making a range of noises like some weird medical orchestra tuning up. Where she hasn't got tubes, she's got bandages, and, between the bandages, there are bruises; it's like a psycho's painting pallet. There's not much of Liz left but what little there is, I try and talk to. It's not easy. I can't talk to people in hospitals when they're awake, so I've no chance here. Besides, idle chit-chat would only make her irritable, and, if she can hear me, that's the last thing she'd want.

So I tell her everything I've been doing and everything I'm going to do, and then I tell her to hurry up and get better before I make a pig's testicles of everything, and then I get ready to leave. But, before I leave, I search through her locker and take her phone with me. She'd understand. Her laptop's not there. It must be back in the chalet.

I pass Jon in the reception area, which makes me feel better about leaving.

'Phone me if there's any change,' I tell him, then I head back to the chalet.

There's no food, no milk, and no biscuits, so all I can do is phone for a takeaway and drink my coffee black. It'll have to do. While I'm waiting, I look through Liz's recent calls, and I reckon if I wrote them down, they'd cover a roll of wallpaper. It looks like, in the last week, she's phoned everyone she's ever met — and then some. Mostly, they're mobile numbers, but there are a few calls to landlines. I recognise some local codes, but I need to check the others. There are five international calls too — three to the USA, one to Canada, and another to New Zealand.

This is how a workaholic works, I find myself thinking.

I positively dread checking her emails.

There are two phone numbers which catch my attention: one, outgoing, is to a local landline, and then there's an incoming call from the same number. I figure I'll give it a ring. Someone answers straight away like they've been sitting beside the phone, just waiting.

'Hi, my name's Phil Tyler. I work with Liz.'

Bingo!

'Sally Richmond,' she says. 'Have you spoken to Liz?'

I explain the situation, and it's clear this is the nurse who contacted me. She's really anxious, like she's expecting a knock at the door and some unwelcome visitors. I can sympathise with that. I still get a sharp pain in my ribs when I do something silly — like walk or breathe.

I tell her about the accident.

'Are you sure it was an accident?' she asks.

That's not a question I want to hear, but I think of Thomas and Helen, the old couple who ran her down, and I figure I can offer some reassurance on that count at least.

'Definitely an accident,' I tell her. 'It was an elderly couple. She just ran out in front of them.'

'Was she pushed? Was someone following her?'

God, now I can hear alarm bells ringing and claxons sounding. I hurry to silence them.

'No, definitely no. I talked to the couple myself. They saw her step off the pavement into the road.'

I'm about to ask her what this is about, what's happening at Westleigh, and why she contacted me, but she interrupts me before I manage a syllable.

'Have you seen the photographs?'

'What photographs?'

'I took them at the clinic — photos of the equipment and the things they brought in. It's real high-tech stuff. I didn't know what half of it was, not then. There are monitors for everything and even equipment to measure brain patterns — headsets, you know, real sci-fi stuff. I sent them to Liz in an email.'

'I haven't had a chance to check yet. What's this about, Sally? Do you know what's going on at Westleigh?'

'When I realised what they were doing, I had to stop them. I mean, it wasn't right... those poor people. They were treated like animals in a laboratory; I helped two of them escape, late at night, through the rear gate... it was all I could do, but they knew it was me. I had to leave... I...'

That's as far as we get. I just hear this crash and this splintering sound like someone has just run a bulldozer through the room, then there's a stifled scream, a voice, and a scuffle.

Then nothing.

'Sally!' I yell. 'Sally!'

Then I hear someone breathing and a deep voice, which is as cold as iced water.

'Who am I speaking to?' it asks in this deep, Yankee drawl.

I hang up.

Then I call the police, but all I can give them is a name and a phone number.

'And she was definitely attacked?'

'Yes.'

'And this was when?'

'About five minutes ago.'

'Any idea who or why?'

This isn't the time to expound conspiracy theories. For all I know, she could be bleeding to death, so I just say no and save myself an hour on the phone.

'I'll get a car out there straight away, Mr Tyler. I'll phone you back when we know something.'

'Thank you.'

Then I sit back and listen to the blood pounding through my head, and my heart is building enough pressure to run a small factory. My thoughts are out of control, moving in random directions like bacteria — infecting everything. I focus on one thread and then another and try to make them stay still, but they won't; they can't — Sally, Liz, Wendy.

Then I latch onto one and hold fast — Liz's emails. The photos.

Her computer is locked, but I've seen her working on it often enough to know the password — "Evening Post," only with 3s and 1s and 0s and 5s and a £ to start — so I type it in: "£v3n1ngP05t". Then I open her emails and scroll through them. There's nothing from Sally — nothing. In fact, if you eliminate the usual dross, there's nothing much there at all. It's like Liz hasn't used it for the last week, which can't be true. She's never off the damned thing.

Maybe she opened a new email account. It'd make sense because she was sure she'd been hacked. I make a few guesses and try a few passwords, but it's like fishing for sharks with a shoelace, so I give up, and I get this awful feeling of panic.

I don't know what to do.

Chapter 28

I can't sleep. I listen to every sound carried on the night air. I hear voices, and I wonder if they're closing in on the chalet. I hear the breeze blow, and I think it's a vehicle approaching. I stare into the darkness and listen. Even the hush of the sea beyond the dunes carries a menace I've never heard before. Loudest of all, and most threatening and disturbing of all, are my thoughts. It's like there's a football crowd in my head, and everyone wants attention; everyone wants to be heard. And amongst the cacophony of loud shouts, there are quiet voices — scared voices crying out for help. They're being trampled underfoot, and there's nothing I can do. The crowd is just too big.

At three o'clock, I get up and sit in the lounge. If I was at my mum and dad's, I'd make a milky drink, but I'm not. I haven't got any cocoa, and I still haven't bought any milk. I flick open a can of beer; it'll have to do. I've got to think. I've got to make space and time to think. I need to step back and forget about all the plates I'm spinning. You can't spin plates and think about other things, can you? You can't focus on anything except poles and plates.

It's time to stop.

First off, I've got to move Wendy. If someone was following Liz when she was hit by that car, maybe they know where she is. I reckon the chalet is still secure, so I'll bring her here. No choice. There's nowhere else.

Second, it's time I levelled with Mel. I'm sure — really sure — I can trust her. I don't believe she knows anything about the seedier side of the people she works for; if she did, she wouldn't stay there. I reckon if I level with her, tell her what's going on, and show her how much I trust her, she'll help me. I could really do with someone on the inside right now.

And I've got to find those photographs.

And write everything down the way Liz told me.

And talk to Slattery.

And find out what's happened Nurse Sally Richmond because the police haven't phoned back.

I need someone to talk to. I feel like I'm caught in a spotlight and everyone's looking, waiting for me to do something — sing and dance maybe — but I can't think of what to do so I just stand there and wait for the slow handclap.

More than anything, I want Liz to wake up.

Next morning, I go back to the hospital and spend an hour saying nothing much to Liz. I take her laptop and memory sticks with me just in case, but her condition hasn't changed. The doctor seems to think she's doing okay, but he's trying not to commit himself either way. I root through the cupboard where they've stashed her stuff, but there's no sign of the photographs — there's no notebook or diary either — not a thing that might help me.

'Come on, Liz,' I murmur. 'I really need your help right now. You've got to come back to me.'

Then I watch her eyes for the slightest flicker. I want it to be like in a film where I turn my back and start to leave and she murmurs my name.

But she doesn't.

And the machines bleep and whirr, and liquid drips down tubes, into her and out of her, and time passes.

'What were you doing there, Liz? What was in the photographs? What have you found out?'

I listen to something which measures her pulse, and I watch something measure her breathing, and the lines which measure her life keep on moving.

'Was someone chasing you? Was that why you walked into the road?'

A door opens and a nurse enters. It's time for me to leave.

Back in my car, I phone Mel, but I haven't got a sentence out before she interrupts me.

'The doctor asked me to call you,' she says. 'And guess what? You're to have a private tour of the clinic, just like they promised. They want you to see the whole place now our first residents have started to arrive. You'll never guess who drove in this morning...'

It turns out it's some soap star who's taken time out from filming to get herself back on track and a retired footballer who can't hack life out of the limelight. I don't watch soaps and I prefer Rugby, so it doesn't mean much to me, but I try hard to sound enthusiastic.

'Why are they giving me a preview when I haven't got a newspaper or a job?'

'The doctor said they promised. She said you could sell an article freelance.'

'I really doubt the Evening Post would buy anything from me,' I tell her. But then again, if it was sufficiently sanitised, I guess they might. Either way, it's not going to happen.

'You'll come, though?'

'Of course — when?'

'Thursday at two.'

She's so pleased, I decide not to spoil it by applying a veneer of cynicism. They're not going to show me what I want to see. They'll flatter me and expect to be flattered in return. I'll get to meet a couple of guests, and they'll expect me to swoon at the sight of some second-tier actress, be struck dumb by the presence of a dribbling superstar, and forget everything else. Still, it won't do any harm to take a look. What they don't show me might be interesting, and I can ask a lot of nasty questions and get right up their sanctimonious noses. Maybe I'll prise a reaction out of them and get some hint or some clue about what's going on.

'That's great news,' I say to Mel. 'I'll look forward to it.'

I try to wax lyrical but it's difficult without inducing a nosebleed, so we arrange to meet for lunch before the event, out near the railway. Then I hang up. I haven't even asked her about Sally Richmond, the disappearing nurse, or the new equipment she told me about. That can wait until Thursday. In the meantime, I've got to see Wendy and then phone Slattery. It's going to be a busy day.

I get the feeling I'm still spinning plates — still trying to reach a point where I can stop and think. I haven't mustered a useful thought in days. It's starting to irritate me. I want to do the whole Poirot bit — sit back in a chair, completely alone, and think for ages until I come up with something — but

I doubt it's going to happen. I haven't even had time to go to the bathroom yet.

I phone the police to ask about Sally Richmond, and Stan puts me through to the new DCI. He's as much use as a bikini in a snowstorm. I come away with nothing but frostbite. He has nothing to report and nothing to share — nothing, no comment, zilch. False alarm. Waste of police time. Waste of space.

'I heard the door splinter,' I remind him.

I didn't realise until that moment that it's possible to hear someone sneering. The line goes dead. I phone Sally's number, but that line is dead too, so I head out to Winston's place.

But even there I'm thwarted. Winston is out, and Patience is immovable.

'The girl's fine here. Nobody's going to trouble us, Phil. Winston put some more locks on the doors for me.'

That's certainly true. The front and back doors have more bolts than the local hardware store. It took five minutes to get in. He's even drilled a hole at the right height for Patience so she can see who's outside. All that's missing is a secret password and a sawn-off shotgun for Patience to hold across her lap.

'Besides,' she says, 'Wendy and I are getting along fine. I don't want to lose her. I never knew what her old self was like but I'm betting we're getting close to finding out. Ah, here she is now. Come on in, girl. Here's Phil to see you.'

A smile breaks out on Wendy's face like sunshine, and it's all for me. Her eyes are bright and clear and blue — so blue. It's like looking at a tranquil sea.

'Phil wants to move you out of here, but I'm telling him we're getting on fine, so there's no need.'

'Why do you want me to move?' she asks. She slips onto the sofa beside me. A subtle fragrance touches me like a hint of mist.

'I'm not sure it's safe here.'

'Is anywhere safe?' she asks.

'I'm telling him it would take someone special to get past that door, and, if they did, they'd not get past me,' Patience says.

'I just think... for the moment, you know... you'd be safer somewhere else.'

'I feel safe here. I don't want to move again.'

'See,' Patience says. 'You see what I'm saying. We're more than a match for those sons of bitches,' and she reaches across and holds Wendy's hand.

I concede defeat. They're too much for me.

'Let's give it a day and see how things go,' I suggest. 'If anything happens, we move you out. Okay?'

A synchronised nod. These two have bonded like sisters.

'Stay there, honey,' Patience tells me. 'Talk to Wendy. I'll put the kettle on.'

As soon as the kitchen door closes, my powers of speech desert me and silence descends. Eventually, 'How are you?' I ask.

'Better,' she smiles, 'much better. You can tell Heather.'

'Can I ask you something?'

'Of course.'

'It's about Liz.'

'How is she? Has she regained consciousness?'

'No, not yet, but we're hopeful. You remember she was here the other day? You were playing rummy, all three of you. Can you tell me what you talked about just before she left?'

A frown wrinkles her forehead, and I want to kiss it away, but I resist.

'I keep remembering things,' she says, 'nothing clearly — just moments. There's a face seen briefly against a light, a man in round, steel glasses with a mask over his mouth, a smiling nurse, and a syringe. Then darkness and then something... something... I was telling Liz. She showed me a photograph of a building — the one I was in. There were people carrying boxes and pushing trolleys stacked with equipment.

'Do you know what was in the boxes?'

'No, I don't know... or maybe... I can't remember.'

'Was there anything else?'

She turns to hold my hand, her eyes sparkle, and she smiles.

'Sasha,' she says. 'Sasha was there. She had a clipboard. She was checking the boxes. I recognised her at once.'

'Did you tell Liz?'

'Yes.'

'And she left soon after?'

'Yes.'

There's something like a nuclear reaction taking place in my stomach, and I've got this really bad feeling again. I take a deep breath.

'Did Liz recognise Sasha?' I ask.

'I don't know. I don't think so. She didn't say anything, but perhaps.'

My heart's still beating like a piston.

'Patience says she was acting kind of weird before she left. Do you know why?'

'No, she seemed okay to me.'

'So nothing unusual?'

That intense frown reappears for a moment.

'Well...'

'Yes?'

'Maybe she saw something in the photograph,' she says. 'She kept staring at it.'

'Sasha?' I ask.

She shakes her head. 'She didn't say. I'm sorry, Phil.'

She's looking anxious now, so I change the subject, and we talk about other things — happier things that have nothing to do with Westleigh and Sasha and Marcus. Then Patience joins us.

'You want to help me with the coffee tray, Philip?' she asks.

Ten minutes later, the cards are out, and I'm playing rummy. An hour passes.

'Time for me to go,' I say at last. 'Are you sure you'll be alright?'

Patience lets her hand fall on mine.

'Don't worry about us, honey,' she says. 'We're more than a match.'

'I'll come back soon. Tell Winston.' I'm about to leave when I think of something. 'The photograph, Patience, was it on Liz's laptop?'

'No, honey, she'd printed it out.'

There's another mystery. Where the hell could it be? It wasn't with her stuff at the hospital.

God, I wish she'd wake up.

Wendy goes with me to the door and watches as I fumble with the keys and bolts.

'Winston does nothing by halves,' I say. 'I hope there isn't a fire.'

'There are always the windows,' she says, and then, quietly, almost in a whisper, 'Thank you.'

'For what?'

'For caring.'

And she leans forward and kisses my cheek.

I want to say something meaningful that fits the moment — something perfect — but it's all too complicated, so I just mumble, 'Anytime.' Then I leave.

And I feel really good because I'm doing something nice and kind, and I feel really bad because I couldn't think of anything better to say than "anytime".

I mean, inadequate just doesn't cover it.

And I feel guilty too.

About Mel.

Chapter 29

The next day is Thursday. I meet Mel and we sit outside the hotel at a table overlooking the river. There are just a few solitary wisps of cloud, and the sun is shining. A moorhen scuttles into the cover of reeds, as a canoe glides by. There are people relaxing on the grass, and, further along, two people are preparing a yacht for an outing. I'm watching Mel closely. I don't like what I'm thinking, but the thought just won't go away.

'Have you ever come across someone called Sasha at Westleigh?' I ask.

'No shop talk, remember,' she smiles.

'It's important, Mel.' There's no point in holding back now. I've got to know. 'Liz had this photograph, you see. She showed it to Wendy, and she recognised someone — a woman with a clipboard who was checking stuff as it was unloaded from a van.'

'Called Sasha?'

'Yes.'

'I knew one Sasha. But she didn't work for us, and she certainly wouldn't be checking deliveries.'

'Can you tell me about her?'

'I thought we agreed...'

'Yeah, I know. It's just... well, Liz was looking at this picture with Wendy, and, afterwards, there was something that she wanted to tell me — something that spooked her so much, she walked out in front of a car. If you knew Liz, you'd know how bad that would have to be.'

'You think it's this Sasha?'

'Yes... no... I don't know.'

'We called her Princess Sasha. She turned up one day as part of a publicity shoot, and she expected everyone to treat her like royalty. She stayed for three days; they filmed her in different locations doing different jobs — in the office, with the doctor, in the guest rooms, and even in the kitchen. You know the sort of thing — the glamorous beauty queen playing the menial. Then she did the voiceover and a piece from the lounge for our target audience. I was really pleased when she left; maybe they were filming her checking the boxes.'

'You're sure she wasn't there longer?'

'I booked her ticket to London and then to New York.'

'What about before she came here?'

'She came from Italy. I remember that clearly because she moaned endlessly about everything on the plane — the tourists, the food, or lack of it, the noise, the children, and having to travel like an ordinary mortal. She was a pain in the arse.'

'I wish I knew what spooked Liz.'

'Can't you look at the photograph? It must be with the rest of her stuff.'

'I've searched. I can't find it.'

'Maybe she dropped it when she had the accident.'

'Maybe.'

'You think someone took it?'

'I don't know what to think.'

'Listen, I know we said no shop talk but if you want to talk to me, I'll listen.'

'You might not like what I have to say.'

'I'll risk it if you will.'

'I'll get us another drink first.'

While I go to the bar and order our drinks, I'm thinking quickly. There's no way Liz was looking at a photograph of Mel or that Mel was Sasha. No one could act the way Mel did, or respond the way she responded, and be hiding something. I believe her — totally. And now I feel guilty for even harbouring a suspicion.

Do I tell her everything?

Liz would say 'no.' Slattery would say 'no.' I bet my mum and dad would say 'no' too, if they were in on the story. I get the feeling the only person who'd be shouting 'yes' would be me.

'Yes,' I say out loud.

'Excuse me?' the barman asks.

'Nothing,' I tell him, 'just talking to myself.'

'We get a lot of that in here,' he says.

When I get back to the table, I start straight away, before I have time to change my mind. I tell her everything — well, nearly everything. I skip Winston's reason for being out at Westleigh, and I omit the monumental erection — out of delicacy. I stick to the not-so-bare facts. By the time I've got to the part about Rigg, I know I've made the right decision. When I tell her about Wendy and how she evaded kidnap, she's gone as pale as the clinic walls, and her mind is whirring so much, I can almost hear it.

I even tell her about the Home Office guy and the research programme. Her eyes widen. 'No one has spoken about any research project,' she says. 'I would know. It's part of my job.'

'There are a lot of secrets hidden within those walls,' I tell her. 'Maybe they don't want you to know.'

I can see she believes me. It's as though I've removed a series of veils, and, step by step, she's seeing things more and more clearly, and she's scared of what she sees.

I take her hand. 'I need your help,' I tell her.

'Of course,' she says. She looks out across the river, and her eyes are moving as if she's following the flight of random thoughts, which dart like insects over the water. Eventually, they turn back to me, dark and deep. She hugs my arm and leans close. 'I'll do anything to help,' she says. 'We've got to find out what's going on.'

I look at my watch. We've just time for another drink before we head off for my grand tour of the clinic.

'The office at the Lodge will be empty,' she says. 'Doctor Harris will be with you and so will Mr Wigmore. I'll take a look and see what I can find.'

'Be careful. I don't want you to get hurt.'

'No one would suspect me,' she smiles. Then she turns to me as a sudden thought startles her. 'Headsets?' she asks.

'Yeah, high-tech headsets and headphones too.'

'You mean like virtual-reality headsets?'

I get this cold prickling on my neck, and I feel a pulsing of blood evacuating my face. There's a rush of coins falling into slots, and something is starting to move. All I can do is stare at her.

'What's the matter?' Mel cries. 'You look like you've seen a ghost.'

Chapter 30

I have to wait for the doctor, so Mel entertains me with coffee and biscuits and the sort of professional chit-chat we're comfortable having on a hidden camera. Eventually, she wanders over to her desk, and I pass ten minutes reading a health and wellbeing magazine. It's full of adverts for supplements which will make you live forever. As you get nearer to death, you just take more. There are a couple of pictures of elderly people who are so fit and healthy, they don't look a day over 50. They ooze smugness. They have rosy, glowing faces and big smiles.

Then Doctor Harris glides through the door, towing Clive Wigmore in her wake, and they both switch on smiles that are so wide, you could cross a river on them. We shake hands, and there's more pointless chit-chat. Then we get down to business. We drive down to the Hall, and I'm led directly into a room where there are rows of chairs and a screen. As if by magic, it turns on and the lights dim. I'm surrounded by music which sounds like it's been specially commissioned to induce nausea.

The music fades but doesn't disappear entirely, the screen brightens, and there it is: Westleigh Hall Clinic. The music is replaced by a friendly voice, which sounds remarkably like Meryl Streep but isn't, and it tells me everything I don't want to know about Logrum Research, from its foundation twenty years ago up to the present day. Words like "caring," "exclusive," "compassionate," "quality," and "cutting-edge treatment" ooze like a thick slime. I glance conspicuously at my watch just in case they think I'm swallowing this sickly ooze. When the music rises like an oil slick and the credits start to roll, lights come on. Doctor Harris takes me by the arm, and we swirl synchronously from the theatre. Clive treads behind us like an antidote to frivolity.

'It's a little theatrical for my tastes,' Doctor Harris whispers. I get the feeling we're sharing a tasty secret. 'But it gives you an idea of what we're about.'

'Not really,' I smile.

The tour continues under Clive's watchful eye.

'Two of our clients have agreed to speak to you,' Doctor Harris confides to me. 'You may recognise them. They're quite well known.'

'*I doubt it*,' I think, but I don't say anything. She wheels me into this private suite that has a lounge, bedroom, and shower room, and there's this ferociously blonde woman who's nearing 60 but trying really hard not to be. She offers me a delicate hand with nails painted a vivid red. They look like they've been used to rip open someone's stomach.

She spends five minutes waxing lyrical about the clinic then gets bored and allows us to leave.

'That's an impressive testimonial from someone who's only been here a few days. What did you do, offer her a discount?'

I make it sound like a joke, but I get the feeling they're beginning to think this tour was a bad idea. By the time I've been singularly unimpressed by the footballer, Doctor Harris is beginning to fray a little.

'Will I see other clients?' I ask. 'Maybe a couple of less famous ones?'

'There are only two other patients at present, and they prefer to remain anonymous. We must respect that.'

'Of course.'

We look at a sauna, a swimming pool, a restaurant, a fitness suite, a theatre, and a games room, and then I'm given a whistle-stop tour of some of the medical facilities, which are as interesting as a wet loaf — just chairs, couches, and monitors. All the time, Doctor Harris is filling the vacant spaces with accounts of the pioneering work at their US clinics, their incredible results, their wonderful clientele, and the testimonials they've received from everyone rich enough to receive their treatments.

I'm getting bored.

And irritated.

'Where are the headsets?' I ask.

'Excuse me?'

'The virtual-reality headsets.'

'I'm sorry; I have no idea what you mean.'

I widen my mouth into a big smile as if I've just stunned them with a wonderful joke.

'You've got everything else in here; I was sure you'd offer virtual reality.'

They laugh, but it's without a trace of humour, and their eyes are as dead as a shark's. I'd love to know what they're thinking.

'You mentioned pioneering approaches,' I say, 'and the video presentation talked about "cutting-edge techniques". Could you tell me about them?'

'I think you might find them rather tedious,' Clive smiles, 'and a little technical.'

'Try me,' I smile back. 'You explain them to your clients, don't you? I'm at least as bright as the two specimens I just met — no offence.'

Clive smiles; Doctor Harris bristles. I don't know which is the least poisonous.

'Let me be frank with you, Mr Tyler,' Doctor Harris explains. 'Our techniques are tailored to individual needs. They're developed from the very latest insights into the conditions from which these poor people suffer. It would be too complex a process to explain in any meaningful way.'

'Just a broad brushstroke, then,' I suggest. 'Is it some form of behaviour modification, for example?'

'All our work is to do with behaviour modification, Mr Tyler,' Doctor Harris says with a voice as sharp as a slice of lemon. 'Every establishment which deals with mental health issues is concerned with some aspect of behaviour modification. It goes without saying.'

'But, here specifically, are you undertaking research work that relates to new techniques of behaviour modification?'

'We aren't a research establishment, Mr Tyler.'

'So Logrum Research doesn't do research? That's rather ironic, isn't it? Besides, the Home Office says you do. They say it's something hush-hush.'

'There are many facets to Logrum, Mr Tyler,' Clive interrupts. 'Some are sensitive — for commercial and political reasons — I'm sure our associates explained this to you.'

'That I should keep out of it, yeah.'

'Then, perhaps you should.'

I ignore him and step forward like a man with a mission.

'Does your research involve virtual reality? I mean, just for clarity, is this facility developing behaviour-modification techniques based on virtual reality?'

'There's nothing innovative about VR,' Clive snaps. 'Lots of clinics use it. We've explained exactly what we do here. You've seen two of our clients. Please do us the courtesy of believing what we tell you.'

'The guy you put me on to at the Home Office was at pains to warn me off because you were involved in some pretty exciting, world-changing research.'

'All the research developed in our clinics is approved by regulatory bodies.'

'That sounds like a cutting from a glossy brochure.'

'Now, if we can move on...'

'Do you want to tell me about Wendy?'

'I can't discuss the details of individual cases with you, Mr Tyler; you know that.'

'Can you confirm you were treating her here at a time when you assured me you had no patients?'

'As I said...'

'Yeah, you can't discuss individual patients. Was she part of your research project?'

'As I keep repeating, Mr Tyler, we respect our patients' privacy, and we maintain absolute confidentiality,' Doctor Harris snaps. The threads of her patience are unravelling. 'And we do not discuss any research programmes. We've explained all this.'

'Let's go back to the VR headsets,' I say. Hell, am I a dog with a bone or what? 'Did Wendy's treatment involve VR?'

Clive stops and fixes me with a look that could melt lead. 'If you're ready, Mr Tyler, I think we're finished here.'

He indicates a doorway and ushers me through it into a long, white corridor. There are doors to the left and right with opaque half-windows.

'What are these?'

'Storage rooms.'

'Storing what?'

'Equipment, cleaning materials, and all the things necessary to the smooth running of our establishment.'

'Where does the research take place? The east wing? Only, I saw some pretty weird shit through the window there. Some guy who looked like he was on an airbed.'

Ooh, Clive is getting really testy now, and Doctor Harris looks like she wants to inject me with something toxic. We're accelerating. Any minute, I'll have to break into a jog. I don't think this is going the way they planned. When we reach reception, it's time for the final onslaught.

'Doctor Harris, did you lose a naked man recently? My source tells me he'd just escaped from this clinic.'

'Your source is mistaken,' she says, and I feel my cheeks frost over. Wow, that was a cold blast.

'We've been over this,' Wigmore says.

'Yeah, but he was seen lying on the backseat of a four-by-four that was being driven by one of your security men. Can you explain that?'

'He was seen by whom? Another of your reliable sources?'

'I have a whole team of them.'

'You mean the two men who tried to burgle Westleigh Lodge?' he says. 'Do you think we don't know? We know everything. They're hardly reliable witnesses.'

Doctor Harris has had enough. She waves her arms and retires with a flouncing of colourful silk. It's a cue for Clive to discard the last vestiges of diplomacy.

'He was a fucking burglar,' he snarls. 'No one will believe a word.'

'What did you do to him? One of your experimental techniques, was it? You had no right.'

'He was a burglar — a common thief.'

'So you thought you'd be judge and jury, did you? You figured he didn't count and that you could deal with him how you liked. That's really arrogant, Clive, if you don't mind me saying.'

You have no idea who you're...'

'Yeah, yeah, I've heard that at least twice before. It's getting really boring, Clive. The thing is, I have a pretty good idea who I'm dealing with, and I don't give a shit. I want to know what happened to Wendy, and I want to know what's so important that you're willing to go to any lengths to get her back. You threaten people, you follow them, you bring out a whole troupe of performing legal and medical monkeys, you beat me up, and then you try to buy me off with this sick pantomime. I mean, Clive — what the hell? You couldn't have handled this worse, could you?'

'That's enough, Mr Tyler. We're finished.'

'What's so special about Wendy, Clive? What's the big secret?'

He clicks his fingers, and two guys stride over from reception, trailing their knuckles. The first gorilla reaches for my arm. I shrug him off, but it only takes a second for them to get me by both arms and drag me to the door.

'I've not finished,' I yell. 'You won't stop me, no matter what.'

But threats lose some of their power when they're delivered by someone stumbling forward and collapsing on their face in the gravel.

'You can find your own way back,' Clive snarls from the door. Then he comes down the steps and gets close enough to whisper, 'Remember, Mr Tyler, you had an opportunity to walk away from this. Whatever happens now is your responsibility. You can't beat us; we're way too big for a pathetic little out-of-work hack like you. You really have no idea.'

'Marcus Van-Doren,' I manage to spit out, along with a mouthful of sandy stone.

'What?'

'I know about Marcus Van-Doren.'

He just laughs and walks away.

'Goodbye, Mr Tyler,' he says. 'I doubt we'll meet again.'

Chapter 31

After my exciting afternoon at the clinic, the next day is a disappointment. All the adrenalin it awoke just shrugged its shoulders and slouched back to bed, ready for the next time. I type up everything, ready for Liz's critical eye, and then I go and visit her and watch her sleep. I phone Winston and listen to him complaining about the turn his life has taken, then I try to contact Mel, but she's out or not answering. I decide to get an early night — alone.

The next day, things liven up a bit. I realise I'm being followed again; it's the same guy, but he has a different newspaper with him — a tabloid daily. He's not reading that either. I entertain myself by taking him on a tour of the Sefton low spots and then losing him in the park. He doesn't really worry me. I've spent my life in Sefton; I have access to hundreds of backdoors. I slip through one of them when I get bored, and I head to Maggie's for a coffee and cake. Then it's time to go back to the chalet.

I see the smoke long before I reach the caravan park. There's a plume rising in the distance and drifting out to sea, where it fades and disappears. It doesn't look like much; it's like someone burning garden refuse has let the fire get out of control. It happens all the time in Sefton. When I turn into the park, however, I realise it's close by — maybe in the dunes or out on the beach.

I don't imagine someone's set fire to the chalet. Not for one minute. I mean, it's broad daylight, and there are security cameras all about the place. There's one outside the site shop, another at the entrance gate, and a couple on the main roadways. Besides, there are people everywhere. This is Sefton in mid-summer. Even though the place is in a bit of a decline, you still can't move without bumping into a tourist. And no one knows about the chalet.

It's our hub, our refuge, and our centre of operations — me and Liz — and, at the moment, it's my home.

Or it used to be.

The fire brigade is there, but the fire is already dying down. They're still hosing it, but there's only smoke now and no flames. Three of the firemen have given up. They're just watching the others and talking — about the state of the van probably. It's like it's been hollowed out. Everything that could burn has been reduced to ash. Even the paint has gone.

PC Jim Davey is there, talking to a woman I recognise. She's on holiday in the neighbouring van with her husband and a sinister-looking terrier which barks a lot. I wish she didn't look excited, as if my home burning down was something designed to make her holiday memorable. Still, she has the decency to lower her head and look sad when she sees me. Jim thanks her and closes his notebook as she walks away. She smiles at me sympathetically. I think she might pat my arm if I don't steer away.

I wonder if she took photographs. I bet she did. Business comes first.

'The chalet belongs to Liz's sister,' I tell Jim. 'She's going to be seriously pissed when she sees it.'

'You were staying here?'

'Yes, with Liz.'

'Shit,' he says.

'Yeah, it wasn't easy.'

'So why were you staying here? You've got a flat, haven't you? You weren't... you know...'

'Give over, Jim. She's older than my mum.'

I give him a brief version of our adventures.

'You think the fire was started by these Logrum people?'

'I'm sure of it. But don't waste your time trying to prove it. And don't report what I've said. Your boss thinks I'm a paranoid sociopath already. Do you know how it started?'

'We'll know more later, but it looks like a gas cylinder.'

'Any witnesses?'

He shakes his head.

'They must have come from the beach,' I say. 'Someone would've seen them if they came through the park. They could've made their way from the south car park. They'd need two heads to stand out among the tourists.'

'There's no camera down there either,' he tells me. 'It's been turned off — cutbacks.'

'Well, there's a surprise.'

'You're sure you don't want me to report your accusations?'

'Yeah, quite sure.'

He scratches his head and then shakes it, casting a professional eye over the ruin.

'The trouble is, at the moment, it looks like an accident.'

'Yeah, but I bet you a week's salary you'll find an accelerant.'

'You haven't got a week's salary. You were sacked, remember?'

'Safe bet, then.'

'What will you do?'

He sounds almost sympathetic.

'That's a really good question. I've been asking it myself. The simple truth is, I don't know. I'm running out of options.'

'Maybe you could go back to your flat.'

I drift away. There's nothing to be gained from hanging around here. I'll go down to the station tomorrow and make a pointless statement, but, before then, I've got to find somewhere to sleep for the night — somewhere safe.

A cold fear has got a grip on my throat, and it won't let go. I feel nauseous. It's as if someone has just opened a box, and all the horrors of my situation are flying out, filling the air around me.

Bacteria? That's a joke.

I really am one inconsequential speck of plankton in an ocean ruled by whales. This isn't David and Goliath. David was always in with a shot, no matter how the odds were stacked against him. I've no chance. Liz is in a coma. The chalet and everything in it is gone. I'm standing on the edge of an abyss, and I'm wobbling. I'm not safe anywhere. I've nowhere to hide, and, without the chalet and the computers, I've no way of fighting back. Worse still, Wendy isn't safe, no matter how many locks Winston has fitted to the door.

Well, isn't this just wonderful? I think I'll go and jump off the pier and cut out the middle man.

There's something else too. I've got all these thoughts nibbling away at my brain like caterpillars on a leaf. I can't make sense of them. I mean, why all this fuss about a few VR headsets? Why is there so much secrecy about some new technique for helping people? It hardly comes as a surprise that there are new projects trialling the benefits of VR. Why not? If you can use it to reconstruct a traumatic experience, to help them relive it, and to take control, isn't that a good thing? New ideas must be emerging all the time. I could even be persuaded that the naked rambler and Wendy were part of some trial if it wasn't for the lies and the violence. Maybe their research *is* "cutting edge"; maybe they want to keep a lid on its precise nature. Maybe the research has economic implications and maybe it merits a degree of secrecy — but it hardly warrants arson, assault, and kidnap, does it?

As far as I can figure, there's only one sensible explanation, once you rule out incompetence on a monumental scale. There's something's going on which they want to keep quiet. Even the Home Office is involved. Suddenly, I'm thinking about those films where a corrupt politician gives the nod and people start dying.

It's not a pleasant thought. Maybe someone is nodding right now. *He's called Tyler, Phil Tyler. Make him go away.*

Whoever they are, it's clear they're scared of what Wendy may tell me. They want her back under wraps, tucked away in their clinic and under control before she has a chance to remember something they don't like. The answer to everything lies with Wendy. Once she's secure, locked away in their clinic, they've nothing to worry about — except me, and I'm just a minor obstacle — something they need to neutralise, like an annoying insect buzzing in their faces — something to be swatted.

I don't fancy being swatted. I'm too young. I want to meet someone nice, get married, have children and a dog, and grow boringly old surrounded by books, music, friends, and family. I want to die at 90 with a bottle of beer in my hand. They may not be earth-shattering ambitions, but they're mine. I'd be seriously pissed off to miss out on all those years of stultifying obscurity.

No, I don't want to be swatted. But I do want to be the buzzing insect which gets in a bull's ear. That's the sort of damage I want to cause. Trouble is, there's no bull — except Slattery — and he's an ageing bull who likes to bellow a lot, and he can do a fair bit of damage if he's riled, but he's no match for Logrum, even with me in his ear.

I suddenly realise I've driven twice around the town without seeing anything. I'm surprised I haven't left a trail of dying pedestrians in my wake. I guess some part of my brain must've remained in charge of the car while the rest of it went for a walkabout. I pull into a parking space on the promenade, facing the sea. It's late, and the sun is sinking towards the horizon. An ominous bank of cloud lies in wait, ready to draw it down into the shifting sand of the night. There are plenty of people about, strolling up and down, but no drunks yet; I guess they've still got their heads in their troughs. They won't be out for a couple of hours, adding pools of vomit to the decor, so it's kind of nice and peaceful. I glance in my mirror and then all around me, just in case some mad axeman is waiting for an opportunity, then I open the window and breathe. A gentle wave of voices rises and falls over the ground bass of the sea. I like it, and, for a few minutes, I just sit there, and it feels good.

I just don't get why people want to spoil things like this. I don't understand why they have to fill the world with noise and violence. I don't understand why money and power are so important. I mean, none of us have any power really, no matter how big and important we think ourselves. We're just dust on a cosmic wind.

Then I remember I'm naïve, sentimental, and prone to introspection and melancholy. My mum told me that.

I'm also in immediate danger.

I told myself that.

I close the window. The sun has disappeared now, swallowed by the sullen clouds. It feels like a premonition.

I phone Patience, but everything's quiet there. They're watching a film. Winston is upstairs listening to music because romantic comedy isn't his scene. Wendy comes to the phone, and we talk for a minute or two, and I'm reassuring and lighthearted and cheerful and all the things I'm really not. I don't tell her about the chalet or my visit to Westleigh. There's no point in spoiling the film. I don't speak to Winston either.

'I'll see you tomorrow,' I tell her. 'I'll call early.'

'That's nice,' she says. 'I miss you.'

Then we hang up, and, when the warm glow subsides, reality kicks in.

I need help. I need somewhere to sleep which isn't my car, and I need to feel safe for a while. I've no choice. I call Slattery.

I don't know where he is, but the music is loud, and the voices are hysterical. It sounds like he's found the doorway to hell and opened it wide.

'Wait a minute,' he says. 'I can hardly hear you. I'm in The Lucky Seven.'

That explains the noise.

'The Lucky Seven?'

'Yeah.'

'Jesus, Slattery, you know how to live, don't you?'

We've got a history, The Lucky Seven and me. I haven't been back since I played my part in getting its owner sent down. The club is under new management since George Mackie, but the place hasn't improved. Police cars speed up as they go past and so does anyone else with sense. It's packed every night. Bloodshed is its biggest attraction.

'I'll go outside,' Slattery shouts. 'I can't hear a thing in this place.'

It takes him so long to get to the door, I figure he's stopped off in the gents, but, eventually, I hear him, his dulcet tones rising above the sound of accelerating traffic. I tell him everything, and he snaps a few questions.

'Philip,' he says eventually, 'you're in deep shit.'

It's not the reassurance I crave.

'What am I going to do, Slattery?'

'Have you got somewhere to go tonight?'

'I could phone Mel.'

'Better not. You're toxic at the moment. There's no point in adding her to the casualty list. Meet me down here. You can stay with me while we figure out our next step.'

Then he's gone.

For the first time since I met him, I realise Slattery must live somewhere. He must have a home like a normal person. Maybe I thought he lived on the street or slept under the pier or just moved from bar to club to bar throughout the day and night. I don't know. I just never imagined him in a domestic setting.

I try to picture the place Slattery calls home, but I can't get beyond a bedsit above a pub in a red-light district. I hear melancholy piano music in a smoky bar — Tom Waits.

Hell. Imagine that! Slattery has a life elsewhere.

I park a few streets away and walk down to The Lucky Seven, where I spend an anxious few minutes hoping none of Mackie's staff still work there, especially Manny, who's six foot four and built like a troll. He used to work the door and acted as Mackie's back-up muscle. He couldn't hold his arms straight at his sides because his biceps got in the way. We never quite hit it off, Manny and me.

Fortunately, there are just the usual groups of rowdy kids, loud drunks, and women who don't seem to understand that heels and alcohol are a lethal combination.

Then a taxi pulls up, and, as if it is to order, Slattery emerges from the club doorway and we both disappear inside it.

'Windsor Gardens,' he says. He looks out of the window, left and right. 'You weren't followed?' he asks.

'I've been wandering round for hours,' I tell him. 'There was no one.'

'Good.'

'Windsor Gardens?' I ask.

'Yeah, I bought it last year when I retired. Somewhere quiet, I thought, just for a change.'

'Windsor Gardens is certainly quiet. People in Windsor Gardens sit at windows and watch funerals go past. It's *schadenfreude*. There's nobody under 70 within a mile. You like it there?'

'It's like death's waiting room,' he says, 'halfway between the hospital and the crematorium. People talk about nothing except their grandchildren, their ailments, and their dead relatives.'

'No wonder you go out.'

'I've got a garden, lawns and flowers, and vegetables. Can you believe that?'

I don't see you kneeling on a mat with a trowel in your hand — no offence.'

'I thought maybe I'd like it,' he says. 'I don't.'

We pull into the drive of a detached bungalow in a neat little plot with a rustic brick wall you could sit on. There's a bench under the window, a couple of flowering cherry trees, and bedding plants in borders.

'I got a gardener,' he says. 'I prefer it like that.'

He opens the door, and we step inside. It's like stepping into Slattery's mind – untidy with stuff scattered around, vinyl albums spread on the carpet near an old-fashioned music deck, and a table with unwashed mugs and an empty polystyrene takeaway packet on it, stained with yesterday's curry.

'That's more like it,' I say. 'I was getting worried.'

'Go and make a coffee,' he says. 'I'll check the spare room.'

'What for, vermin?'

But it's okay. I catch a glimpse of a bed with a clean sheet and duvet, a small chest of drawers, and a built-in wardrobe.

'No one ever comes here,' he says, 'except the kids once a decade.'

We sit down with our coffee. He pours a slug of whisky in each mug.

'To help you sleep,' he says.

Then we talk.

'I don't know what to do,' I tell him. 'It's like I've reached a dead end, and there's no way out; it's like a horror film where you reach a wall and it's too high to climb, so you've got to turn and face whatever's coming behind you.'

'Sooner or later, Wendy's going to remember things. She's the key to all this. First thing tomorrow, you've got to move her from Winston's. And start thinking, Phil. It's what you're good at, and, so far, deep thought has been in very short supply. You've been running around like a hamster on a wheel. It's time to get off and look around. This guy in Rigg, Tim, you think he knows something?'

'I'm sure of it.'

'Then we need to find out what. You think Wendy was part of some dodgy research project?'

'That's my guess.'

'Was she a willing participant, do you think?'

'She wanted out; that much I know.'

'And they didn't want her opting out?'

'They made that pretty clear.'

'What about Liz? You think she was onto something?'

I think back to the urgent text messages. 'Yeah, there was something in the photograph the nurse sent her. Maybe there were other things too... I don't know. She'd been making a lot of calls.'

'But the photo's gone and so has the nurse?'

'Yeah, her room was trashed — no phone, no computer. I got that from Jim Davey.'

'What about her relatives? Aren't they beating the door down trying to find out what happened?'

'I figure someone's reassured them she's okay; maybe there was a phone call, an email, or a text message, who knows? Maybe she'll turn up as a singer in a nightclub — and happy.'

'That's one sick sense of humour you've got there, Phil.'

'Pay no attention. It's how I get by.'

'You've still got Liz's phone?'

'Yes, I keep it in my laptop case.'

'Make a few more calls. See who she'd been speaking to, and find out what they said. There might be something. What about Mel?'

'What about her?'

'It seems to me, whether you're right or wrong, you've decided to trust her. You think she'll help?'

'I'm certain.'

He yawns and drinks the last drops of coffee. 'Time for bed.' He stumbles through to the backroom, and the door closes — no ceremony. Next morning, there's a note on the table and a set of keys, but no Slattery — seems he left early.

Help yourself to anything. I'm off to Rigg to meet Tim.

There's something reassuring about Slattery's philosophy in life: *if you can't reach the ring in its nose, just take the bull by the horns.*

I feel this surge of energy, like it's contagious or something.

He's right, though; I've got to start thinking. I'm worse than a hamster on a wheel. I'm the wheel. The hamster's in control.

It's time to stop spinning and think.

Poirot — yeah!

I phone the hospital. The nurse tells me there's no change in Liz's condition and that they're still waiting for her to wake up, so I root though Slattery's albums for a suitably mellow jazz number, put it on the turntable, and sit back.

And think.

And think.

And think.

And it does no good at all.

I need to talk to someone — anyone except Winston because talking to Winston is like having a conversation on a fairground ride. Mum and Dad? No, that won't do. There'd be too many questions. It'd be a dialogue, and I don't want a dialogue. I just want someone to listen.

Then the answer comes through loud and clear, and it's obvious, so I head down to the hospital, and I talk to Liz. I tell her everything, and nobody interrupts me or contradicts me or tells me to get out of here or that my ideas are stupid.

Two hours pass like ten minutes.

'Thanks, Liz,' I say, and, as I head out of the hospital, I feel as if my head is clear for the first time in days. It's time to act. And it's time to get everything on paper because, second to thinking, I can write. I know what I'm going to write too.

This is going to be Wendy's story all the way, and it's going to be so close and personal, it'll rouse people to fury. They'll be out on the streets looking for blood. There'll be a media storm.

Yeah!

Chapter 32

I check my watch. It's just after midday, and I'm running late. I should have checked on Wendy long before this. Slattery says we should move her — find her somewhere else, somewhere safer, where Logrum's team of hired thugs can never find her. It's a pressing issue to Slattery because he trusts Winston as far as he could lob a curling stone. Normally, I'd share his anxiety; Winston doesn't have a track record of reliability. The only thing you can reliably predict about Winston is that he won't be reliable. He's made a career out of it. This has been the longest period of sustained reliability I can remember. I think it's because of what they did to Benny.

I'm inclined to clamber out on another branch and trust him. I figure it would take an act of outstanding bravery — or stupidity — to do something Patience wouldn't like. Winston's not that brave or stupid, not when his mum is concerned. There's a heady mix of respect and fear in that relationship, which will be acting like a damn on Winston's usual stream of heedless chatter.

Nonetheless, the longer she's in one place, the more likely it is they'll find her, and that wouldn't be fair on anyone. Patience might see herself hanging on to her walking frame and demolishing her adversaries with a variety of kitchen utensils, but it's hard for anyone who isn't Patience to believe the outcome would be favourable. As for Winston, he'd do his best, but he's spent all his life, since he acquired the power of speech, talking his way out of trouble. I doubt the Logrum guys would be in a listening mood.

No, it's time I found a new place for Wendy. Unfortunately, there's one boulder-sized obstacle to this, and I can't see a way round it. I've nowhere to move her. My flat certainly isn't safe, the chalet's gone, and Slattery's bungalow only has two bedrooms. For a minute, I flirt with the idea of taking her to my mum and dad's, but I know what they'd be like. They've been waiting for years for me to settle down and father a child or two. I think they mark the dates off on a calendar in anticipation of the big moment. If I mention a girl's name to my mum, it's like I'm throwing something to keep her afloat when she thinks she's drowning.

No, I can't raise false expectations — I'll hold Mum and Dad in reserve.

It's at moments like this that I realise how few friends I've got who own houses, have wives or partners, and have more than one bedroom.

Then I get this really weird idea, and the more I think about it, the more I reckon it might work. Jon, my ally at the paper, has recently married his long-term partner, and he lives out in a nice, modern estate in a three-bedroom semi, which they bought in expectation of raising a family. More to the point, he knows enough about what's going on to want to help. He shares my strange and incomprehensible loyalty to Liz, despite the fact that she treats us both like we've got special educational needs and a contagious skin infection.

I phone him, and he checks with Lindsay, his partner, who says it's okay, so it's with a lighter spirit that I head off down to Winston's. I just hope Lindsay isn't the jealous type because Wendy is enough to make anyone jealous. Shit, I feel pangs of jealousy even leaving her with Jon, and he's prematurely balding, overweight, and has a moustache.

Now all I have to do is prise Wendy out of Patience's defensive arms. It's not going to be easy. I picture her holding on to Wendy and beating me with a walking stick while Winston tries to calm her down.

'Hey, chill, Mum.'

But his mum doesn't chill, and we're both laid out on the floor while Patience takes Wendy back to the rummy table.

'That chilled enough for you, honey?'

As it turns out, they've already been talking, and Patience is ready to compromise.

'No point in arguing with the old lady,' Winston warns me, 'once her mind is made up. They're going to a show in town, and that's that.'

'You've got to talk her out of it, Winston. Think of the risks.'

'Hell, man, they've been planning this since Tuesday. It's like a military campaign — a taxi takes them from here to the theatre, another taxi brings them back, and they've got me and Benny riding shotgun.'

'You've got to tell her...'

'If you want to tell my mum she can't take her new friend to a theatre, Phil, you go ahead.'

'Shit, Winston, I've got enough to worry about.'

'You think you've got problems. Benny and I have got to watch two hours of crap cabaret in a theatre full of happy tourists. She bought us tickets — didn't even ask. "You got nothing better to do", she says. I mean, I've no choice in the matter. You get me?'

I get him alright.

I've already conceded defeat when I speak to Patience and Wendy. But I gain a concession: I'll be outside the theatre when they go in, I'll be there when they come out, and I'll follow them home. I won't sleep otherwise.

'And tomorrow morning,' I say to Wendy, 'we move you somewhere else, okay?'

It's agreed, and I phone Jon to confirm.

All I have to do now is hang about a bar opposite the theatre for a couple of hours, watching holiday-makers laughing too much, getting loud, and getting drunk — my idea of hell. But it turns out I know the guy behind the bar, so the time passes quickly enough, and I'm there as they emerge. Winston and Benny go to left and right and watch the street like something out of a bodyguard film. Winston's even got his hand inside his coat like he's holding a firearm, and Benny's sporting dark glasses. I'd laugh if it wasn't serious.

People are watching too. It's like someone's forgotten to lay out the red carpet. I can see people nudging each other.

Who are those people?

Then a taxi rolls up, and they're whisked away before anyone asks for autographs.

I follow them, and I watch as Winston and Benny usher them indoors and turn the lights on. Wendy stops at the door and turns to wave and smile before she disappears. It gives me this warm feeling which stays with me all the way back to Windsor Gardens.

There's a light on in the lounge when I get there. Slattery's back. He's wearing a dressing gown and sitting with his feet on the coffee table and a bottle of beer in his hand. The dressing gown gapes to reveal a substantial paunch. He rests the beer on it while he scratches his head and yawns.

'You got her moved?' he asks.

'Tomorrow,' I tell him. 'It's a long story.'

'She remembered anything else?'

'Nothing. What about Tim?'

'Let's just say we had a frank exchange of views.'

'Did it involve blood?'

'Only the threat of it; he's not a brave man. I went to his workshop so we could be alone. As soon as I started with the questions, he got defensive; when I told him what I thought I knew, he suggested I should leave. I didn't. He doesn't have a particularly high regard for you, by the way — not at all. What was it he called you, "a sanctimonious do-gooder who should keep his nose out of things that aren't his fucking business"? Yeah, that was it.'

'I'm not sanctimonious.'

'If you say so. Anyway, he tried to take me by the arm, which I didn't think was very friendly, so we got into a momentary tussle.'

'What did he tell you?'

'Apparently, these legal guys turned up at his business one day. They knew everything about him — his family circumstances, his business dealings, and the state of his finances. They made him an offer he couldn't refuse.'

'What was that?'

'They promised his family wouldn't come to any harm if he cooperated.'

'That's some way to open a negotiation.'

'They also said they'd clear his debts and make sure his cash-flow problems disappeared. There were also some hints about more work coming his way.'

'They offered him all this in return for what?'

'A signature — he had to witness Wendy's signature on a document approving a new, experimental treatment they were offering.'

'Is that all?'

'He had to sign another document too — non-disclosure. They also explained he was subject to the provisions of the Official Secrets Act, but that might have been a bluff. More to the point, they made it pretty clear that they couldn't guarantee the safety of his family unless he complied; as I said, he's not a brave man.'

'Tim isn't even related to Wendy? How could he sign anything?'

'He forged Heather's signature and then added his own to witness it.'

'Did he know what it involved, this new treatment?'

'He says not.'

'You believe him?'

'I think he preferred not to know — once he got his money.'

'Maybe they told him the treatment was her best chance of making a complete recovery and that he'd be doing her a favour, to ease his conscience.'

'That's a very generous interpretation, Phil. It does you credit. Personally, I'll stick with the cynical version. The bastard was paid to make sure she didn't back out.'

Chapter 33

'Fuckers are out there, man.'

The call comes through just after eight the next morning. I'm in the kitchen, brewing coffee and grilling toast. Slattery hasn't emerged yet. He says he can't get used to regular hours.

'They're in a four-by-four down the corner of the street, wearing shades on their foreheads like mob hitmen — *Goodfellas,* you know, like the film. They're watching the house through binoculars.'

'How many of them?'

'Just the two — I saw them when I went for the old lady's paper; they're just sitting there. I can't tell Mum, Phil; she'd be down there waving her walking stick at them.'

'I can imagine.'

'You figure they know Wendy's here?'

'They're checking you out, just in case. It wouldn't have taken them long to link you and me. How long have they been there?'

'Just this morning; I've been pretty damned careful, man, especially with Mum having the temper she has. I check the street for cars every time I go out the door.'

'Have they seen Wendy? Has she been outside or stood at the window or anything?'

'She's in the kitchen with Mum, making some egg-and-spinach thing for breakfast. They expect me to eat breakfast every day. All this healthy stuff is making me ill. They've got a recipe book and everything. It's getting out of hand, man, I mean... spinach? It's got to stop. You've got to get her out of here. Mum's talking vegetarian.'

'Never mind your sodding diet! Just keep them away from the windows. I'm coming straight down. I'll park behind the house and come in the back.'

'Make it quick, man, before I have to eat this spinach shit.'

'Jesus Christ, Winston.'

Slattery appears at the door, unshaven and wearing shorts and a T-shirt — not a pretty sight. He yawns and stretches and pours a coffee into a stained mug.

'Nectar,' he says. 'Nothing can beat the first coffee of the day. I can't function without it.'

'Today's an exception,' I tell him as I take the cup from his hands and put it on the table. 'Winston says there's someone watching the house — two guys in a four-by-four. Get dressed; we've got to get down there.'

Slattery picks up the mug and slurps.

'A moment,' he says.

He clicks his fingers and indicates the phone. I pass it to him, and he enters a number clumsily with one hand.

'Stan?' he asks. 'It's Slattery. Listen, I need a favour... yeah, another one... yeah, I know, I owe you... listen, there are some suspicious-looking guys I need you to go chat with, just check them out...'

When he's finished, he strolls through to the lounge, sits down, and rests his coffee mug on his paunch.

'Give me five minutes,' he says.

Between him and Winston, I don't know how I've survived this long, especially given my genetic aversion to stress.

Ten minutes later, I'm driving through the town towards Winston's, and I'm having difficulty keeping to the speed limit. I hit the morning traffic, and every traffic light is on red. By the time we pass the end of Winston's street, my hands are raw from gripping the wheel, and I've ground my teeth to a stump. Blood is pulsing in my ears like it's trying to erupt.

'Bloody traffic, bloody cars, bloody people, bloody lights, bloody roundabouts, bloody hell,' I mutter.

'My, we *are* tetchy this morning,' Slattery yawns.

At the end of the street, there's a police car pulled up in front of a black four-by-four with tinted windows. Two policemen are talking to the driver. They've got notebooks out, and they're asking questions.

'They'll keep them busy for a while and then send them on their way,' Slattery says. 'There's no hurry. You've got to learn to relax, Phil. You'll end up with an ulcer.'

'Another one?' I mutter.

I park down the street behind Winston's, and we cut down an alleyway and clamber over a locked gate into the garden behind the house. The gate has four shiny silver bolts — new. Winston's been taking no chances. I slide them open, ready for our getaway.

The kitchen door is unlocked, and Winston is waiting inside. I feel a cold blast of air because the front door is wide open, and Patience is heading out to meet her adversaries. I can hear her as she opens the gate.

'You tell those sons of bitches...' she's shouting, '...coming around here and harassing an old lady. You let me near them; I'll show them...'

Wendy is in the kitchen. She has a bag packed and looks ready to go.

'I had to tell Mum,' Winston apologises. 'Spinach, man...'

There's no time for further explanations. I take the bag from Wendy as Slattery goes to the back gate and checks.

'Come on.'

'It'll be okay,' I tell Wendy. 'I've got somewhere safe for you.'

She looks at me, her eyes searching me for answers.

'But nowhere is safe, is it, not until I remember?'

'It'll all be over soon. I promise.'

That's one hell of a promise to be making under present circumstances, but she smiles, reassured, so I figure it was worth it.

'Cheers, Winston,' I say.

'No worries, man. I'd better go and get Mum before she does some damage.'

I can still hear her occasionally as the breeze catches her words and carries them through the house.

'For someone who doesn't like you swearing, that's one hell of a range of obscenities she's using.'

'When she gets going, man... she taught me everything I know.'

'See if you can keep them busy for a few minutes, yeah?'

We slip out of the gate and down the alleyway to the car. When we pass the end of the street, one of the police officers is making an effort to calm

Patience while the other is alternating between the two guys in the car and Winston, who's got this big grin on his face. They look seriously harassed.

'A policeman's lot,' Slattery says with a wry smile. 'They'll give me hell for this.'

It's only a mile or so to Jon's, but I take a trip along the length of the promenade first, and I'm checking my mirror like I'm taking a driving test and want the examiner to notice. It's stop-start all the way, but I don't notice anyone following us.

'I think we're clear,' I say to Slattery.

'Once you lose the blue Fiat,' he says. 'Take a right up ahead.'

'It's a one-way street.'

'Bravo,' he says.

I half-close my eyes and then accelerate because the street's empty, and I'd kind of like it to stay like that until I reach the end. I glance back, and there's a blue Fiat following us, just like he said.

'How the hell did you see that?' I begin, then I swear because there's a people carrier heading towards me. From the blasts on the horn, the driver's none too pleased.

'Now left and then right.'

I turn left and listen for a squeal of brakes, but it's disappointingly quiet. The right turn takes me down another one-way street with cars parked on either side. I accelerate again.

'Do you know any prayers?' I ask Slattery.

'For what we are about to receive,' he says, 'may the Lord make us truly thankful. Now sharp left.'

There's another blast from an approaching Mini; people are so intolerant once they get behind the wheel of a car.

'That should slow them up,' he says, and I guess he's right because, once we've taken another couple of turns, he takes me back to the promenade, and we head straight to Jon's.

'Leave the engine running,' Slattery says, 'and take Wendy inside. I'll take the car and keep driving for a while, just in case they're cruising, looking for us. I'll give them a tour of the sights and then park up at the police station. I owe a few apologies, I think.'

Wendy opens the door and slips out. She follows me to the door, where Jon is already waiting. Lindsay is standing beside him, and she takes control at once. Within a few minutes, Wendy has left her bag in the room they've set aside for her, and we're partaking in the British solution to every crisis — a cup of tea. I've already explained the situation to Jon. Now it's time we told Lindsay.

'Are we safe?' she asks.

'I can't promise that. I wish I could. They didn't follow us, so I think we're okay, but I can't promise.'

'What do they want?' she asks.

It's Wendy who answers. Her voice is soft, like a distant bird song. Maybe it's returning from some distant place in her memory, somewhere with Marcus and Sasha. It brings a hush to the room. Jon is melting — like me. Even Lindsay is touched.

'They don't want me to remember what they did to me,' she says. 'They want to take me away and lock me in their clinic so I never remember — so I can never tell anyone.' Then she turns and looks at me, and those blue eyes strike deep. 'But I want to remember.'

'You will,' I tell her. 'I'll help you.'

She turns to Lindsay. 'I don't want to bring danger to your home. We can find somewhere else, can't we?'

'Of course,' I tell her, though I've no idea where she could go, except maybe with Mel.

'No,' Jon says. He turns to Lindsay. 'We can't let them win, can we?'

Lindsay only needs to think for a moment. 'No, of course not. You're welcome to stay here.' Then she pauses for a moment before she continues. 'I think you should stay here too,' she says to me. 'Maybe you can help Wendy remember. At the very least, you'll be here if she does.'

Jon is nodding like some wind-up toy.

'You can use my office for your writing,' he says. 'I can help you.'

I've got to admit it's a good idea — just for a night or two. I've spent too long acting the part of a headless chicken. If I stay here, I can make those calls to people on Liz's phone. I can set up a new email. I can start writing and putting together the things I already know or guess. And I can spend time with Wendy, get to know her better, talk to her, and start my story.

'Thank you,' I say. 'Just a couple of nights. I'd like that.'

Chapter 34

'Tim was with me when I went to the clinic,' Wendy says. 'I remember that. I didn't understand why it was Tim and not Heather, but he said she was busy with a portrait which had to be finished. I was disappointed because I wanted to say goodbye.'

We're in the lounge at Jon's house. It's mid-morning, the sky outside is overcast, and only the occasional ripple of sunlight stirs the foliage on the floral wallpaper. Wendy is sitting with her legs curled under her on the warm leather sofa, and I'm beside her, my arm resting along the cushioned back. Jon and Lindsay are at work, so we have the place to ourselves, and we have time to talk.

'I remember this strange feeling — like I was back in the sixteenth century, and I was setting sail for the Americas, and I might never see her again; it was like the distance between us would be so vast, my letters would take months to reach her, and we'd live separate lives forever. It sounds silly when I say it now, but, at the time...'

'It was a big step you were taking.'

'Tim kept reassuring me. He told me it was what Heather wanted for me and what I wanted for myself. He said I'd made the decision. There was no going back.'

Do you remember anything about the treatment they promised you?'

'No details — nothing concrete. They said I'd get better, I'd be happy again, and that I was lucky to be able to take part. Most of the time, they spoke to Tim. It was like he was responsible for me and was making the decisions I couldn't make — like I was too ill to make them. I felt like I'd handed control of my life over to him.'

'But you signed the contract.'

'I think I wanted to sign it because I wanted my life to change, and Tim said over and over how it was my best chance and how I was lucky to be offered this new treatment.'

'And Heather?'

'He said she agreed with him because she wanted me to be happy.'

'But she wasn't there when you signed.'

'I think they'd talked it over; Tim said...'

'Did you believe him? Did you trust him?'

'Then — not now.'

'Did you meet Marcus at the clinic?'

'I think I'd known him for a long time, though I remember he was there with me sometimes.'

'And Sasha?'

'We'd been friends since university, I think — best friends. I'm sure she came to see me at the clinic. Sometimes, I remember seeing her at my bedside with Marcus, and they were holding my hands, but it's like peering into a mist, Phil. Shapes and shadows come and go. For a moment, I seem to see them clearly, but before I can reach out and touch them, they fade and drift away again, and I'm left with nothing, just swirling mists and strange shadows.'

'And the treatment — what do you remember about that?'

'Nothing.'

'What about the doctors and nurses, other patients, or the room where you stayed?'

'Nothing; from the moment Tim left the consulting room and the door closed, my mind is a blank.'

'What about just before? Can you remember who else was in the room?'

'I remember a nurse, just an ordinary nurse; she was about 25 and had dark hair — she was nice — and a man, an American with a deep voice. He was like an administrator or a manager, not a doctor — maybe a solicitor. He had a final contract for me to sign.'

'Clive Wigmore,' I tell her. 'He's called Clive Wigmore; I've met him.'

'There was someone else too. He sat at one side of the room near a corner, just listening and watching. He was older — maybe in his late sixties or seventies, with thin grey hair and a trimmed beard. He never spoke, not once, but the others kept glancing towards him — I remember that. They were checking with him like he was a consultant or something — someone important. He never said anything to them, though, and when we signed the contract, he just stood up and left.'

'Do you remember how you came to leave the clinic?'

'I remember a lane and a cottage and a woman in a garden. I remember that I felt alone — unbearably alone. It was as if I was grieving, you know; it was a feeling so deep and painful I was overwhelmed by it.'

'What about before that? Do you remember anything about how you escaped from the clinic?'

She shakes her head.

'Do you remember why you left?'

'I just knew I had to. I knew I had that one chance. I don't understand why I felt like that. I just did.'

Then she turns to me and she grasps my arm.

'I remember a nurse,' she cries. 'Yes, there was a nurse — maybe the same one I met on that first day, I don't know. I think she helped me. Yes, I'm sure of it. She opened a gate, a gate at the end of a long path. It was dark and cold.'

'Sally Richmond,' I murmur. Then I say it louder. 'She's called Sally Richmond.'

'I wish I could remember.'

'Don't worry about it, and don't try to force it. It'll come back to you in time and of its own accord. You just need time and a bit of peace and quiet.'

'And someone to talk to,' she smiles, and she rests her head on my chest. 'I'm glad you're here.'

'Where else would I be?' I say, and, before I know it, I'm stroking her hair, and then I kiss her head, and I feel her snuggle close against me. I have to remind myself that I'm a mug for anyone who's being victimised or oppressed and that vulnerability brings out the best and the worst in me. To make a move and take advantage would make me as bad as them, and I'm not like them — not one bit. Maybe in time, when this is all over and the passage of time makes everything clear... but not now, not here. No.

'Coffee?' I ask.

'Mm,' she says, so I slip free and head to the kitchen.

And while the kettle boils, I phone Mel. Maybe it's guilt; maybe I want to prove to myself I'm with Mel and that I'm being open and honest, or maybe I just feel the need to show her I trust her. I've decided I want her to meet Wendy.

'They've moved me from the office to reception,' she tells me. 'It's like they don't trust me anymore.'

'Don't take any risks,' I tell her.

I explain what's happened and tell her how these guys turned up at Winston's and how we moved Wendy somewhere else. I even tell her about Patience and Winston and the stand-off in the street.

'I don't know how they got to Winston, but it'd be easy enough to link us, I guess. The least you can say about Winston is he's conspicuous.'

'I checked all the files I could access,' Mel tells me, 'but it's not easy with the camera watching everything. There's some correspondence between Westleigh and other clinics, and a couple of files have been shared between us and the U.S., but they're encrypted. Apart from proving a link between Westleigh and some corporation in the States, there's nothing.'

'Can you copy the files?'

'Not now I've been moved.'

'Never mind; it's probably better you don't get any more involved.'

'I've noticed one thing since I've been moved, apart from the ridiculous number of security guards; there's a section of the east wing which is sealed off. Nobody goes in there except for Doctor Harris and a couple of others — secretive types who are definitely medical staff and definitely American — a man and a woman.'

'Do they sign in? Do you know their names?'

'Doctor John Cox and Ms Jane Bull.'

'"Cox and Bull" sounds about right. At least they've got a sense of humour.'

'It doesn't show. They haven't cracked a smile since they've been here.'

'Okay, listen, Mel. Don't do anything else. Keep out of this now; leave it to me. Can we meet later, after work? It's time you met the person this is all about. I'll collect you.'

We arrange to meet at her home just after seven, and I spend the rest of the morning making calls to numbers on Liz's phone. Most of them are journalist colleagues or news outlets. When I tell them about Liz, the shock is palpable.

"A formidable lady" is a regular comment, as is "one of the best journalists I've ever worked with."

There's a hell of a lot of respect out there.

'You'll let us know how she gets on?'

'Of course.'

'When she comes around, tell her we're thinking of her.'

'Yes.'

'If anything comes of her story, make sure you copy me in. Anything for Liz, you know.'

'Thanks. I will.'

The calls to the U.S. are a blank wall; it's just one receptionist after another, at one corporation after another, who can't recall anything. They all tell me to have a nice day. There's only one thing that connects them, and I discover that after a lot of searching and enquiring; they're all owned, one way or another, by Marcus Van-Doren.

Only one call, to Memphis, turns up anything.

'Why yes,' the woman tells me. 'I remember because I have friends in Sefton and my husband and I visit on vacation every few years, when we're touring the UK. I sent her some archival material she wanted for her research. Did she find it useful?'

I explain the situation.

'That's truly awful,' she says. 'You tell her she's in my prayers. With God's help, she'll be on the road to recovery in no time.'

'I'd like to make headway with her research while she's in hospital,' I say. 'Is there any chance you could forward me the same information?'

'Sure, that's no problem. It'll be later in the day because I'm a little busy just at the moment — tomorrow at the latest.'

So I give her my new email address and move on.

And get nowhere.

I spend an hour at the hospital, and I tell Liz everything. I wonder if she'd be pleased.

We'll make a journalist of you yet, Philip. Well done.

Or whether she'd be disappointed.

Is this it? Is this the best you could do? Sometimes, Philip, you drive me to despair.

In her absence, I figure I'll go with the optimistic version.

When I get back, I sit with Wendy and we talk, and, all the time, I'm thinking about the article I'm going to write, how I'm going to shape it, how it's going to lead with a photo of Wendy, how it's going to tear at the heart-strings, how it's going to provoke outrage and fury, and how I'm going to bring this whole edifice crumbling down.

Then I write, and the words flow like they've been set free, and they're running so wild, I know I'll need to harness them before they race off into the sunset. That's a job for later; for now, I'm just enjoying the experience. Eventually, the door opens, and Lindsay appears. Not long after, Jon turns up, and we pitch in together to get some food on the table.

It's hard to imagine, under these circumstances, that a day could feel perfect. But this one does, and now, to round it off, I'll go and collect Mel and bring her here to meet Wendy.

I take a round-about route to her house and a different round-about route back, but I'm sure no one's following us because the final stretch is down empty streets, and there's no one. I tell her about my article and the calls I've made, and she tells me again about Cox and Bull.

When we get to Jon's, the door opens, and Wendy is standing there, caught in the glow of the hallway lights. We don't get more than halfway along the path before Wendy runs towards us and throws her arms round Mel's shoulders, hugging her.

'Sasha,' she cries, 'I thought I'd lost you forever. I've missed you so much.'

Chapter 35

I don't know if shock is contagious, but, at that moment, it's hard to know who is the most shocked. Jon looks up and down the street as if he's expecting a squad of mercenaries. Lindsay looks at Jon and then at me, and I can see a whole army of questions lined up, ready to burst out. As for me, I'm pretty sure I haven't a drop of blood left in my face, and I'm staring, open mouthed. I can't find one sensible word to say.

But Mel — Mel looks worse than any of us. She looks like she's suddenly aged ten years — like someone's opened a pit beneath her, and she's hanging momentarily before she falls. Her arm slips round Wendy, and she holds her tight, but when she turns and looks at me, her eyes are wide and frightened. She tries to shake her head, and her lips start to move to formulate words, but nothing emerges. She just stands there, and Wendy holds her tight, as if she's never going to let go. It's like we're trapped in a still-frame from a horror movie where our worst fears are revealed and captured forever.

We don't have time to do or say anything. Wendy has only just released Mel when two cars pull up and doors open. A nurse, a doctor, and a couple of men in suits emerge and walk towards us. One of the suited guys slaps a paper on my chest and mumbles some legal jargon which means they've every right to take Wendy, and they're going to do it.

I take a step to get between them and Wendy.

'If you want to get in the way, that's your funeral,' the first clone mutters in my ear.

Behind me, I hear Mel. It's like she's just woken up, and she's trying to fight her way out of some nightmare world she's been living in.

'Get inside,' she yells at Lindsay and Jon. 'Get inside. Call the police. Get a camera, Jon, quickly. Phil, don't let them get past.'

Easier said than done.

I hold my ground for about two seconds before a blow slams into the side of my face and sends me spinning; it's like someone just impounded my brain. There's blood in my mouth and strange things going on in my head. I think I get kicked a couple of times and someone treads on my chest, and I can hear screaming and shouting.

That's about it. The next thing I can truly remember is Jon standing over me with Lindsay at his shoulder. In the distance, I hear a police siren. It comes closer and gets louder until a car pulls up at the gate. I try to clamber to my feet, but I guess I'm kind of punch drunk because I'm wobbling all over the garden like a puppet with broken strings. Eventually, I collapse on my face on the lawn.

'Wendy?' I try to say.

'Gone,' Jon says.

'Mel?'

'She's gone too — she left straight after.'

I have enough strength left for one final groan, then I close my eyes, and I just let go. The last thing I remember is the sound of an ambulance turning into the street and pulling up outside. I want Jon to tell them to shut up because I want to sleep.

I think they must've given me something at the hospital because it's dark when I open my eyes the first time and light when I open them a second time. When I eventually get around to moving, I'm aware that I've got more than my share of bruises, a tooth has gone walkabout, one of my eyes is malfunctioning, and my ribs feel like they've been put together by someone using pliers, nails, and a hammer. But that's nothing to the desperation I'm feeling deep inside. The groan which brings the nurse running has nothing to do with bodily pain, and the flurry of expletives I emit does nothing to help.

Jon leans over me.

'Welcome back,' he says.

'Have you been here all night?' I slur. It's like my tongue, teeth, and lips have severed all contact with my brain.

'No, I just got here half an hour ago. How are you?'

'How do I look?'

'Like the remains of last night's sweet and sour.'

'Any news?'

'They're going to charge you with kidnap, obstruction, perverting the course of justice, and a few other things. Those two guys were authorised government agents.'

'What the fuck?' I try to say, only, it sounds like "wob the thuck", so I guess it loses some of its poignancy.

'They're outside now.'

'No police?'

'These guys get first shot. The police come later.'

'Wendy? Mel?'

'Nothing. I tried the clinic, but no one's answering. The guys outside have the communication skills of crustaceans. After you left, they made it clear they were acting well within their rights. They had papers which proved it.'

I want to tell him people like them could prove the sea was made of lemon curd, but it's too much effort. I think he knows already.

'Anything I can do?' he asks.

'I need to get out of here.'

'You can't, not yet. Besides, there's someone who wants to see you.'

'Who?'

'Liz. She woke up last night.'

'Oh, shit.'

'Yeah, she was asking for you.'

'Oh, thuck.'

'She wanted to know if you'd made any progress with the investigation. That's Liz, straight to the point.'

'What did you tell her?'

'As little as possible — I thought I'd leave it to you.'

'Thanks. I think I'll sleep now and build up my strength. Maybe I'll be ready for her by November.'

Only, I don't get the chance to sleep. First, it's the doctor, who tells me I'll live, although I might feel some discomfort for a few days. He prescribes paracetamol, which feels like an insult to the quality of my bruising. He says I can go home soon, but I'm to take it easy.

I get the feeling even four hours constitutes bed-blocking round here.

Can you crawl?

Yeah.

Then why are you here?

Because I'm in pain.

We need the bed. Buy yourself some paracetamol and piss off.

He leaves the door open for the rock-face who's been sitting outside. He lumbers through and settles beside me like a landslip. I swear I hear the chair groan.

'Where's your friend?' I ask. 'Getting an oil change?'

'Funny man,' he growls. It's like distant thunder. Then the door opens, and his colleague appears, casting a shadow on the walls. Suddenly, I understand the meaning of claustrophobia. It's like a film where the hero wakes up surrounded by trolls — only, I'm no hero, and these guys would scare the shit out of any troll.

One of them leans forward.

'You have the fucking right to remain fucking silent — which I would strongly fucking advise — because anything you fucking say will be taken and rammed down your fucking throat until you fucking choke. Do I make myself clear?'

'As thucking day.'

The other one sits on the bed, and the mattress sinks until I think I'm in danger of rolling towards him.

'That's the formalities over with,' he says with a smile that's as sincere as a dentist's drill. 'Now, let's get down to business.'

His approach to business doesn't involve negotiation. He's at lengths to show me he's not just holding all the good cards; he's got the whole pack. I don't even have the joker, and, if I did, my face would be on it.

The argument goes roughly like this:

Wendy was detained under section 2 of The Mental Health Act 1983 with the agreement of her GP and the clinician involved in her case. She was transferred to Logrum Clinic with the agreement of her medical team and her family representative in order to take part in a trial of a new therapy. The details of this therapy were explained to her family representative and to Wendy herself, and their agreement was obtained. When she subsequently removed herself from the clinic in a disorientated state, it was necessary for the medical staff to detain her for a further six months under section 3 of the said act. This course of action was considered essential to prevent any harm from coming to her, whether it was self-inflicted, unintentional, or at the hands of others. She is now in Logrum Clinic and will remain there until she is well enough to be released. Her condition will be regularly assessed, and her family — or, in this case, her adopted family — will be kept fully informed.

There's a sub-text:

This is what's going to happen, so get used to it. We have the legal power to do this, and that should be enough. However, we also have other powers, and we aren't afraid to use them. Get in our way and you'll suffer indescribable pain. Make no mistake.

'You burnt down the chalet I was staying in. Why did you do that?'

He smiles, if you can call that bare-toothed grimace a smile. 'You would have great difficulty proving that, Mr Tyler.'

'You've hacked computers, blocked emails and accounts, deleted data, and tapped phones. You've had me followed; you've had Wendy's sister followed. Whoever followed Liz drove her to step out in front of a car.'

'I think you overestimate our power. To be honest, it sounds like paranoia.'

'Perhaps you should have me sectioned.'

'Best not make jokes, Mr Tyler.'

'You've attacked me, put me in hospital, broken my tooth, and made me sound like a thucking puppet; I haven't got time for jokes.'

'You kidnapped and illegally held a vulnerable young woman. You obstructed us when we came for her, and you used force to prevent us from performing our duties. We were well within our rights to use reasonable force.'

I'd laugh if it wasn't painful, and I'd give vent to a whole world of expletives if I wasn't already struggling to manage long sentences. I sound like I'm talking through a mouthful of carpet tacks.

'This doesn't feel particularly reasonable.'

'You should think yourself lucky I didn't carve my name into your face,' his colleague, Troll Junior, snarls.

'Can you spell your name?'

I think the medication is numbing my natural caution.

'Now, Mr Tyler,' the smoother troll rumbles, 'we have some good news for you. You'll be pleased to hear we're not pressing charges at this time. I think you understand your situation well enough. There's nothing left for you to do; you're finished. If we...'

'What's happened to Sally Richmond?' I interrupt.

'Who's Sally Richmond?'

'She's the nurse who helped Wendy escape from the clinic. She got a visit from you or some of your colleagues. I know because I heard them; they didn't sound friendly.'

Troll Junior leans on my ribs until I groan, then he presses his thumbs down on my eyes. Agony doesn't do it justice.

'I don't think you're listening to us, Mr Tyler. Let me make this totally clear — no more questions, no more enquiries — not so much as an email. You are way out of your depth. You're in the mid-Atlantic in a typhoon, and you're floating on a rubber dinghy with a leak and no oars. There's nothing you can do without us knowing; there's nowhere you can go where we won't see you. You can't even think without us knowing about it.'

He lets me go and just leans on my ribs.

'I hope you haven't bugged my bathroom, not with my bowels the way they are...'

Shit, these guys don't do humour. I think another rib just cracked.

'Where's a nurse when you want one?' I groan.

'There are a lot of pressures on NHS staff,' Troll Junior growls. 'We're one of them.'

Troll Senior looks at his watch.

'Time to go,' he says.

'Already?' I try to smile, but my mouth won't stretch that far.

His junior colleague leans forward and whispers in my ear.

'Nurse Richmond is back at work, Mr Tyler. She has no idea what you're talking about and made a statement to the police to that effect, just today.' He stands up. Big smile.

'The detective chief inspector didn't seem happy with your conduct,' says Troll Senior. 'I'd avoid him if I were you. Consider yourself lucky we're not pressing charges. Remember this: we can do anything to anyone in any way we please. There is no law that can touch us. There is no power in the land greater than the power you see before you. I am God All-Fucking-Mighty, Mr Tyler, and I will come down on you from one almighty height if I hear your name again. You are as significant as a fly.'

Now that does make me smile.

'What the hell are you smiling about?'

'Yeah,' I murmur. 'Yeah, I'm a fly, just a fly...'

'Yes, Mr Tyler — hold on to that thought.'

They turn to leave. I hear their footsteps disappear into the hygienic distance, and my smile is transformed into a painful, dribbling laugh.

'A fly in an elephant's ear. Try and swat that, you bastards.'

Chapter 36

It's around four the next afternoon, and I've been discharged. The doctor makes it clear he's too busy with genuinely sick people to worry about someone who clutters up his corridors with policemen. He more or less tells me I can suffer just as easily at home and not be a burden to the NHS. He recommends paracetamol and a period of good behaviour.

Before I leave, I drift down to see Liz. She's propped up on pillows, but she's found her glasses just so she can peer over them at me. She's tried to tie her hair back but not with much success, so her face looks softer, like she could be someone's aunty. She looks weak too, and tired, though she's not going to concede that without a fight.

'You look better,' I tell her, 'but I suppose you'd have to.'

'How did I look before?'

'Like a corpse.'

She looks me up and down slowly.

'You look like you've made a bollocks of everything while I've been asleep. Who's been walking on your face?'

'You should see the other guy.'

'I bet he's smiling.'

'At least I'm going home today — you're not.'

'And where is home nowadays? I hear you've trashed my sister's van.'

'I'm staying with Slattery.'

'Heaven preserve us. Does that old reprobate actually have a home?'

'Windsor Gardens.'

I'm worried the laughter might kill her.

'Windsor Gardens?'

'Yeah. If it's any consolation, I don't think it'll last — he doesn't like the neighbours. Besides, he thinks old age is contagious and everyone round there is infected.'

'Wendy?'

'Logrum have got her.'

'I see; now I understand the bruises. Mel?'

'She's Sasha — and before you come over all smug and say you told me so, remember you've got any number of tubes I could pull out...'

She tries to sit up but fails and lets her head fall back onto the pillows.

'Look in the cupboard, inside the dust cover of the book you'll find there.'

I root in the cupboard and emerge with a hardback edition.

'*And the Wind Won't Blow it All Away* — you're a fan of Brautigan, are you?'

'Just that book; it haunts me.'

I remove the dust cover, and two photographs fall onto the bed.

'Are these from Sally Richmond?'

'Who?'

'Sally Richmond, the nurse.'

'Oh, is that her name?' She's off on her own single track. 'Look at them, and don't ask foolish questions.'

I see at once they can't have been taken by Sally Richmond. They're grainy, strangely-coloured prints; both are decades old.

'Look inside the book — her photographs are there.'

Two colour photographs drop onto the duvet. They were taken recently and printed hastily onto plain paper. They show a white van with Logrum Logistics painted in black on its sides and a couple of guys unloading equipment. There are two people in the background, a woman with a clipboard, and a bearded elderly guy.

'He looks like a man Wendy described,' I say. 'He was watching when she signed the contract at the clinic,' and I explain to Liz about the guy she encountered. 'He just watched, never said a word, and left as soon as she'd signed. She said he was creepy.'

'Interesting,' Liz says.

'You know who he is?'

'Oh yes, but look at the other photographs first.'

'This is just some young guy in a tasteless polo jumper and hipster jeans. The suntan must've cost a fortune. It's the sort of handsome, well-adjusted, confident, manly face I always want to slap.'

'Envy,' Liz says.

'100%' I tell her. 'I've spent thirty hard years struggling to be mediocre. What do you expect? Who is he?'

'That, Philip, is Mark Van-Doren back in the eighties when he'd just started out on his first billion.'

'And the old guy?'

'That was taken just last year, without the approval of the subject, and with a high-powered lens. I believe it was taken from a yacht moored off the island owned by the gentleman in question.'

'So who is it?'

'You're being irritatingly naïve, Philip; that's Mark Van-Doren too.'

Well, that has my jaw dropping fast enough to eject a couple of loose teeth, I can tell you.

'He was in England? At the clinic?'

'Yes, it would appear he was. Now, what are we to make of that?'

Not much, as it happens. The nurse appears with a look which tells me the patient needs her rest and it's time I made myself scarce. I stand up, irritatingly cowed by authority and get ready to leave, but there's something I need to ask before I go.

'Just two minutes?' I ask the nurse.

'Two minutes — no longer,' she says and strides away to another bed and another task and, no doubt, another couple of forms to fill in.

'What would draw a reclusive multi-billionaire from his island hideaway to spend a week in Sefton-on-Sea? It'd have to be something pretty damned big, wouldn't you say? He's hardly come here for the fish and chips, the *cordon bleu* curry sauce, or the baked potatoes.'

'He must have a significant personal stake in the experimental work they're doing — and not just money, either. This research matters to him.'

'This is getting scary, Liz. I mean, what could be big enough to involve a guy like him? And why Wendy, for God's sake? What did she ever do?'

'She crossed his path, Philip. She registered on his radar as just a faint, inconsequential blip that he recognised and made use of.'

'People are getting hurt, Liz, especially me. What are we going to do?'

'I'm going back to sleep, Philip. You're going to find out what's going on, then you're going to find and rescue Wendy and write the most impressive, well-referenced, watertight article you've ever penned; you're going to expose these bastards for what they are. You're going to tell the world what they're doing.'

'I'm relieved. For a minute there, I thought you might suggest something difficult.'

'I have complete faith, Philip. I don't misjudge people. They always live up to my expectations.'

'Or suffer the consequences.'

'Indeed. Now goodnight, Philip.'

'Just one thing before you drift away into a land of peaceful dreams — tell me about your accident. Patience says you were playing rummy, and then you suddenly left. Of course, I put it down to early-onset dementia.'

'Naturally.'

'So why did you walk out in front of a car?'

'There was a young, red-headed gentleman — bearded. I was sure he was following me. He looked like an Ed Sheeran tribute act — not a very good one. By the time I'd realised he was no such thing, I'd started to run. It was only then that I saw the black limousine and the man who really *was* watching me. I recognised him at once.'

'Who was it?'

'Our friend Clive Wigmore.'

She closes her eyes, and there's a smile on her face as if she sees something funny which has escaped the rest of us. It's a secret that she's going to dwell on from the safety of her hospital bed. There's no point in asking what it is. She'd come out with some enigmatic answer which would allow her to smile more and make matters worse.

'Sleep soundly, Liz, and don't go worrying yourself about me,' I say with more than a hint of sarcasm.

'I won't.'

I slip the photos into my pocket and leave. I figure I've got one thing to do before I go back to Slattery's and get some sleep; I've got to speak to Mel. My car is still back at Jon's, parked in his garage while his car takes up the tiled drive, so I get a taxi and spend the journey preparing for the kind of showdown I've only ever seen in films. Mostly, they're the sort of films my nan used to watch, where a private eye gets suckered by a good-looking woman, who turns out to be playing angles of her own. They're never together in the sequel.

Mel's at the door before I'm out of the taxi, and she looks like she's been preparing this speech since Wendy got abducted and I got hospitalised.

'Liz says thanks for the flowers. Love from Sasha — nice touch,' I manage to say before she hits me with a barrage.

'Don't!' she snaps. 'Don't you dare accuse me of anything. Do you hear? Fact: I've never met Wendy before. Fact: I'm not Sasha. Fact: I don't know what the hell is going on. Fact: I wanted to help you, and I put my neck on the line for you. Fact: I've been hit by a confidentiality agreement I signed in order to get the job in the first place. And now, to cap it all, I've given up the job and told them where to stick it, so don't start, Phil, because I'm not in the mood.'

Well, either she's genuine or that's the best bit of acting I've seen in a long and distinguished career as an amateur film buff. My own well-rehearsed attack is beaten before it begins, and I limp disconsolately from the field.

'I surrender,' is the best I can manage.

Only when I get inside and we're sitting together on the sofa do I probe a little further. I have to be careful — it's like prodding a rattlesnake with a very short stick.

'You've got to admit, Mel, this is very mysterious. I mean, why was Wendy so sure you were Sasha?'

'I don't know.'

'Take a wild guess — anything. I admit I'm struggling here. She flung her arms round you like you were her long-lost friend. There didn't seem to be much doubt in her mind.'

'I told you, I don't know.'

'I mean, this is either the worst case of identity theft I've ever encountered or... Jesus...'

'What's the matter? You've gone pale. Don't look at me like that; you're scaring me. What is it?'

'Shit, don't you see?'

'See what? I don't see anything.'

'But that's it; that's what this is all about.'

I'm rambling now, and I know it. It's as if a door has opened and a flood of thoughts have escaped into the room, and they're flying all over the place, round the furniture, across the window, behind the tables — everywhere. It's like a plague of locusts.

'They never existed — none of them,' I say at last.

I'm standing up now and pacing back and forth across the room, and all those random thoughts are cohering like filings to a magnet.

'Who? What are you talking about?'

I sit down next to her and take her hands.

'They were planted in her mind and allowed to grow there — Sasha, Marcus, all those sunny afternoons, that too-good-to-be-true gentle overnight rain, the perfect garden, and the scent of sublime roses. Identity, that's it — identity. Yeah, yeah that's it. They created Sasha from you. You're Sasha. Not you but just enough of you — your face and gestures and maybe some superficial personality traits. The rest she'd fill in for herself as part of her VR therapy.'

'You mean all the things she told you about Sasha and Marcus was a kind of dream?'

'No, not a dream, not at all. Someone created that story for her, fed it to her, and allowed her to live it until it was so real, everything else became the dream.'

'But Marcus?'

'Yeah, I was wondering about that. Who the hell is Marcus?'

'If I'm Sasha, Marcus could be anyone. I mean, he could just be some guy they picked up off the street because he had the right face.'

'Yeah, I know, but I've got this weird thought creeping around my mind, and it won't go away. I keep picturing this narcissist with an ego the size of a planet, who thinks he has the right to play with people's lives. Do you reckon he'd let someone else play Romeo to his Juliet? Imagine entering someone else's life — even as a virtual you — even as the "you" you haven't been for decades. Can you imagine the kick a man like that would get out of seducing a beautiful, vulnerable young woman?'

'Beautiful? I wouldn't have said she was beautiful. Pretty, maybe, in an ordinary sort of way.'

'Okay, a pretty young woman in an ordinary sort of way.'

'If you say so.'

'Jesus, Mel — is this the time for an analysis of male versus female perceptions of beauty?'

'I thought we'd agreed she wasn't beautiful. Anyway, you started it.'

'Started what?'

'Everything.'

I've been in these arguments before. The more you speak, the bigger the hole you dig yourself. It's like walking into quicksand. It's better not to struggle; that only makes things worse.

'Imagine, just for a moment, that Mark Van-Doren has projected a young version of himself into this fantasy. It'd certainly explain why the bastard has been hanging around the clinics, watching everything. Mark — Marcus — it's not too big of a stretch, is it?'

'I still don't understand why anyone would want to do something like that. What's the business motive?'

'Imagine, Mel, that you could use VR to take a person back into their past and reshape it so they could awaken with a control they never had; imagine the abused wife or partner, the sexually abused kid, the victim of violent crime, or the soldier with PTSD — just think how their lives might be improved if you could manipulate their perceptions of themselves and help them come to terms with the trauma they've suffered.'

'That sounds pretty good to me, but I thought they were already experimenting with that sort of therapy.'

'Yeah, but these guys have gone way beyond that. Look at Benny. They acted like they were judge and jury — he was a burglar, a common thief, so they could treat him how they liked. They had the power, and they had the means, and they sentenced him to a lifetime as a happy missionary, and he had no right to object — no right of appeal, no trial, no jury.'

'What's wrong with making someone happy?'

'If you can't see what's wrong, I can't explain it.'

'You think the Home Office has sanctioned this?'

'They must be mighty interested in a therapy which could be incorporated into crime prevention. Imagine it: "I sentence you to six months of VR therapy, at the end of which you will emerge as a happy pacifist who votes Conservative and goes to church on Sundays. You will never make anything of your life, but at least you won't bother anyone else — except to irritate the hell out of them with that vapid smile you get as a bonus."

'So there's a genuine side to their work and then this secret research. And Wendy is a volunteer?'

'Maybe, but if she was, she certainly didn't sign up to six months of Marcus and Sasha. I don't understand why she's so important to them. Their work is going way beyond the official brief.'

'So something else is going on.'

'Yes, but I don't know what it is. I just know it scares the holy shit out of me.'

'And Wendy, what happens to her now?'

'I've got to get her out of there before they send her back to lover boy.'

'No, forget it, Phil. There's nothing you can do. You're just one person — a nobody.'

'A fly in an elephant's ear,' I tell her.

'Who's the elephant?'

That's a really good question. It seems the metaphor doesn't work in my case. I'm just buzzing around a window waiting to be swatted. There isn't an elephant in sight.

Why is there never an elephant when you need one?

Which makes me think of Liz.

Which makes me look at my watch and check the time — ten o'clock.

Which reminds me that the best elephants are the ones you make yourself — like homemade cheese and onion pies and tomatoes from your own greenhouse.

It's time to build my elephant.

'I've got to get this down on paper. Then I've got to get her out before it's too late.'

'You're in no fit state to write a coherent article or to rescue anyone.'

'Well, maybe I exaggerated my injuries just a little...'

'The broken ribs?'

'Bruised might be a better description...'

'Blind in one eye?'

'Swollen... and a touch of concussion which has gone. It felt worse earlier, honest.'

'A possible blood clot on the brain?'

'Maybe headaches and anxiety?'

'You said might never walk again.'

'Bruised testicles; I think you misheard "walk."'

'You need some sleep.'

'I've had all the sleep a sensible person needs. They don't risk you waking up in hospitals, you know. They give you something approaching an overdose of sleeping pills, then they all bugger off home, I'm sure of it.'

'Paranoia.'

'I've got tablets for that too.'

'You still can't continue your article, break into the clinic, rescue Wendy, then bring her back here while you edit and redraft it. It's madness. You'd need an army; besides, they'll be watching, just in case you didn't heed their warning.'

'I know.'

'So it's a really stupid plan. Write your article tomorrow after a good night's sleep, and make sure everyone knows what's going on. There's nothing you can do for Wendy, you know that. Besides, she might come out in a few months, happier than she's ever been.'

'It's the wrong kind of happy.'

'What gives you the right to decide what's best for her?'

'I don't have any right. But I'm sure she doesn't want what they're offering. She's being forced to take part on the back of some dodgy documents and the signature of a guy who doesn't give a shit about her — someone who saw an opportunity to make a few quid. I've got to try, Mel. I just have to. I've got to live with myself for the rest of my life. I don't think that'll be a pleasant experience if I don't at least try.'

'Phone Slattery and ask him. See if he can talk sense into you.'

'Okay.'

I don't tell her Slattery is the one person I can think of who is even more impulsive than me — and he's tougher too, and he's got a grudge against the new DCI, so he'll fancy a bit of covert two-finger raising.

Only, Slattery isn't at home when I get him on his mobile. He sounds like he's drinking in a football stadium. I figure it's the Lucky Seven again, especially when I hear shouts and a chair breaking across a table — or maybe someone's head. Slattery's voice rises above the din.

'Mind my fucking pint, moron.'

The moron obviously minds Slattery's pint because Slattery is edging closer to the bar, where he says it'll be quieter.

Only, it isn't, and Slattery sounds like he's had a few tonight, and he's not entirely in control of his faculties or his temper.

'Fuck off! Can't you see I'm on the phone, fuckwit!' he shouts at someone.

I sometimes wonder how Slattery has lived this long. I try — I really try — to have a conversation, but, in the end, I just tell him I'm going to Logrum at about two, and I'm going to get Wendy out of there, and then I'm going to... oh, bugger it, I'm not even convincing myself. I'm going to what? Ride in on a big white horse and carry away the damsel in distress, and then expose the whole corrupt racket? They'll sue me off the planet — if they don't kill me first. All I can do is make a hell of a lot of noise and hope some really clever journalist picks up on it. Shit, I wonder if *Panorama* will give it a go, or some consumer programme on the radio like the ones that scare my mum about internet banking?

Mel's given up on me; she's given it her last shot, and when the see-through lingerie doesn't do it, she sighs and goes to bed.

I bring up my article on the screen. I reread it and start to write. Slowly, I start to put together the pieces, and I know it makes sense; I know I've got to one root of the story. Trouble is, the taproot is still eluding me. There are still questions — questions without answers that scare me and scenarios that scare me even more. Then there's the all too important question of proof. I don't have any.

So I write everything down, and I keep writing. It's David and Goliath all over again; only, Goliath is the size of a planet, and David is Wendy, a thistle-down seed on a light breeze.

When I look at my watch, it's past one, but I've finished, and I know the piece is good — no, it's not just good; it's way beyond that — it's my personal masterpiece, and if I never write another thing, this article will show anyone who reads it what I can really do.

If anyone ever reads it.

Which they probably won't because it lacks the one thing any serious reader will want to see.

Proof.

It's one thing knowing, it's quite another proving. For that, I need Wendy, and I still have to get her out of the clinic. That's not going to be easy. It's time I was going before I think about it too much and change my mind.

I creep upstairs to Mel's room and sit on the bed beside her. 'Mel?' I ask. She doesn't stir. She's breathing softly, and her lips are pursed like she's blowing out a candle flame. Her hair is a dark halo on the pillow. I don't want to wake her.

I risk a kiss on her head, then I slip down the stairs and out onto the cold street.

Chapter 37

There's no moon tonight, and a fresh wind stirs the branches and leaves. The trees have a full head of hair, and it's waving and swaying. They'll get no sleep tonight, those trees. Their minds are restless and disturbed. Like mine.

The car is parked back down the lane in the same place as before, hidden from the road and invisible from the house. The overarching darkness helps. It's like someone dropped a black dome over everything. I've got a head torch, but I try not to use it more than I have to. I keep to the edge of the lane, one foot on the grass and one on the tarmac, and head towards the gate. Eventually, it looms ahead of me, trapped against the sky; in the distance, beyond it, is a solitary light. Someone's up — a nurse maybe or a doctor called to an emergency.

Or maybe Wendy.

An image flashes through my mind with the force of a lightning strike, and I imagine her, sedated and lying still on her bed, her head encased in a VR headlock from which there's no escape, until someone — some research director, money-man, or maybe even Mark Van-Doren himself, says she's cured, transformed, and ready to be someone else in a brave new world they've prepared her for.

I try to hurry as I follow the wall, but it's a mistake. Tree roots lurch out from the ground, branches swing down at my face, brambles grab at me, and pines shoot hypodermic needles in my arms and legs. I slow down and keep one hand on the wall to my left. I'm counting my steps. Every ten, I risk the light of my torch and capture the image of my next ten steps, and, slowly, I make my way to the corner, where I can make out the shape of the tree and the branch and the razor wire on the wall.

There's no voice persuading me to retreat — not tonight.

Then, as if a malignant deity is looking down on my presumptuous aspirations, it starts to rain, gently at first then more heavily, and the darkness closes in until I can hardly breathe. I've no choice now; I have to use the torch. The trunk and the branches will be wet and slippery. I remember how difficult it was before, but I can't let myself think about how much worse it will be tonight. It's just something I have to do, an obstacle I have to overcome, and it's the first obstacle of many. It's weird, but I have no doubts tonight — not one.

It takes a couple of attempts to get high enough up the trunk to reach the branch, and problem number one suddenly grows in stature. That branch, which I can hardly see, feels like its mossy surface has just been transformed by the hand of God into something smoothly polished and covered in a layer of grease. It's like a fairground challenge which no one can beat.

I turn the torch off, mainly because I'm above the height of the wall, so maybe I can be seen from the house, but also because I really don't want to see what's ahead of me. This is one of those "so far so good" moments.

I straddle the branch and ease myself out into the void. It's like there's nothing around me, just a black emptiness as wide and as deep as eternity. Then a branch catches my head and another snags my leg and nearly upends me. I'm back to reality, and my concentration is intense. Slowly, inch by inch, I ease myself towards the wall. The branch is narrower now, and it is bending, but I can see the razor wire and the top of the wall. I ease forward — calm, not hurrying — and allow my left foot to reach down and touch the stone that is just inches from the razor wire behind me. One slip now and I'll be hanging from it, upside down with blood dripping down my face.

Not a thought to linger on.

Besides, I've got more pressing worries. I've got both feet on the rough stone, but I'm wobbling precariously. If I don't get myself under control pretty soon, the only chance I've got is to jump out into the darkness and hope for the best.

Which is what I have to do because, if I don't, I'm going to spread myself over that razor wire and gut myself like a fish.

So I leap.

And I land.

I hit the ground way before I have time to prepare for it, and I feel like someone just broke both my legs and popped a couple of discs in my spine. I mean, shit, I'm so winded, it's like I've just been hit in the gut by some big guy with a baseball bat.

I crouch down and wait.

Maybe I'll stop breathing and die right here, right now. A minute passes, and I'm still alive, so I congratulate myself and try to stand upright. It's not easy, but once that's done, I figure the next bit will be easier. I just have to walk. A quick flash of the light picks out the bark-covered track leading towards the house. I slip along it, keeping beneath the overhanging branches and close to the trees, and it gets easier. I can see the light at a ground-floor window. It's like a beacon drawing me closer — a lighthouse beam by which I can plan my route.

Over to the left is the main drive; to the right, there's the kitchen garden, a jumble of outbuildings, and the servants' entrance. That's still my best chance, I reckon, despite the Stalag Guard I met last time. I'm just praying I don't have to engage in any life-saving sprints for the gate. I doubt my current limp would get me ten yards before I am overtaken by some hefty, mean-looking security guys. Bruised ribs and a pelvic floor which is in my throat isn't good preparation for a 100-metre sprint.

I crouch down and run until I reach the relative security of the wall by the window. I press my back against it and inch towards the light. Then everything goes black. The light in the room is turned off, and I'm left staring into a void.

Time to edge around the corner of the house, check there's no one watching, and run a few paces to the kitchen door.

Locked.

I'm not expecting this. It was open last time. It should be open now. It should always be open. There's probably someone inside with their back to the door, dangling a key and sniggering.

What now?

God knows.

Look for a window maybe? Or wander round the perimeter and see if there's another door?

And if there isn't?

I don't want to think about that.

Knock on the front door maybe?

Hi, I think you're expecting me. I've come to visit Wendy.

It's not easy moving round the house without finding myself being gazed at by a camera. They're everywhere, every twenty metres or so, and they're looking in all directions. Some of them move, panning an area of the ground. With every step, it's getting harder to believe no one's picked me out. I'm starting to feel like a mouse who thinks he's escaped the cat, only to find the cat is just sitting there, paw raised and claws at the ready.

Mee-ow.

By the time I'm round the back of the house, I figure I might as well step out onto the lawn and do a song and dance act, and, when I see a light go on and realise it's behind a small half-glazed wooden door like you might find on any suburban semi, I just know this isn't going to end well.

But I carry on nonetheless, playing a game that has rules I don't understand and knowing that I can't win because the other guy has all the cards and knows what victory looks like and how you get there. I don't even pause at the door. I just open it and glance down a carpeted hallway to an open door — an expensive one this time — oak, I think — which reveals a dimly-lit office with a mahogany desk, a bookcase with leather-bound volumes, and a red leather sofa and chairs. They're like the ones my mum's friend has, only they're expensive. And about as comfortable as a park bench.

I know without looking that there's someone sitting at the desk. They're just out of sight to the left, caught in the light of a table lamp. I get the feeling this whole thing has been choreographed just for effect — just so I know who's in control here. I bet that face is in half-shadow. Maybe he's facing the other way and will turn as I enter. Maybe there should be dramatic music rising to a pitch as I realise who it is and how hopeless my situation has become. Very James Bond.

But there's no need for the music and no need for the drama because, even before I step up to the door and cross the threshold, I know who's sitting in that chair.

'Hello, Mr Van-Doren,' I say. 'It's good of you to wait up.'

He stands up slowly and moves round the desk, hand extended.

'I see you've parted with the beard,' I say, trying to keep my voice calm. 'I think that's wise. It aged you.'

His face is thin and wrinkled, and his neck hangs in folds like it's been deflated. Even the hand I take is thin and bony, like there isn't enough skin to stretch over it. Veins protrude, and there are blue bruises. The grip is tight, though, like he's keeping a hold on everything, even life. The eyes are bright and cunning too. Here's a man who weighs his opponent to the last gram. Life is a competition to this guy, and he plans to win every game until the one he can't win.

Maybe he thinks he can win that one too.

'Mr Tyler,' he says.

There's no weakness in the voice, even though it emerges with an effort from somewhere deep. I know now that it is his will keeping him going — nothing else.

This guy is dying.

Chapter 38

Two men, black suited, in white shirts and blue ties, appear at the door like something out of a mob movie. They never have names, these guys. They're so anonymous, even their wives don't know who they are.

'Is this all for me? How kind.' I smile. 'A coffee would be nice,' I say.

I wish I didn't do that. It's nerves. It's like I go out of my way to antagonise people, and the more dangerous the situation, the more flippant I get. It really isn't a good idea. I mean, I might be in their hands later — literally.

Van-Holden nods, and the door closes. I imagine the two clones outside with their backs to the wall and their hands crossed in front of them. For some reason, I always picture men like them wearing shades even when it's dark.

Men in black.

'Do take a seat, Mr Tyler.'

I look around and pick the red leather chair which faces the window, just in case I want to make one of those dramatic escapes where I charge through the glass, roll on the gravel, and scarper across the lawn.

Only, it's not a window you'd risk trying to break. It's small, has a wooden frame, and is double glazed. I'd end up unconscious on the floor, looking really stupid.

'I want to see Wendy,' I tell him as he sits down on the sofa and pours brandy in a glass the size of a goldfish bowl. He swills it and peers into it like he can see the future, which must be pretty depressing given the state of his health. He rests his arm across the back of the chair, but he doesn't look at me. His attention is all on the brandy. He pours another glass.

'Here, drink this; you may need it.'

'I haven't come here to share a convivial glass. I want to see Wendy.'

'Humour me, Mr Tyler,' he says, and he looks straight at me. The eyes are fiercely penetrating in that old, dying face. It's like they're holding onto life and power any way they can. They won't let go.

'You'll see Wendy soon,' he says.

I still don't touch the glass.

'Explanations first — can I ask a few questions?'

He leans back, and a thin smile fractures into fissures across his face. Only, the eyes don't change. Shit, that's some fierce fire he's got burning in there.

'Of course,' he says. 'There need be no secrets — not anymore.'

There's something about the way he says this which makes me feel like he's about to make a final, devastating move.

Checkmate.

I try to keep my eyes firm and my will strong, but it's not easy. I feel like I'm melting. Soon, I'll be a pool of quivering fat dripping on the polished leather. I take a sip of brandy, and I imagine Liz's voice emerging from somewhere just behind me. She doesn't sound pleased.

What are you, Mr Tyler?

I'm a journalist, Liz, a good one.

Are you, Mr Tyler? Are you really?

Yes.

Then show me, and stop snivelling in front of this narcissistic, megalomaniacal corpse.

I take another sip, then I put the glass down and start.

'Why are you here in the UK, Mr Van-Holden?' I ask.

'You know why.'

'No, not really. I mean, I know you want to oversee the experiments that are taking place here. I understand that. I also figure there are aspects of your research which only a few people, including representatives of the UK and US administrations, have any knowledge of. You plan to keep it like that.'

'Not even your government or the US administration knows everything, Mr Tyler.'

'So what are you doing?'

He smiles that crocodile smile again.

'Drink up. It's a long story. Cigar?'

I shake my head, but I finish the glass and watch as he pours another from an expensive cut-glass decanter. There's a slight tremor in his hands — nothing more. He glances up at me, and I feel like I'm buzzing perilously close to a web from which I'll not escape. This is the consummate businessman at work, the guy who made a fortune exploiting the idealistic and the naïve. This is the guy who built an empire by clambering over the corpses of his victims. Each move is planned, each step securely placed. He knows what he's doing, and he knows he can't lose. He never loses; he doesn't know how.

'Tell me what you think you know,' he says.

'What's it like being you?' I ask.

'What do you mean?'

'You've got everything a man could want. You're so wealthy, it makes my eyes water just thinking about it. There's nothing you can't have. I mean, what's that like, to have everything and then find it's nothing — just sand slipping through your fingers like a broken hourglass?'

For a moment, a look of annoyance flickers, but it's quickly subdued. His mind is focussed on the task at hand. He's not going to be waylaid by a few well-targeted remarks. Still, it's worth persisting. I like the idea that I can rattle him, even if it's only very slightly — the stirring of a violin string, not an earthquake.

'It must be hard for you. You look round your empire now you're at the end of your life, and, instead of pride, you just feel kind of empty. Yeah, you've got all this, but, hey, it's just stuff, isn't it? It's stolen stuff too, not even your own. You're standing there in your fairytale castle, and you look out of the window, and all there is out there is desolation and death. Jesus, that must hurt.'

'You're wasting time, Mr Tyler. If you want to know the truth about what's happening here, it's time to stop pissing about and tell me what you think you know. This amateur psychology stuff won't work on me, I assure you.'

'I guess you'd like to live forever, Mark, but you're a century or two too early for that. We don't have the cures and the replacement parts in stock — not yet. That's for another generation of money-makers, not you. Some other rich guy, born in the twenty-second century, may well find a way to postpone death almost indefinitely. Imagine that.'

'I don't see where this is leading, Mr Tyler. I'm beginning to think I overestimated you. You know nothing.'

I'm keeping a close focus on those shifting eyes. Whenever he looks at me, I'm there ahead of him, staring him down, not blinking. He's uncomfortable and momentarily weak, and he knows I can see it.

'You can't have any of that, so you focus on power, maintaining control over everything you can until your miserable little life expires and you're just dust like everyone else.'

'You know nothing about me.'

'I know you've been experimenting with VR and not just as a therapy for people who are weak and vulnerable, as a treatment for mental health disorders, or for the excesses of the rich and famous. No, you're way ahead of that game. You've done what you do best; you've seen the opportunities. You've recognised the potential, and you've gone straight ahead. You're into serious behavioural change.'

'That's very good, Mr Tyler, though why you would give me such credit for something which is so blatantly obvious, I can't imagine. And I don't understand why you're so shocked and indulge in this moral outrage. Imagine, if you can — and I confess I don't understand the medical details of these procedures; I am merely a businessman, after all. I take the technology and turn it to the advantage of all — but imagine a mind brought to a perfect, receptive state through the administration of medication. Imagine that mind being directed, by the use of VR, to enter a new reality and live, for a period of time, in a world which is repelled by their previous crimes or perversions — a world where they are valued by the decency of their lives. Imagine the criminal who becomes appalled by crime and is rendered incapable of a criminal act. Imagine the murderer who, tortured by guilt, is brought to see and feel the reality of the crime.'

'VR as the prison of the future?'

'But a prison where the therapy is guaranteed to work — where the behaviour of the criminal is so radically altered, there can be complete assurance of exemplary behaviour in the community. Imagine the terrorist converted from his perverse beliefs and the society that would be rid of their dangerous extremes. This is all within reach, Mr Tyler. I have placed it within our grasp. I have given the world the power to eliminate crime and enforce adherence to a moral code of which we all approve. Can't you see the world that we will soon have at our fingertips? It's Utopia.'

'Your Utopia maybe, not mine. You want to turn people like Benny into God-fearing Christians?'

'Benny?'

'You caught him burgling Westleigh Lodge. He was the guy you subjected to your therapy, the guy who came out of here with a set of beliefs and behaviours which weren't his own, the guy who was convicted and sentenced without the approval of any court of law and without any due process, the guy whose rights were trampled underfoot...'

'He was a thief, Mr Tyler, just a common thief. He deserved prison, not the benefits of the therapy we could offer him. Do you doubt he came out a better person? Can you question that he was no longer a drain on society — someone who was a blight on the lives of others.'

'He was in your way. Maybe he saw things you didn't want him to see, or maybe he was just in the wrong place at the wrong time. You decided he was a risk to your enterprise, so you subjected him to your treatment to shut him up.'

'He was a nobody, a thief.'

'So you can make Benny a model missionary Christian; what if someone came to you who was gay? Would you straighten them out? Can you stop my mate Winston from swearing and being a devious, amoral son of a bitch?'

'Don't be absurd. You're being hysterical. This is a business which will be governed by the strictest moral guidance.'

'Let's skip the moral justifications, shall we? It makes me feel sick. This isn't about the greater good, is it, Mark? This is about power — your power to control everyone and everything until the very last moment of your miserable life.'

'The benefits to humanity are immeasurable; I'll be remembered...'

'You think? It sounds like you've got the key in the doorway to hell, and you're about to turn it.'

'Any technological leap forward carries risks. Mankind has proven adept at restricting the worst excesses. Society continues to progress. Change will come whether you want it or not, Mr Tyler. That is the way it has always been.

This isn't a guy you can argue with. He's got this look about the eyes now, like he's some kind of fanatic leading his children along a road to the perfect world. His eyes are fixed so firmly on the horizon, he can't see the ground beneath his feet or the damage his vision is causing. Besides, he doesn't care.

'And Wendy?'

'Ah, Wendy,' he says, 'my protégé.'

'What do you mean, "protégé"? She's a victim. She wanted out, and you wouldn't let her. What about the guy Winston saw on the road?'

'Yes, yes, Derek Stott, another patient of exceptional talent.'

'Talent? What the hell are you talking about?'

My head's starting to spin. Brandy at this time of the morning isn't a good idea, and, as quickly as I've emptied a glass, Mark has been filling it. There's something else too; the room is getting warmer, and my mouth is dry. I loosen my collar and wipe the moisture from my forehead.

'I apologise for the heat in the room,' he says. 'A man of my age and frailty feels the cold. Shall I open a window?'

'No, just tell me what you mean? What talent?'

'Like you, Mr Tyler. You too were exceptional.'

'Me? What are you talking about?'

'Some of our subjects respond so well and so quickly, they start to inhabit the world we have given them.'

'I don't understand. I don't...'

'I think you do, Mr Tyler. I mean, take a look at yourself; you have bruises and stitches, and you've been punched and kicked until you required hospital treatment. But look at you now. Do you feel any pain or discomfort? Do you really believe you could recover so quickly?'

'I exaggerate; I always exaggerate. Besides, if I move, I can still feel...'

I struggle to my feet but too quickly. Dizziness overtakes me, and I fall back. But he's right — there's no pain, no discomfort, nothing.

'Do you remember the night you foolishly broke into the compound? Do you remember running towards the gate, how it miraculously opened in front of you, how the guards lost you in the woods, and how your car was undisturbed in the place you left it?'

'I was lucky. I ran and hoped, and I was lucky...'

'But as you ran, you knew they were gaining on you, and the distance to the gate seemed to grow with every step. Then, suddenly, you found some energy from somewhere; it was enough for a final burst which took you to the gate and freedom. That's right, isn't it?'

'Yes, but...'

'No, Mr Tyler, you didn't escape. My security guards caught you, injected you to render you unconscious and compliant, and brought you back to the clinic. You talk about power, Mr Tyler; you've been in my power for weeks.'

'Don't be ridiculous. I remember getting in the car and driving back to town. I remember it all...'

'Just as if it really happened, yes. It's remarkable, isn't it, the power of the human mind? You were particularly compliant, you know. It was quite remarkable. You filled the scenario we gave you with images of your own; you peopled our world and made it live — quite remarkable. Yes, you were one of the best. Like Wendy, in fact.'

My head is starting to gyrate like I'm on some fairground ride. I want it to stop, and I want to get off, but it's moving faster and faster, and I'm losing control. All I can do is focus as hard as I can on the face of Mark Van-Doren, the picture on the wall, the brandy glass, or the window.

'This isn't true, none of it. You put something in the brandy,' I manage to gasp. 'You son of a bitch, you put something in the brandy.'

'Just a little something to help you relax, Mr Tyler, nothing more. It's just to help you see things for what they are.'

'You're playing with my mind... I won't let you... I know what you're doing. You think you can control me...'

'You have no idea, Mr Tyler, none at all.' He swirls the brandy in his glass, and I feel my mind swirl with it. He's smiling now, a grim, close-mouthed smile — the smile of a man who holds victory in his hands. 'You really do have a most interesting desire to face and defeat adversity, do you know that? Do you recall how you burnt down your chalet and destroyed everything just to show your resilience in the face of disaster?'

'No, I didn't... I...'

'It was all you, Mr Tyler. It was all your own invention — all in your mind. You create an impossible scenario and face the most improbable of challenges, then you're beaten back, seemingly subdued and utterly defeated, and emerge like a phoenix and rise splendidly above everything. It's remarkable, truly remarkable. If only it were true. We gave you a simple virtual world; we wanted you to be content, but your imagination was powerful, and you made it your own. You've been a most interesting subject, Mr Tyler.'

I can feel perspiration on my forehead, and my hands are clammy. My breath is breaking from my lungs in painful gasps. All I can do is reach for my collar, get some air, and fight off the panic that's assailing me. I try to get to my feet, but I fall back once again, and Van-Doren's voice goes on and on. He's seen his advantage and taken it; he's attacking now, and he won't relent until I'm beaten.

'You like to see the best in people too, don't you? Do you recall how your friend Winston changed almost overnight? Do you remember how, one minute, he's turning his back on his friend, pursuing his own selfish interests, and, the next, he's part of a rescue? Really, Mr Tyler? Can you not see? Can you really imagine Winston living at home, caring for his dear, invalid mother? Please, it's too absurd. Your burglar friend too — do you really think a bitter, malignant individual like Benny is the victim of a deep, personal tragedy? Do you believe he has a dead son, a departed wife, and a daughter he no longer sees? No, Mr Tyler; they are the people you *wish* to see. They are your creations. And then there's... well, see for yourself.'

He presses a button on the desk, a door opens, and a figure swims into view and then fades and then emerges again like it's inflating and deflating before me.

'Mel?' I cry out. 'Mel!'

'Sasha, Mr Tyler. This is Sasha; have you learned nothing? The girl who dumped you for some spotty youth with a car — the first love of your teenage life, projected onto the face of an actress hired to fill your emptiness and make you content. We planned for you to marry, to have children, to grow old together — in our VR world, of course.'

'But why?' I cry out. 'Why?'

The face has disappeared, and I'm left facing Van-Doren. He's closer now, his face almost pressed against mine. The eyes stare unrelentingly, and I feel as if I can see in their depths some nightmare from which I'll never awake.

'Because I can,' he snarls. 'The floor beneath your feet, Mr Tyler, is it real? The walls, the windows, are they really there? What about me? You asked what brought me from the States to this miserable little blemish on the face of the planet. Do you understand now? Can you see why I'm here?'

'You're not here at all. It was me,' I gasp. 'I did it...'

'Yes, Mr Tyler, you brought me here...'

'Wendy,' I gasp. 'Where's Wendy?'

'She has gone,' he says, and he thrusts the final knife deep in my heart. 'She has gone where she has always wanted to be. She is with Marcus and Sasha, and she will never come back. That was the deal, Mr Tyler. Did you really think I was so shallow that I would spend billions to rehabilitate a bunch of offenders? Did you think this was all about money? I have money, Mr Tyler. I could burn more money than you could ever imagine, and I would feel no loss. It's nothing to me.

'No, I am creating worlds. I am offering an eternity of contentment — a life filled with everything a person might desire; in a matter of days, there will be no more pain, no more despair, no more unhappiness. I have that power, Mr Tyler.'

'She didn't want it. She changed her mind. She didn't know...'

'It was a one-way ticket. There was no way back. She exchanged her current existence for a new one, a new reality, a new life. The past never existed; there has only ever been Sasha and Marcus and a life of love and contentment. What could be wrong with that, Mr Tyler?'

'Everything.'

He laughs a wide, cavernous laugh, and his pale gums move towards me and throb like some monstrous, glistening, salivating lifeform. Then they recede, and the room spins on.

'You too became ours, Mr Tyler,' he says, 'the very moment you chose to enter our clinic that night.'

'No! No, I didn't!' I cry out, but I feel my legs give way beneath me, and all my strength and resistance collapses with them.

'Where am I?' I cry out.

He doesn't answer, just rings a bell again. Two white-coated guards emerge from nowhere and gather like a shroud around me. Then I'm moving, and all I can see is the darkness beyond the window, and all I can hear are Van-Doren's words. I try to focus, but there's nothing there.

Only the window.

Only the window and the darkness.

Only the window and the darkness and the movement of trees.

And Winston.

And Slattery.

Out there, peering in through the glass.

And that big, stupid smile on Winston's face, like this is some silly game he's invented.

'Bunny...Bunny...' he mouths.

And Slattery is holding something, and I can't make out what it is, but I know I want to laugh, so I do. I laugh and laugh and laugh until tears are pouring down my cheeks, and, as I laugh, I feel something like strength pulse back into my legs, and I can take my weight, and my mind is suddenly, momentarily clear.

'I've won.' I cry out. 'I've beaten you.'

The two wardens pause and glance at Van-Doren, but he doesn't know what's happening either. He's looking as bewildered as they are.

'Do you hear me, Mark? I've beaten you.'

For the first time, there's a look of fear on his face.

'Do you not understand, you stupid fuck?' I say to him. 'It hurts.'

'What? What hurts?'

'My face, my ribs, my whole life — they hurt — and not some in madman's dream world. The pain is real, and it's mine.'

And I laugh until I cry.

Chapter 39

Even as they lead me from the room and Van-Doren turns to leave like the ghost he'll soon become, I hear the distant sound of Slattery making an entrance; somewhere in a distant corner of the house, there's splintering wood and shattering glass. I get this surge of panic as I think again that maybe it's not really happening; maybe it's just something deep inside my head, making its wishful presence felt.

Then I think of the pain in my ribs and my eyes, I remember Winston's face at the window and Slattery peering over his shoulder, and I'm sure, really sure, that no amount of wishful thinking would conjure that image.

At least, I *think* I'm sure.

I tell you, it's disorientating, this reality shift Van-Doren is laying on me. I don't know if I'm here or in a bed somewhere, under a helmet, or travelling slowly through my own intestines. Feels like all three at once. The drug he's fed me doesn't help. It's like an acid trip — all lights and movements and dancing shapes. I have to try really hard to stare through it, to keep my mind on what's happening, and to keep my wits as sharp as I can. Trouble is, I feel about as sharp as a pound of those sausages my mum buys from the butcher's in town. I'm just slithering about, like I'm falling from a wet paper bag.

'Goodbye, Mr Tyler,' Van-Doren says. 'We shan't meet again.'

'Except in our dreams,' I say, and I give him a big wink. I'm not letting the bastard think I'm sinking under his drug cocktail, no, sir. I know where I am, I know who I am, and I know Slattery is bringing the cavalry.

Well, he's bringing Winston.

That'll have to do.

It's hardly "Ride of the Valkyries", but what the hell. You take what you can get.

'Playing the hero to the very end,' Van-Doren smirks as he disappears behind the door. I want to stumble after him and punch that narcissistic, smug face as hard as I can, but it feels like he's slipped not just out of sight, but out of existence, as if the house and the trees, the fields, and the railway are just figments of some ghastly imagination.

One of the apes at my side grunts, 'Time for your medication.'

I think he's trying to be funny.

'Then you can lie back and watch TV,' the other says.

Their laughter is a sound you'd usually associate with drains.

'Well, damn me,' I manage to smile. 'You're a double act.'

There's another crash, closer now, as another door gives way under the pressure of Slattery's mighty shoulder. My warders hurry me down a couple of corridors and into a side room which I recognise at once. It's the partitioned ward I looked in on, days ago, when I came here before — if I came here before — it's where I saw the sleeping figure on his moving bed. The jigsaw pieces, which had floated apart into the ether of my drug-induced state, slowly gather and fit together again.

In the distance, Slattery demolishes something. I hear the crash of glass. Ape One looks worried.

'Nothing for us to be concerned about,' Ape Two rumbles. 'Security will be onto them.'

'They're probably not even real,' the other says, and the drains gurgle again.

'The guy in the bed by the window,' I say. 'Where did he go?'

'No one goes anywhere.'

We're deeper in the room, and I can see six of the ten beds hold patients, who are wired up to drips and catheters. Electronic equipment bleeps their lives away as they pitch and roll in their private worlds. Their faces and heads are buried in headsets.

I realise, with a sudden shudder, that these people signed up to a new life; they signed away their mundane, maybe tragic existences for something else, something they were told would be so much better, which could be delivered through an all-immersing screen and a cocktail of drugs. An eternity of phoney, unbridled happiness.

'Where's the guy who escaped — the guy who went walkabout down the lane?'

'Some we win, some we lose,' Ape Two says. 'He's back now; he won't be going anywhere again.'

And I know that in bed three our naked rambler is sharing eternity with Bunny, the love of his life.

'You bastards,' I say.

It earns me another painful bruise as they drag me to the end of the ward.

'Want to say goodbye?' Ape One asks.

And there's Wendy, and she's sitting in a bed. She's not wearing a helmet; she's just facing the end of the bed in a dreamy kind of trance. Her arms are strapped to the bedside, but her eyes are free, and they meet mine, and a smile spreads like sunlight.

'I remember everything,' she says, 'everything.'

For a moment, all I can do is stare, then...

'I'm here to rescue you,' I tell her.

We look at each other for a moment, and we start to laugh.

'Are you okay?' I ask.

'Yes,' she says, 'just waiting for tomorrow...'

I don't want to think about tomorrow. I've got my hopes pinned on Slattery and — God help me — on Winston. I know they're back there somewhere. I just wish they'd hurry up. I want to stop thinking about what happens if they don't get through. Everything will be lost. Game over.

I listen, but there's nothing now — just the ticking of a round-faced clock on the wall. The only movement is the pendulum slowly measuring out this weird, unreal time we're passing through. Ape One is standing by the window while Ape Two holds my arm. I can hear a deep thrumming coming from outside as a helicopter rises from behind the house.

'Van-Doren,' Ape One says, 'going to the airport.'

'Creepy kind of guy,' the other says. 'He made me shudder with those cold eyes. I wouldn't want to cross him.'

'Something of the corpse about him.'

'That's what I said,' I tell them, but no one's listening.

'Private plane, no expense spared. How the other half...'

'Kind of makes you think of rats and sinking ships, doesn't it?' I say. 'Keep listening, guys. The police will be here soon.'

No one's coming, shithead,' Ape One says. He turns back from the window and throws me on a bed opposite Wendy. 'Mr Van-Doren says you can be together until the final curtains close. He says to tell you it's your reward.'

'Reward for what?'

'He says "for being a model patient and a pleasure to work on."'

A laugh like a rusty chain, like gravel on a drum.

'He's a real tease, your Mr Van-Doren,' I say, 'a laugh a minute. I'll miss him.'

'A joker to the end,' he sneers. 'It won't do you any good.'

He's right. This is just bravado. I can't help it; it's just the way I am. When things can't get much worse and I'm chin-deep in sinking sand, I keep looking at the stars. I say something stupid, something annoying, and I hope for a happy ending. That's my way. But out of sight, somewhere deep inside me, I feel a surge of panic. I feel nauseous. I can't fight the drugs anymore. I can't fight anything.

'He said you'd understand.'

'Yeah, I understand.'

They're still laughing as they leave the room.

I look at Wendy. This is my last chance. I've got to say it, no matter how stupid I sound, no matter how pathetic.

'I love you.'

She doesn't hesitate.

'Me too,' she says.

There's no pain now; I can't feel my hands or feet. But I can turn my head and fix my eyes on Wendy, and that's enough for me. I hold them there like I'm grasping a sliver of rock, and I'm hanging over a crevasse, and there's just Wendy above me, looking down and reaching for me. There's just her between me and...

...Between me and what?

I don't know.

I don't know.

I feel myself slipping, falling away.

'Don't leave me.'

Her voice slips across the space between us like a thread of mist.

'Don't leave me,' she calls again.

I reach out and touch the thread, and it's strong, very strong. I feel her pulling it, and, as she pulls, it becomes stronger. The thread is a string and the string a rope and the rope a chain.

'Don't leave me.'

I scramble back up the bed, and I clench my hands into my ribs until the pain surges back.

'I'm going nowhere.' Anger rises inside me like a volcano.

I stumble towards her bed. I tear the straps from her arms, and I hold her close, like I'll never let go. I'm still holding her as we clamber to our feet and struggle towards the door.

...which opens.

And there's Winston with that same grin on his face, like this is just one big adventure, and he's having the time of his life. Only, he's got blood dripping from his nose.

'That guard guy took a swing at me,' he says. 'Shit, man, it could be broken. I could be deformed or something. If Slattery hadn't stepped in, I'd have killed him.'

'Yeah,' says Slattery, 'I could see him quaking. You two okay?' he asks.

I'm holding Wendy, and she's holding me, and we both look like we'd fall down if we weren't.

'We're okay.' I look at Wendy, and we share a special smile. 'Yeah, we're okay.'

Winston's eyes widen.

'Mel ain't going to like this,' he murmurs, then he says, 'Can we go home now? Mum's waiting up to hear whether you're alright.'

In the distance, I hear sirens, and they're coming closer.

'They took their time,' Slattery mutters. 'That new DCI can't hold his dick without getting orders in writing.'

Then a big smile widens, and something like the cracks in a rock wall creases his face. He's dangling something on a lanyard in front of me.

'I've still got it,' he says. 'I don't know what it is, but I've still got it.'

I reach out and grasp the object. It's a tiny micro-recorder.

'You heard it all?' I ask.

'Every word, Phil, every god-damn word.'

Chapter 40

The sirens cease just beyond the gate, and Slattery, who's at the window, looks worried.

'They're turning,' he says. 'They're going back.'

There's an uncomfortable silence. Not far away, I can hear footsteps approaching along the corridor. I reckon we've got seconds to make a move. Winston's instinct for self-preservation kicks in.

'Run!' he yells. He's down the ward and away through the double doors at the end before I've drawn breath. Seconds later, we're yards behind him, and we're heading out towards the kitchen door and the garden. Wendy is leaning against me, and the two of us barely have the stability of a moth in a gale, but Slattery, behind us, pushes us on, looking back over his shoulder all the time.

When we reach the garden, there's no sign of Winston. The night seems to have swallowed him whole. I point towards the low wall of the kitchen garden, which leads along the side of the lawn, and we run, heads low, towards the relative safety of trees. There, we pause and peer back towards the house. Then we hear them.

'They've got dogs,' I gasp to Slattery.

'Shit,' he says, 'I'm too old for this.'

There's a blast of light from the kitchen door. Torches emerge and disperse like fireflies.

'Where are we heading?' Slattery asks.

'I have no idea,' I tell him.

'That's alright, then. Let's go.'

A car engine hums into life, and its lights flash over us as it heads towards the gate.

I lead the way through the trees. It's slow, painful progress. Roots seem to leap from the ground to snag our legs, and branches appear from nowhere to crack our heads. Only when we reach the dark path can we move easily.

'Where does this go?' Wendy asks.

'To a gate,' I say, 'but don't get your hopes up. It's locked. There's a push-button code.'

'I remember that gate,' she says. 'That's the way I left.'

'How did you get out?'

'The nurse — the one I told you about — she let me out. I think maybe... I remember the code. It's Marcus' birthday.'

Well, that gives us a boost, I can tell you — albeit in a sickening kind of way. His birthday, for God's sake. I barely have time to feel contempt. If we can get out of the gate, and if no one is waiting outside, we can disappear into the wood, which is the best news I've had for a while.

'Where's your car?' I ask Slattery.

'Where no one can find it,' he smiles grimly, 'not even these bastards.'

By the time we reach the gate, I can hear people behind us. They're shouting, and, not far behind them, dogs are barking. They sound hungry.

And angry.

And in no mood to be messed with.

'Let's get out of here,' I say.

Wendy is standing in front of the push-button. She's got her eyes closed, and she's thinking hard. Then she punches in a code. Slattery tries the gate.

Nothing.

'Try again.'

She punches in the numbers once more.

'And again.'

'I'm sure these are the right numbers,' Wendy says. 'They must have changed it.'

'Maybe it's the day he's going to die,' I suggest. 'Try tomorrow.'

The voices are coming closer. I can see torch lights flickering through the branches, panning left and right through the trees. The dogs are louder now too; they're close behind. Then there's another sound, even closer, almost beside us, like a wild hog charging through the undergrowth. I turn to face it, fists clenched and heart beating like a frenzy of thunder.

Winston bursts through the trees.

'Shit, Winston, you scared the hell out of me.'

'Where the hell have you been?' he says. 'This way! Quick!'

And he's gone again, and all we can do is follow him. The branches tear and scratch our heads, but there's no time to think about that now. The voices are louder, as if they've seen us and know they've got us cornered. Even the dogs are louder. I can picture them tearing at their leashes, snarling and dripping saliva.

Bloodlust.

It's the sort of noise that spurs you on, way beyond your normal capacities. The thought of teeth tearing into my legs is enough to encourage one final spurt. I grab Wendy's hand and pull her forward. Ahead, I catch a glimpse of Winston snaking round the trees. Behind me, there's Slattery — somewhere — I don't know where. I can't hear him anymore.

Then, suddenly, we're in the open, and we've reached the corner wall where the branch hangs flimsily over the razor wire.

And there's a short ladder — maybe eight feet — extended almost to the top of the wall, and Winston's up there, grinning down at us.

'Where the hell did you find a ladder?' I manage to gasp.

'I found it while you were pissing about in the house,' he calls. 'It's a walled garden, isn't it? How did you think they'd climb the walls?'

That's all there's time for. Winston leaps in the air with a wild cry and drops out of sight over the wall. I guide Wendy onto the rungs and climb behind her. When we get to the top, there's no sign of Winston; there's no sign of anything. The ground below us might as well not exist. There's just this void — this endless, dark emptiness.

'You've got to jump,' I tell Wendy.

I look behind me.

Where the hell is Slattery?

'You've got to jump,' I repeat. 'There's no alternative.'

There's a movement ahead of us, and Winston emerges from the darkness.

'Come on, man, what the hell are you waiting for?'

Wendy lets go of my hand. She's not giving herself time to think about this. She tenses, her jaw sets firm, and then she's gone, over the razor wire and down onto the ground below. I see Winston gather her and lead her into the trees. Then he appears again.

'Come on, Phil.'

'Get her somewhere safe,' I call. 'I'll wait for Slattery.'

The voices are close now, and the dogs are loud. I can hear them disturbing the branches of the spruces not far away.

'It's too late. You've got to get out,' Winston calls.

'He's got the recording. I'm going back for him. Get Wendy somewhere safe.'

I'm at the foot of the ladder when Slattery emerges from the trees like a stampeding bull. He's trailing a branch, and his hair is full of needles, and he doesn't look happy — no, not one little bit. Just behind him, the advanced guard emerges. It's a guy in an anorak, and he looks like he's just won the big prize. I make out the look of elation on his face as he reaches an arm to grab Slattery.

The elated look doesn't last long. Slattery is in no mood for surrender. He turns with impatience and plants a fist directly in the face of his adversary.

'Fuck off!' he snaps, like he's swatting an irritating insect. The guy in the anorak falls back like a felled tree and lies motionless.

Slattery mutters something under his breath, but I don't catch it.

There's someone else approaching now. Slattery backs towards the ladder. He's got his fists at the ready and his legs apart, bracing himself. He might be heading well into old age, and he might not be in the best of conditions, but Slattery is still a force to be reckoned with.

But even Slattery can't beat off an army of thugs with ravenous dogs.

'Get up the ladder,' he snaps. 'I'm right behind you. And take this.' He hands me the recorder on its lanyard. 'Just in case...'

The "just in case" emerges from the trees, and his torch catches us both in its beam, but I'm already approaching the top, and I don't plan to stop now. As I take a final glance back, I see Slattery level a punch that could demolish a statue.

Then I jump, and I land and roll into the grass beneath the trees. As I look up, there's Slattery at the top of the wall, heaving his not-insubstantial frame over the razor wire.

It's then that I hear the gunshot.

Slattery turns in the air as he falls. He drops heavily beside me and groans.

'Slattery? Come on, Slattery, get up. We're nearly there.'

Only, he doesn't move, and, when I raise my hand, it's sticky and wet with blood.

Chapter 41

'Jesus Christ, he's dead.'

That's Winston. He's just reappeared from the trees. I make out Wendy a few yards behind him. She sees Slattery, lets out a gasp, and runs forward.

'Get out of the way,' she says, and she pushes us aside to lean over him.

'What the hell are you doing back here?' I snap at Winston. 'You were supposed to get Wendy somewhere safe.'

'Slattery's got the car keys,' he says, 'and I'm not sure where we parked. All these trees look the same, man.'

'You're something else, you know that, Winston?'

'Yeah,' he grins. 'Get the keys.'

Wendy is pressing down on Slattery's shoulder and talking, saying something to him I can't hear, but he's not moving, and his eyes are closed. I reach towards his trouser pocket and reach inside for the keys. Any minute, the gate will open, and the hunt will be on again. But as my hand reaches the keys and grasps them, a hand takes a firm hold of mine, and a voice says,

'Move another inch and I'll break your fingers.'

Slattery's eyes are open. He looks up at Wendy, who is kneeling beside him, looking down.

'Heaven,' he murmurs.

His grip tightens on my hand.

'What are you doing in my trouser pocket,' he says, and his grip tightens until I want to cry out.

'Just getting the keys,' I try to tell him. 'Can you move?'

'Get the keys,' Winston's saying. 'Leave him. Come back for him later.'

'You don't know where the car is, remember?'

'Oh yeah.' He leans over Slattery. 'Come on, man, you can make it.'

Slattery rolls onto his side and then his knees.

'Help me up,' he says.

Wendy has pulled an old handkerchief from his pocket. 'Keep this pressed on your shoulder,' she says, and we help him to his feet.

'That handkerchief is more dangerous than a bullet,' I manage to mutter before he grabs me with his good hand and pushes me forward. 'That way.'

We move slowly through the trees, making frequent stops. Supporting Slattery is no easy matter.

'You ever think of going on a diet?' Winston complains.

'No,' Slattery says. 'You ever think of going straight?'

'I get your point, man.'

It takes half an hour to escape the torment of the trees. It feels a lot longer. Eventually, we're on a forest track, and, ten minutes later, Slattery stops.

'Car's around the corner, back off the track. Better go slowly now.'

'I'll go ahead,' Winston says. He holds out a hand.

'Maybe I'll keep the keys,' I tell him, 'till you get back.'

Then Slattery's legs buckle, and we have to lower him to the ground.

'He can't go any further,' Wendy says. 'He's lost too much blood; you'll have to fetch the car, Winston.'

Well, here's a predicament. I reach into my pocket for the keys. Then I hesitate.

'Come on, man, you can trust me,' Winston says. 'For Benny, yeah?'

I risk a smile.

'Yeah, for Benny.'

I throw him the keys, and he disappears into the darkness. I turn off my head torch. No point advertising our presence. Then we wait.

'Will he come back?' Wendy asks.

'Yeah,' I tell her. 'You can trust Winston.'

And I laugh very quietly to myself because I reckon it's true.

Five minutes pass before I hear a car engine, and then subdued lights turn the corner towards us. Winston pulls up, and we help Slattery inside. Wendy sits beside him on the rear seat and presses his handkerchief against the wound. I check the glove compartment and hand her some tissues.

'Here, try these. That handkerchief has more germs than pond water.'

'Shit, man,' Winston is saying, 'how do we get out of here without being seen? The road will be crawling.'

Slattery's voice emerges from the back.

'Follow the track. It comes out... somewhere...'

'Where?' Winston asks.

'How the f... should I know? Just... drive the car.'

I think Winston fancies himself as a rally driver because as soon as we start to move, the beam is on full, his foot hits the accelerator, and my back is pressed into the seat. I hear a gasp from Wendy in the back and a groan from Slattery. My hand reaches for the brake, and my feet press invisible pedals, but the best I can do is close my eyes and pray.

I don't know how he does it, but Winston avoids the trees, swerves past holes in the ground deep enough to swallow a pony, brakes sharply enough to turn without flinging us out of the doors, and accelerates like a rally driver. When I dare to open my eyes, I glance in the wing mirror. There's no one following us. Eventually, just when we're wondering if we can survive another corner, there's an opening and a grass verge and an unmetalled road.

'Get me to a hospital,' Slattery groans, 'before he kills me.'

Two miles down the lane, we meet a bigger road. Another mile brings us to a junction, and we join the main highway into town. There's a police car, lights flashing, parked at the end. There's no way past. A police officer is standing there, waving us down.

'Shit,' says Winston.

Shit indeed.

As we slow up and draw to a halt, I recognise Jim Davey, and something approaching relief surges through me. I lower the window, and he looks inside at me and Winston, Wendy, and Slattery.

'I've got to arrest you,' he says. 'It's orders — aggravated burglary, assault, criminal damage, kidnap, and attempted murder. I reckon they'll add industrial espionage, treason, and dangerous driving too. Have you got a license, Winston? How about insurance?'

Winston's grin is answer enough.

'They'll add that too. What's up with Slattery?'

'They shot him,' I say. 'We need to get him to a hospital, Jim.'

'Jesus.'

'And then I need to get to a laptop before they catch up with us.'

'If we see you, we have to stop you and arrest you — orders from on high.' His colleague is standing not far behind him. They exchange quick looks. 'Lucky for you, we haven't seen you,' he says. 'You must've gone some other way.'

'Thanks, Jim.'

'Take the backroads. There are cars all over the main routes. There are some friendly faces out there but not all of them. Be careful.'

With that, he disappears, and the police car reverses off the road. Winston eases us forward and turns first left then quickly right. We're on home ground now. No one will catch us.

'Where will you find a laptop?' Wendy asks.

'I'll drop in on Liz while we're at the hospital. No one's going to bother me there.'

We pull up outside the main entrance to A & E, and, within minutes, Slattery is being wheeled inside on a trolley.

'I've got to see Liz,' I tell Winston. 'Can you take Wendy somewhere safe?'

'Trust me, man,' he says for the second time tonight.

'Don't push your luck,' I tell him.

'We'll be at Benny's,' he says.

Liz is asleep when I enter her room, but she wakes up at once, and she's obviously back to normal. A nurse appears.

'I'm afraid you can't visit at this time of day,' she tells me.

Liz hits her with a look that could kill a bull. 'My dear young woman,' she says, 'whether you understand it or not, we are engaged in matters of life and death. We have no time for your rules and regulations. If you want my visitor to leave, you will need to call the police and prepare for bloodshed. Do I make myself clear?'

She does.

'Make sure you're gone before the doctor makes his rounds,' the nurse says to me. 'Do you work with Liz?' she asks.

I nod.

'God help you,' she says.

One minute later, the curtains are round the bed, the laptop is out, and Liz has brought up the article I sent her.

'I've edited it,' she says.

It sounds like heavy criticism.

'Now,' she says, 'the recording, please.'

We listen to it twice through. It's not clear, and there are sections we can barely hear, but there's enough to bring a smile to her sculpted features.

'Well done, Slattery,' she says. 'I do hope he doesn't die before I congratulate him. Now, we'll download it and copy it.'

She starts to type, adding a paragraph here and a sentence there, deleting the odd phrase, and tutting now and then as she sees something she still doesn't like. I feel like I'm back at school. She's marking my homework and showing me how I can turn it into something tolerably good (for my age).

'Sentimental drivel,' she mutters and deletes a couple of lines. 'I have a reputation to maintain.' She looks up. 'The facts alone convey all the emotion you need. Give your readers some credit. Some of them can fill the spaces with their own feelings.'

'Yes, Liz.'

'Three adverbs in one paragraph! What have I told you?'

'Be sparing with adverbs, Liz.'

'And look what you've written here.' She stabs a finger towards the screen. 'Totally unnecessary words — space fillers — it's like hanging earrings on a cockatoo: pointless decoration.'

'Yes, Liz.'

'And stop saying "Yes, Liz."'

'Okay, Liz.'

'Now,' she says, 'read it through. It's your name going on it.'

'I thought we'd share the credit.'

'Dear me, Philip, I don't want my name associated with such bleeding-heart material.' Her face widens into a smile. 'Besides, you've earned it. Well done, young man, well done. As soon as you press enter, this article will be ready to be released on our very own online news-sheet. Next, we send it to an old friend who works on one of the national broadsheets. Within a day, phones and keyboards will be melting all over the country, and every headline will be printed blood red.'

'Avoid hyperbole,' I murmur.

'What?'

'Something else you one told me, Liz. Avoid hyperbole. Don't get carried away with your own narrative.'

'It's *my* rule. I can choose to break it.'

'Okay, Liz.'

'And stop saying "okay, Liz."'

'Yes, Liz.'

Liz lies back. She looks ten years younger. I'm envious because I feel about 80 at the moment. It's like I'm sitting here waiting for the explosion my detonation must cause. Only, nothing happens. I just age rapidly and sink onto my chair. I realise I'm more tired at this moment than I've ever been before.

And there's still no time for sleep. There are things to be done.

'What about the papers Van-Doren controls?'

'To hell with them — he can't control them all. We can expect a shitstorm of fake news and counter-attacks, but he'll know when he's beaten. It's all rear-guard action for him now. He'll retreat to one of his many sanctuaries to lick his wounds.'

'And the government?'

'Will deny all knowledge, talk about the dangers of these therapies, be full of righteous indignation and moral outrage, and set up a committee to think about setting up a committee to think about investigating something sometime. There's a lot of long grass out there.'

'So what now?' I ask.

'Now you phone Heather, and then you go back to Wendy and prepare her.'

'Prepare her for what?'

'A media storm.'

'I get the feeling she's a lot tougher than I gave her credit for.'

'You sound disappointed.'

'I was hoping I'd finally found a woman who wasn't tougher than me.'

'That may require a long search, Philip.'

The nurse reappears, and the grin on Liz's face is replaced by a scowl.

'You really have to go,' the nurse says. 'I can bend the rules; I can't break them.'

I just have time for one last question.

'What about Tim? Do I tell Heather?'

'No, let the bastard sweat. Wendy can tell her if she wants to. She may choose to keep him in her power. I would. I'd have him quaking every time I looked at him. I've always thought I deserved a servant.'

'Sometimes you really scare me, Liz.'

'Good.'

'When will they let you out?'

'In a day or two.'

'I bet it'll make their week. What'll you do then? I mean, you've no newspaper.'

'I think we can live off our fame for a while until something turns up. There are a lot more articles in this business — maybe even a book. What do you think?'

'Me and you?'

'Yes.'

'I'd rather chew my arm off,' I grin.

'Cheeky sod; you'll not get a better offer.'

'In that case, I'll think about it.'

It's time for me to leave.

Chapter 42

Wendy's asleep when I get to Benny's place. Winston and Benny are sitting with beers in their hands. The TV is on, and there are plates on the floor — bacon and eggs from the look of it. I feel faintly nauseous. Maybe it's fatigue, maybe it's hunger, or maybe it's the sight of congealed egg and fat or the pervasive smell of bacon.

'You look like shit,' Winston says.

'Thanks.'

'You want to sit down before you fall.'

'How's Wendy?'

'On Benny's bed, out for the count.'

'I keep checking on her,' Benny says. 'She's so...'

'Benny's in love,' Winston tells me, 'head over heels. I've told him it's hands off.'

'She's so...' Benny says again.

'Yeah, she is...'

'Yeah.'

'I think we should leave her a while,' I suggest. 'She's been through a lot. And maybe I'll take a nap... just for a while... just...'

I don't know if I start that sentence, get partway through, or finish it. I know I wake up an hour later because Winston is tugging at my arm. He's saying something which sounds urgent. The clock inside my head is telling me I need another seven hours at least, and I'm trying to resist opening my eyes, but, eventually, I have to stir.

'Hey, wake up, Phil. She's asking for you. Benny's with her, but he's got no idea, man. You better go rescue her before he sends her to sleep again.'

Benny's showing her the photo of his ex and the kids, and there are tears in his eyes. Yeah, this is just what she needs after what she's been through. She's looking at the photo, though, and saying something which makes Benny smile, so I suppose she's okay. Like I said, she's tougher than I thought. When she sees me, she's on her feet, and we're holding each other close. I want to bestow a conquering smile on Benny, but it doesn't seem fair to gloat.

'I remember everything,' she says. 'I want to tell you before Heather gets here.' So I usher Benny and Winston from the room. I shut the door on them, and we sit together on the bed.

'They said they could cure me,' she says. 'They said they could make me happy again, like I used to be. They said they'd take me back and show me how to take the pain away and how to face up to what happened. Then they'd make a new life for me and give me a future not darkened by the past. It sounded perfect, just what I wanted, just what I needed. I couldn't go on as I was.

'There was a man with them — an old man. He sat by the window and didn't speak, but, every time I looked up, he was watching me. The doctors seemed nervous, as if they wanted him to leave, as if they were being checked up on. That was when they said I could have a whole new life — a new future.'

'Was Tim with you?'

'Yes, he was very keen that I should accept their offer.'

'Did you know it was a one-way ticket?'

'No, but I think Tim did. The way he looked at me... he was nervous, and he couldn't look in my eyes.'

'Yeah, I'll bet.'

'I'd already met Marcus and Sasha by then, you know. I didn't remember that until yesterday. They were part of the treatment they'd started. They were kind and loving. Even after a few days, and even though I knew they were just part of my therapy, I thought of them as my friends.'

'They were preparing you all the time. Van-Doren said you were remarkably responsive. He must have got a message to say you were the client they'd been looking for. I bet he was on the first jet over.'

'Why would he want to do such a thing to me?'

'He wanted to control you and to have power over you. He wanted to know that, deep inside your new reality, you were his. He got a kick out of it. Van-Doren, or a young version of him, was Marcus.'

'So that's all it was, just power and selfishness? That's insane.'

'Maybe, but I've got to say, this technology scares the shit out of me. Everything seems to be spiralling away from us, like we invent and create powerful new forces way before we've got the ability to control them. And it's not the government that holds the reins either; it's monster business empires and people like Van-Doren. He's one scary guy. As soon as I met him, he started playing these mind games with me, like I was an opponent in some game he had to win. Within minutes, the board was out, the pieces were in place, and he was persuading me I was part of the programme, that everything — you, me, Liz, the fire — was part of my new reality, something I'd created to make my life mean something, that nothing was real.'

'You didn't believe him?'

'For a while I did. He really freaked me out. He put some hallucinatory shit in my drink — something to make me responsive, I suppose. I mean, for a few minutes there, I was really going for it. I was scared and totally disorientated. It was like trying to grasp shapes in the mist.'

'But you came back — like me.'

Yeah, only, it wasn't someone as nice as you who brought me back. It was Winston and Slattery at the window and a nasty pain in my ribs. There's no way I was going to give myself a pain like that in my virtual world, and I doubt Winston would feature. That's when I knew I could play his game and maybe even win.'

I don't tell her that even now I'm not sure of anything. It's too ridiculous. But I mean, he could be right, couldn't he? I could be lying in a bed somewhere, plugged in, sucking food through a drip, and pissing in a bag. I mean, for all I know, I might be a seventeen stone lump of body fat wallowing on a waterbed. I wouldn't know. I'd have no idea my life was just pictures on a screen, a good imagination, and a drip pouring drugs into me. I mean, I could be...

I shake the thought away.

There's no way I'd dream up Winston and Slattery.

Shit, no.

'With me, it was Heather,' Wendy is saying. 'I knew there was something beyond my new world — something I was hanging on to, and I couldn't let it go. Even when I was with Marcus and everything was just perfect, there was something there, holding my hand. When we talked about leaving and going to the States, I just woke up. I don't know why. It was like I opened my eyes and knew it was all something I didn't want. I dragged the headset away. I didn't know where I was or what I was doing. I think I screamed.'

'And the nurse helped you escape.'

'Yes, she was so kind. She understood. But if it hadn't been for Heather and you, I don't know if I'd have ever recovered.'

'Yeah, you would. You're tough. You wouldn't let them win.'

'What'll happen now?'

'We'll get those people out of Westleigh and somewhere safe, where they can be looked after.'

'That's good.'

'And you've got a decision to make about talking to the national press. It's up to you. No one will make the decision for you.'

'Tell me what you think.'

I take a deep breath.

'I think, if you feel up to it, you should do it. If you tell everything, Logrum and Van-Doren will have no hold over you. You'll be free of them. They'll lie and prevaricate and accuse us of all sorts of things, but they won't dare touch you.'

'Will you be with me?'

'If that's what you want.'

She nods. 'Okay. I want to put an end to this. We can't let them win.'

'One for the little guys,' I say.

'Yes, a victory for us.'

There's a knock at the door, and Heather arrives, so I vacate the room to give them space for the hugs and tears and everything that goes with a reunion like this.

'No Tim?' I ask Winston.

'He's outside in the car. Looks like he didn't want to come in.'

'I think maybe I'll go and say hello.'

'Yeah, I'll come too. Introduce myself.'

'I'll make tea,' Benny says.

'Yeah.'

So Winston and I go down to where Tim is sitting in his van, looking anxious. When he sees us coming over, he looks even more anxious and fumbles with the locks on the door. He's not quick enough. Winston pulls back the door, and I clamber in the passenger seat. Then Winston climbs in the back and leans forward, his head close to Tim's.

'Hello, Tim,' I say.

I've never seen a face go so pale so quickly.

Winston rests a hand on Tim's shoulder. 'Is this the guy?' he asks, his voice at least an octave deeper than normal.

'Yeah, this is him.'

'The guy who sold Wendy like some animal to be experimented on?'

'Yep.'

Winston's arm has closed round Tim's throat. He pulls his head back and stares down.

'He doesn't look much,' he says. His arm tightens until Tim's eyes start to bulge and he kicks out his legs. 'You think I should break his neck or just strangle the fucker?'

I think Tim might need a change of underwear if Winston carries on like this. For someone who cries at sentimental films, he's doing a pretty good impression of a tough guy.

'Not here,' I say, doing my best to play the mob boss. 'We don't want some innocent bystander catching a glimpse.'

'I'll take him down the old quarries — those deep pools, you know.'

'Yeah, no one will find him down there. Fossilise him.'

Tim's struggling becomes frantic, and I start to seriously worry that someone might see us. This is like a scene from *The Godfather.* I'm Al Pacino, and Winston is a dark version of the guy who ends up sleeping with the fishes. I'm almost sorry for Tim.

Almost.

But not enough to stop just yet.

'The guy who beat me up the night after we met — a friend of yours, was he?'

He goes even paler, and he's trembling like a *blancmange* in an earthquake.

'I just wanted...' he gargles.

'Yeah, I thought so. You figured it'd scare me off if you set your thug mate on me.'

Winston looks from me to Tim and back again.

'That was this weasel?' he asks, and he inserts a range of expletives and imaginative threats which are vast even by his standards.

'He's all yours, Winston,' I say, and I start to climb from the car. That sets Tim off again, kicking and grunting and waving his arms about like a demented puppet, but he's going nowhere, not with Winston's arm locked around his throat.

I shut the door behind me, but, as I disappear into the house, I glance back to see Winston clambering into the passenger seat. He looks up briefly, and, through the misted window, I see this huge, silly grin on his face. Winston is enjoying himself.

Tim isn't.

When Winston climbs from the car ten minutes later, Tim has done everything except wet himself, and I feel no sympathy — none at all. Winston isn't the violent type, but if you want to beat a victim to death with words, Winston's your man. His vocabulary in settings like this is as vast as an ocean.

By the time we walk back to the flat, we're both feeling pretty good, and Winston has a grin on his face as wide as the car park.

'What a shithead!' he says.

'Indeed he is, Winston.'

'You going to write about him?'

'I doubt it. Liz says I should use words as if there's a price on them. He's not worth a paragraph.'

'You'll tell Heather?'

'Not me — that's up to Wendy. She may want to leave him living in fear. I would.'

'What are you going to say to Mel about all this?' he asks as we reach the stairs.

'Oh shit,' I say. 'Mel!'

Chapter 43

I'm sitting at Slattery's bedside. Judging by his mood, I'd say he's getting back to normal. The doctor says it's the first transfusion he's done where he added a bottle of scotch to the blood just to keep the balance right. He's only half-joking.

'Have you seen the food in this place?' Slattery complains. 'It's designed so you don't have to chew. You could eat it through a straw. They warm it up by putting it on a windowsill. What do they think, that I'm going to choke or burn myself to death?'

'Makes you want to get better and leave,' I tell him. 'Food aside, how are they treating you?'

'Like an invalid.'

'When will they let you go?'

'As soon as we can,' a voice chirps up from not far away. It's one of the nurses.

'Can't even have a private conversation,' Slattery snaps. 'And I haven't had a cigarette in weeks. If you want to smoke in this place, you've got to take a bus ride to the precinct.'

'Maybe you'll give up?' I see the look on his face. 'Yeah, maybe not. Winston's coming later,' I tell him.

'Winston? What does he want?'

'He thinks you're are big buddies now you've shared an adventure — friends for life.'

'In his dreams. Shit, Phil, what I'd give for a decent fry up and a pint of Guinness.'

Like I say, he's on the mend.

'What about you and Mel?' he asks, changing the subject, 'how's that going?'

'Going, going, and gone,' I tell him. 'I'm relieved, to be honest with you. We were good together for a while, you know; but I'm an out-of-work, poverty-stricken, homely idealist. I want to stay here in Sefton and grow old with friends around me, familiar streets, familiar faces, and maybe someone to share it all with. She's not. She's ambitious — London, Paris, New York. She'd already met the equivalent of a spotty git with a car, only, this time he was a senior executive with a Porsche.'

'Story of your life.'

'Yeah, but I guess the writing was on the wall after everything that's happened — and Wendy.'

'How about you and her? I always figured you'd be a good mix.'

'Yeah, we're good — better than good, but she's been through a lot. It'll take time.'

'Still the story of your life. It's not really your strong suit, romance.'

'Yeah, I guess.'

'Still, got to keep trying.'

'I suppose.'

I don't tell him that Wendy and I are growing closer every day, that it's like we've known each other forever, and that I can't imagine my life without her. I reckon she feels the same. But she's got a lot to work through yet, so I'll just stay by her side, and one day maybe...

Yeah, I'm sure of it. One day...

The door behind me opens, and Winston interrupts my reverie like a football hitting the side of my head.

'He's dead,' he says.

He throws a tabloid on the bed next to Slattery.

'Who's dead?'

'Van-Doren. Page five. Cancer.'

Slattery picks up the paper, flicks through it, then folds it open. 'I hope it was a painful end,' he says.

Winston drops onto the bed and starts eating chocolates Jim Davey brought earlier.

'Help yourself,' Slattery says, 'don't stand on ceremony.'

He gets that grin Winston saves for moments like this.

'When do you get out?'

'I don't know, next week maybe.'

'We'll go for a drink,' Winston says, 'and a Chinese. What do you say? A celebration?'

'I'd rather eat with an eight-foot slug, is what I say.'

'I'll get it planned then,' Winston continues. 'You in, Phil?'

'You couldn't keep me out,' I tell him.

Winston looks around.

'I don't like hospitals. They're full of sick people. No offence,' he adds to Slattery, 'only, you never know what you're going to catch, do you?'

'Dead right,' says Slattery. 'People die in these places. Have you seen the food?' He indicates a half-congealed plate of mince and mash. 'Looks like someone's already chewed it.'

'Pre-digested,' Winston nods. 'What are the nurses like?'

'Tyrants.'

'Doctors?'

'Sadists.'

'Other patients?'

'Snore and fart all night; I can't get a wink.'

'I'll plan a coming out party.'

'Yeah, do that. It'll give me something to look forward to.'

Something really weird is happening in my head. It's like I'm swirling away, caught in some strange vortex; they're way down below me and I'm just looking on. Winston and Slattery are talking like friends.

'You okay, Phil?'

'Yeah, yeah, I'm fine.'

'Looked like you were drifting there, for a minute, man.'

'Time I was going,' I say.

I can't admit the truth, not to Winston and Slattery. Only with Wendy can I open up because she understands, because she's been there, and because she doesn't think I'm losing my mind. Everyone else would.

'It's like Van-Doren got in my head, and he won't go away,' I tell her. 'He's buzzing in there like a fly in a jar. Sometimes, it goes away for days on end, but then something — I never know what it'll be — a smell, a sound, even a few words — takes me back there, and, suddenly, I'm caught up in this spiral, like a tornado, and I can't get out. I mean, I know it's not real. I know that here, now, with you, sitting on this chair at your side, is as real I can ever feel or ever want to feel. I know that. It's just... I don't know... It's just...'

'A doubt,' she murmurs, 'a question. Am I really here? Is this my one true reality? Or is this all a dream manufactured in some clinic and fed by my own desires and imaginings...'

'For a moment, I just don't know. I think perhaps what Van-Doren said is true. Perhaps the clinic hasn't closed, and it's just my dream telling me it has. Perhaps those people are still out there, experimenting on more and more people; perhaps...'

'Shh,' she says. 'Shh, this is real — here, now, you, me, everything we feel and share.' She looks at me, and those blue eyes penetrate my soul. 'Nothing else matters.'

And I know she's right. She lays her head against me, and we sit in silence as the darkness slowly falls, and shadows cast by the table lamp flicker and stir like strange, unknown lives.

Did you love *Shifting Sands*? Then you should read *Waves Break (on Unknown Shores)*[1] by Barry Litherland!

[2]

Past events cast shadows you can't outrun. Wayne and Phil knew that better than anyone, after Stevie died, way back when they were children. A pebble dropped in a pool. Ripples spreading outwards. Who knew where they would end?

Read more at www.bleaknorth.net.

1. https://books2read.com/u/49QoDW
2. https://books2read.com/u/49QoDW

Also by Barry Litherland

The Hand of Ronan Hawke
Waves Break (on Unknown Shores)
Shifting Sands

Watch for more at www.bleaknorth.net.

About the Author

Barry Litherland is an author of crime and paranormal crime mystery thrillers. He lives and works in the far North of Scotland where he lives with his wife and two energetic springer spaniels.

Read more at https://www.bleaknorth.net.

Printed in Poland
by Amazon Fulfillment
Poland Sp. z o.o., Wrocław

57945811R00155